RACK AND RUIN

JESSICA RANEY

Third Wheel Publishing

CHAPTER 1

DELILAH MONROE WAITED in the parking lot of the Burger King. She drummed her fingers on the steering wheel and stared up through the open top of the Jeep. The summer air was heavy and thick in the late afternoon sun. Del tucked a sweaty strand of blonde hair behind her ear and blew out and upward to dispel some stagnant air. She didn't run the air conditioner. Usually she preferred a little sweat; it felt good when the Jeep was rolling, but she'd been waiting in the parking lot for thirty minutes and the perspiration beaded up on her skin, soaking her t-shirt in strategic places and making her antsy. It annoyed her to sit and wait, but she gripped the steering wheel and willed herself not to fidget. She gritted her teeth and practiced patience, even though the smell of the flame-grilled meat nauseated her and the waiting induced a slight rage in her guts.

Her patience was rewarded when a 1997 Ford Focus pulled into the parking space beside her. The car had seen better days. The back bumper was caved in and the headliner, having long ago lost the will and adhesive to stick tight to the roof of the car, hung down in several places. Its exhaust was trailer park loud, signaling a hole in the muffler, and it sputtered a bit when it stopped. A tall, bearded man wearing a black polo shirt and black jeans got out of the passenger side. He waited until the driver exited before moving to the Jeep. The driver was a thin young man with sparse facial hair and a nervous shake. He looked down at the ground instead of at the Jeep, and he had to shut his door twice. The bearded man nodded his head, pointed to the Jeep, and waited for the skinny man to climb in.

"Ah, hey, Del," the skinny man said. He wrung his hands and looked at the floor mat.

"What took so long?" Del asked. She wasn't in any mood for pleasantries or small talk.

"Yeah, well, I-I had to come on back around and you know I didn't want to look too suspicious, just in case," he said.

"That's fucking stupid. This ain't a Mission Impossible movie, Barry. You was just confirming that kid was in there selling shit," Del said.

"I-I just didn't want the law to catch me," Barry said. He looked Del in the eye once, then around at the man with the beard, then back at the floor.

"The Law around here couldn't catch a cold," Del said. "Let me see it." She held out her hand, palm up.

Barry rummaged around in his jeans pocket and pulled out a little bag. He placed it in Del's hand. The bag was slick and wet, and Del could smell the rank stench of Barry's nasty blue jeans and sweat coming from it. She could also smell drugs. She opened the bag and took a quick sniff. It was 40% cocaine and 60% baby laxative, easy. She couldn't care less that it was a shitty cut and bad coke. She did care that the punk ass kid was using some outside supply, and that he was dealing without her blessing.

"That's shit," she said as she handed the bag to the bearded man in the back seat. "What's his name?"

"Evan Combs. He's working drive thru. You just order the number 11," Barry said. "Can I go? I did what you asked."

"So you did, Barry," Del said. She nodded at the bearded man. "Cal will make sure you get home safe."

"Oh, well, that ain't necessary Del. I-I-I ain't in no danger," Barry said.

"Better safe than sorry," Del said. She smiled at Barry and patted his leg. "Now look here, Barry. I'm going to knock a grand off what you owe because you done good today. But Cal here is gonna be back in a week and if you don't have my money, or if you try to freelance anything again, you're gonna have yourself a real big problem. You take my meaning?"

"Sure... sure, Del. I'll be okay from now on. You won't have to worry over it no more," Barry said.

"That's good. Real good, Barry," Del said. "Now get the fuck out of my vehicle."

Barry didn't have to be told twice. He yanked at the handle and shoved the door open hard, then nearly fell over himself getting out. He slammed the door shut behind him and scampered into the Focus.

Del turned to Cal. "He ain't gonna pay, and he's a fucking idiot. Take him out to the Holler and have Frank turn him. He might be able to cook."

"You sure? He's real dumb," Cal said.

"No need to waste a warm body, so to speak," Del said. Barry wouldn't be warm after they turned him. He'd never be warm again, not even if he blew himself sky-high cooking meth in one of the labs.

"He'll blow himself up in a week," Cal said.

"Well, if you feel strongly about it, pop his dumb ass, and take him out to the Ring Brothers."

Cal's face grimaced in a rare expression of feeling. "Them two creep me out."

"They're fucking disgusting, but useful. Nobody will miss Barry, and nobody will ever find him if you take him to see the Boys."

"I'll let you know how it goes," Cal said. He got out of the Jeep.

"Nah, I couldn't care less either way," Del said.

Cal got in the Focus, and it took off in a plume of white oil-burning smoke. That smell mixed with the scent of the cheap grilled meat made Del even sicker. She started up the

Jeep and steered it through the drive thru. When she pulled up to the speaker and looked at the menu, she smiled. There was no number eleven. The combo meals only went to ten.

"Welcome to Burger King, Home of the Flame-Grilled Whopper. What can I make for you today?" a young man's voice came through the speaker, garbled and bored.

"Yeah, I'll have a number eleven," Del said.

"What to drink with that?"

"A large Coke."

"One number eleven with a large Coke. Please pull to the second window."

Del smiled as she pulled through. She held out a folded stack of twenties. The kid in the drive-thru didn't smile. Brown, greasy hair hung down and obscured his long, sullen, acne-riddled face. He handed her a large Coke, took the cash, then handed Del a bag. Del took the bag and looked inside. There was an order of kid's fries and a little baggie of drugs. She supposed it worked for this dumbass, but it was short-sighted. Sooner rather than later, even Jacob and his local dipshit cops would figure it out.

The kid didn't know who she was. When he looked at her, his face held no fear, no look of recognition at all. To him, she was just some junkie.

Del smiled at him. "Can I get some ketchup? And a straw?"

His face was blank as he reached down and grabbed a handful of ketchup packets, then handed them out the window.

"A little closer?" Del said.

He leaned a bit out the window, and Del grabbed his uniform shirt. She yanked him out of the window, then took off. He clawed at the side of the Jeep. Del sped up. She had a good hold on him. He wasn't going anywhere. She grinned at his screaming and scrambling. A screaming, pimply kid hanging out of the side of her Jeep would attract attention. She didn't care much, but she liked to avoid shit with the Sheriff when possible. In this case, it was possible. She drove about a half a mile down the road, to one of the river put-ins, a make-shift boat launch that was little more than a worn-down slope of grass in a flat section of riverbank. Del spun the Jeep in a circle for good measure, just to make sure the kid was scared enough, then she tossed him aside, stopped the Jeep, and got out in one smooth, graceful motion.

Del was big and lanky, over six-feet tall. Her people were all big people, but Del was big even for them. She was fifty years old but looked twenty-five. Few lines creased her forehead, and even fewer were visible at the corners of her eyes or the draw of her mouth. Her blonde hair had not even a hint of fading or grey. Her aging had slowed to a crawl, which was normal for her kind, but aging at half, even for them, was unheard of. She was all corded muscle and annoyance, and the kid scooted backward on his ass through the trampled down grass as she stalked over to him. His face finally had some expression, and that expression was terror. Del sniffed him, then looked at his crotch. He'd pissed himself. She grinned. She wondered if she could induce a number two.

"Hello, Evan."

"Who-Who are you? What is this?" Evan stammered as he cowered.

"Well look at you, Evan. Asking questions like you're workin' for the school paper," Del said. She reached down and grabbed his shirt, then yanked him straight up into the air. She held him, his feet dangling six inches above the ground.

"What do you want? Money? I-I ain't got—" Evan stammered.

"Oh, you got plenty from what I hear," Del said. "That seems like a real smart little operation you got going there, in the fucking Burger King drive-thru window."

"It's... It's cool lady. I-I just..."

Del shook her head, then tossed him backward. Evan landed a solid fifteen feet away and stayed on the ground. Del picked him up again and slapped him. His head snapped to the side, and he blinked his eyes, dazed from the blow. She dropped him, then squatted down next to him in the dust.

"Evan. You are gonna stop dealing blow out of that fucking Burger King. You understand me?"

"What? Why? You ain't a cop. What do you care?"

Del kicked him in the ribs, then grabbed him by his greasy hair and pulled him around in a circle. Evan screamed and clawed at her hand, but she held tight.

"I ain't a cop, that's for sure. I'm much worse. So, let me

tell you what will happen to you if you keep slinging that shitty coke. I'm gonna take you way back up in a holler. I'm gonna tie you up. I'm gonna light a blow torch and burn holes in you until you don't think there's no more space for a hole. Nobody will help you. Nobody will ever find you. All for some shitty coke deal in a fucking Burger King. Is that what you want to happen?"

"Who the fuck are you, lady?" Evan said, sobbing as he held his bruised ribs.

"I'm the one who says what gets dealt in this county and where it gets dealt. And I say that you ain't dealing that shitty coke out of that shitty restaurant," Del said.

Evan's eyes got wide, and he stopped sobbing. Del sniffed the air and smiled. The hot odor of feces hit her nose. She had indeed induced a number two in the kid. Good.

"You're... you're—" Evan whispered. His face was white, and he sat still, flattening himself to the ground.

Del nodded. "Yep. I'm her. Are you gonna keep on being a dumbass, Evan?"

"No. No ma'am. I'll stop. I won't deal no more. I swear."

Del held up her hands. "Let's not be too hasty, there, Evan. I ain't trying to crush a dream. You're gonna deal, you just ain't gonna do it out of that Burger King."

"Huh?"

"Tomorrow, you start work down at the Lion's Den," Del said.

"The porn store?"

"The very same," Del said. "You'll get a bag of shit a week.

You turn that, I give you more. It's easy pickings dealing out of there. Smart kid like you can make a name for himself, in a good way. I get my cut, you keep making money, and I don't have to burn holes in you. Everybody wins."

"Yes, ma'am."

"It's Del. Not ma'am. That's for old ladies."

"Yes, ma—I mean, Del," Evan said.

"Great. One last thing. Where did you get that shitty blow?"

"Um… lady name of Karen. She works at that check cashing place on Elm."

"Very good," Del nodded. She knew Karen. She'd make sure Karen got a message too and find out where the cheap cut was coming from. "Go on home now. Be careful, Evan. I'd hate to see anything happen to a young man with your potential."

Del climbed back in the Jeep, started it up, then spun around Evan in a cloud of dust, the deep tread of the tires spitting clumps of dirt everywhere. She left him there, in his shitty pants, pondering his life choices as she sped off toward the payday loan place on Elm, where she would lead Karen to a similar epiphany.

CHAPTER 2

DEL RELAXED in the chair across from Karen's desk. It was a cheap particle board thing, and Del hesitated before propping her feet up on it, afraid it would collapse with the weight. It was appropriate for the office. Pay Day loan places were paperboard businesses, prone to collapse at any minute. She'd let Karen run this one for a cut, but Del had never liked the business plan. Juicing degenerates was one thing. Del did that all the time. It was another to squeeze working folks who thought they were getting a helping deal. Del knew not all the patrons were good people, down on their luck. Some were just shitbags. She knew better than most the amount of shitty people in the County, so she was under no illusions about the purity of the patrons, but still, something about the FastCash2Go had always seemed dishonest to her, which was ironic, even to Del.

"I was gonna cut you in Del, I swear I was," Karen said. Her hands shook as she put a cigarette to her lips and tried to light it.

"No smoking. I fucking hate that smell," Del said.

Karen dropped the cig and sobbed. She'd started crying the minute Del walked in the door. Karen's heavy Maybelline had white ruts running through it now where the tears traced canyons in the thick application. Her mascara was black around her eyes and clumpy.

"I'm sorry," Karen said, crying. "I swear I'll stop."

"In my experience, Karen, second chances never work out so good," Del said. "But tell me where you got this shitty blow and I'll think on it."

"I-I can't. They'll kill me."

"Like I fucking won't?" Del said. She gave a little snort laugh. "Tell me. Or don't, and we take this meeting offsite." She looked hard at Karen, and Karen sobbed.

"Guy named Spider."

Del rolled her eyes. "What else about Spider? Where's he out of?"

"He's in a gang. Bikers. He comes out here from California."

A California biker named Spider sounded like a pain in Del's ass. She knew gangs. Most steered clear out of respect and a dose of fear. She occasionally worked with a few out of Barstow, but as a general rule, she didn't deal with them. They were usually Neo-Nazis and almost always whacked out on PCP. That wasn't a combination Del cared to manage.

"Okay," Del pulled Karen's cell phone out of her jacket pocket and slid it across the desk. "Call him. Set up another pickup. How do you normally do it?"

"I call, then go pick up the half."

Del rolled her eyes. "No shit. Where?"

"At the Motel 6 off 77," Karen said. "But look, Del, I ain't sold the stuff I got last week. He'll be suspicious."

"You must be a shitty dealer, you can't move that much coke in a week." Del narrowed her eyes and looked at Karen for a second, then grinned. "You ain't got his money or you owe him more, huh?"

Karen cried harder, her face in her hands as she nodded.

"All right. Quit your crying. Call him. Tell him you got all his money and you want another brick." Del rapped the table with her knuckle to get Karen's attention. "Fucking stop crying and get it done. I ain't got all day.

DEL SAT outside the rundown Motel 6 and watched the first-floor room, 103. That was where Spider stayed, according to Karen. She'd called him and set up a meeting, and Del could hear how angry he was at her over the phone. Karen had been skimming coke and was short on cash for sure. She'd left Karen back at her office, under the watchful eye of Cal. She'd deal with her in good time. Right at the moment, she needed to go deal with a coke-pushing skinhead biker.

Del walked up to room 103. A tricked-out Harley sat outside the room. It was an expensive bike, but not clean and maintained. The paint job was a woman with huge tits spreading her leg so you could see her tonsils and everything else. Spider was a charmer, for sure.

Del didn't bother knocking. She kicked the cheap door in and strode into the room. Spider shoved the hooker off his crotch and stood up from the ratty loveseat but tripped over his pants. He was bald and covered in tattoos, even his dick, and he yowled and sputtered as he tried to stand up and extricate himself from his pants. Del helped him by grabbing him by the neck and throwing him against the headboard. He hit it so hard he cracked the cheap wood.

Del looked to the hooker. She wasn't one of Del's and she had enormous bruises and angry cigarette burns all over her. One eye was swollen over. Del helped her to her feet.

"You don't work for me. Who you work for?" Del asked.

The girl pointed to Spider, who moaned on the bed. "Him."

"Huh. He's a pimp too? What's your cut?"

"25%."

Del laughed. "You gotta be kidding me. He takes 75%? How old are you?"

"I'm twenty-two," the girl said. She looked down at the ground.

"Bullshit. How old are you?"

"Sixteen."

"Fucking piece of shit." Del growled and picked Spider up. She choked him against the wall. "What's your name?" she asked the girl.

"Darla."

"Darla, get in Spider's wallet. He got cash?"

"I-I can't…"

"Sure you can. He won't mind, will you Spider?" Spider didn't answer because Del squeezed his windpipe. "How much he got?"

Darla looked through his wallet and pulled out a wad of cash. "It's a bunch."

Del nodded. "Okay. You take all of it and get on out of here. I don't want to see you turning tricks again." Del threw Spider down and stomped his crotch with her boot heel. He screamed and writhed on the floor. Del rummaged in the nightstand and pulled out a pen and piece of the complimentary motel stationary. She wrote down a phone number and handed it to Darla. "You want work, call that number. Charity. She'll find you something legal to do. Stay away from pieces of shit like this." Del pointed to Spider, who had vomited all over himself.

The girl nodded as she dressed. Del grabbed her and looked her in the eye. "I mean it, Darla. I say who tricks here, and I say underage don't trick in this county. I'll know if you do. You believe me?"

Darla nodded. "I-I won't."

"Good girl. Now get out of here. I need to have a brief discussion with this old boy."

Darla took her money and ran. Del turned her attention to Spider. He had recovered and rummaged around in a bag. He pulled out a gun and shot Del in the shoulder. The bullet stung, but she'd been shot before in more painful places. She'd heal when she turned in a few days, but even so, she could feel her accelerated healing kick in as the bleeding slowed, and the flesh rippled and itched. The healing was slow, but a hundred times faster than a human, and she'd be fine, only now, she was mad.

Del grabbed Spider's wrist and squeezed until she heard the bones crack. He shrieked and dropped the gun. Del yanked on his wrist again and popped his shoulder out of joint. She let go and grabbed him by the throat again and slammed him against the wall. He left a body-sized dent as the drywall caved in.

"Now look here, fuckstick. You're gonna answer some questions."

"Fuck you," Spider hissed as he slapped at Del's hand with his good arm. Del grabbed it and pulled back on it, snapping his wrist back. She dropped him on the couch, screaming.

"Who do you work for?"

"Big mistake, bitch. They'll kill you for this."

"For a pedophile pimp? I doubt anyone's gonna go to war over you," Del said. She punched him in the mouth. "I'm gonna keep breaking shit until you ain't got no more shit to break." Del grabbed his dick and squeezed. His eyes bugged out of his head and he screeched.

"I will break it right off. So tell me who sent you here."

"He'll kill you, hillbilly."

"Uh-huh. Who?"

Del doubted Spider dealt with the head of the organization. She squeezed his dick again and tilted her wrist up, bending it.

"I-I call my President. I'm just a courier."

"Just a courier, huh? That's good, 'cause I got a message for your mysterious boss." Del let go of his dick and found his leathers. She examined the patches. The main patch was a bloody red hand, palm out. His club wasn't one she was familiar with, but she wasn't an expert in Cali motorcycle thugs. She knew some though, and they might have information.

By the time Cal arrived, Del had broken several more things on Spider and squeezed two important things until they popped. Spider was a bloody writhing mess. Cal grimaced and stepped around him.

"Jesus. What did he do?"

"He's our shitty coke source, and he tried to run underage girls in my town." Del chucked Spider in the back seat of Cal's big truck. "Take him to San Diego. I called Jose. He's gonna meet you. He'll make sure this sack of shit gets back to deliver my message."

"What's the message?" Cal asked.

Del looked at the motorcycle. She grabbed the front end and ripped it off, then bent it in half. She picked up the rest of the bike and smashed it on the concrete until it was a mangled ball of metal. Del tossed the whole thing in the back of Cal's truck.

"The message is, please kindly refrain from doing business in my territory." Del looked in at Spider, who cried and moaned at his ruined balls and bike. "Spider, be sure and say please."

CHAPTER 3

DEL STOOD up and smiled when the old man walked in the office. She came around the desk as he grinned at her and spread his arms wide.

"There's my girl."

Del hugged him. "Looks like you ain't dead yet, Paulie." She pulled back in the embrace and looked him over. He'd worn his hair the same way for thirty years, a silver, slicked up pompadour. He was stooped and his face worn looking as the wrinkles stood in relief against his spray tanned skin. Del thought his eyes looked tired. Paulie had been one of the first Jersey guys she'd dealt with back when she started. He'd been a good partner and ally, but he was Jersey, he wasn't from home and Del never forgot that. Today, she smelled a bit of fear on him, mixed in with the heavy scent of old man cologne.

"Not dead, but look at you, still a hot piece of–"

"Okay, enough of that, less you wanna lose a couple somethings of value," Del said. She laughed, but she learned a long time ago that while you had to play a little to get these guys in your corner, you also couldn't take shit either. They respected her and wanted her at the same time. She'd worked hard for it. She motioned for him to sit down. "You come by yourself?"

"No, Tony's outside. He drove." He handed her a white paper bag. "I brought you some of those bialies you like.

Del took the bag, sniffed it, and grinned. "Well, you want something? Coffee?"

"Nah, thanks, doll."

"Wanna get to it, huh?" Del asked. "Okay. Paulie. What's this shit about my missing booze trucks?"

Paulie's face got red, and he held up his hands. "Yeah, about that. Couldn't be helped."

"What do you mean? You missed the last three drops. You left Cal and my boys looking like assholes over in Hagerstown."

"We had to divert 'em. Sorry, Del."

"Look, Paulie. We been doing this for a long fucking time. You ain't never had an issue before. What's the issue now?"

"It's only temporary, Del. I had a last-minute request and filled it instead of yours. I get more stock, I'm sending a truck this way. Hey. To make up for it, how about a half a truck of drug store shit? Tampons. You know you can take them to Mexico for big bucks."Del wanted to roll her eyes.

He ditched her for somebody else and thought a pallet of Tampax would make up for it. The bigger question was who had more muscle than her to make him give up the booze?

"Yeah. I'll take the Tampax. And you're gonna have my two trucks by Tuesday."

"By Tuesday? No way. Can't be done."

"Oh it can, and it will, Paulie. Two. By Tuesday."

She crossed her arms and growled at him. Paulie slid back in his chair and pressed himself against the back rest.

"I'll do my best."

"See that you do." Del relaxed. "Now, seeing as how you're in a bind, I'm gonna help. I got three trailers ready for you over in Pittsburg. Have your guys get 'em. I promise, ain't no law gonna stop 'em. You can haul whatever you like."

He eyed her, but he knew she could move whatever she wanted and she'd been doing it undetected for ten years now. Del had helped him before, but was stingy with the trailers, and she could tell by his face and the excited smell he gave off that he wanted those trucks bad.

"I got one condition."

"What's that?"

Del leaned forward in her chair and stared at him for a second. "I wanna know who you dropped me for."

Paulie's face reddened, and he sputtered. "Now come on, doll... you know I can't tell you that."

"I think you can and if you want them trailers, you will."

It was more than that. She liked Paulie. She had done

business with Jersey for years, but a change was in the air, she could feel it. She wanted ahead of it. She'd burn him and every goon in Newark to ash if she had to.

Paulie knew Del well enough to know she meant business. He threw up his hands. "Out west. He took the booze and helped us with some girls out in Vegas. It couldn't be helped, Del."

"I coulda helped too. But here we are." Del leaned back and smiled. Out west. Just like her biker friend. Del didn't believe in coincidences. Actions had consequences, and things happened for reasons. This was the second move on her from the west and it was getting to be tiresome.

"Hey, doll, we're still friends. Good friends. But this outfit... it ain't so easy to say no."

Del nodded and patted Paulie on the knee. "We're still friends, Paulie. Of course." She gripped his knee with her hand and squeezed until the old man was red in the face. "You ever short me again, and I'll figure out how many dead Jersey boys I can fit in a 48-foot trailer. You take my meaning?"

Paulie nodded and sputtered. "Easy, Del. Easy."

"I asked if you understand."

"I understand, doll. I understand."

Del let him go and patted his swollen knee. "Good. Now tell me more about this old boy from Cali."

"I'm telling you, Del, he's bad business."

Juan's hand shook as he downed the shot and slammed it on the bar. He was afraid. Dell could smell it on him, even through the choking smell of cigarettes and Monostat 7 cream that pervaded the dirty, run-down Reno strip club. Del wrinkled her nose and downed her own drink.

"So am I, Juan."

Juan shook his head. "Not like him. Look, that Red Hand? They took over five other MC's. Know how?"

"Punch and Pie at the meetings?"

"They came in and took out the Presidents. Guys went nuts. One shot up an In and Out. One jumped off a bridge. All of 'em lost their shit."

"Huh. Well, whatever works," Del said. She motioned to the bartender for two more drinks. A stripper with braces and pigtails and a big cesarean scar hovered around her. She turned to the girl and handed her a twenty. "That's to not fucking come back, get it?" The girl pouted but took the money and left. Del turned back to Juan. "So the Red Hand is some bunch of motorcycle fucks. That's what he's got? Gotta be more."

Juan nodded. "There's more." He shifted awkwardly, looked around and then back at Del as he whispered. "They're all weirdos."

"Yeah? Like how weird?"

"I-I don't know, but," Juan crossed himself. "Not... well..."

Del nodded. He meant not human but couldn't bring

himself to say it. "Yeah. I catch the meaning, bud. Look. Everything is gonna be fine."

"No, Del, it won't. The Red Hand was mad about their boy, you sent back. He ain't ever gonna be able to use his hands right again."

"Good. That was my goal." It really wasn't. Her goal was to make them stay away, but based on what Paulie had told her earlier in the week and what Juan was spilling now, it was a pipe dream. "You done what I asked. You and your crew should just steer clear of 'em. I'm sending Cal out with a half shipment of guns and a couple kilos of Crank. No charge."

Juan nodded. "Thanks, Del. You know I wanna help, but…"

Del nodded. "Yeah. I know, man. It's fine. I'll handle this old boy and if he wants to come out to my holler and dance, we'll dance."

"I don't think you're gonna want that. He took over all the Mexican Cartels. Runs 'em from San Diego."

Del furrowed her brow. How did a bunch of motorcycle jerks and some slick West Coast punk take out the Sinaloa bastards? Wasn't possible.

"All of 'em? Sinaloa? Jalisco?"

Juan nodded. "Todo. Everything goes through them now."

"Huh," Del said. "Well, it ought to be an interesting ride then."

"Don't make it your last, Del."

Del shrugged. "Gotta come sometime." She slugged back her whiskey and handed another stripper a twenty to leave her alone as she contemplated the chess board and hoped she was choosing the right gambit.

CHAPTER 4

"Boss, ah, there's some... umm... folks here to see you," Cal said. He waited by the door and fidgeted. Del sniffed the air and smelled the fear coming from him in waves, which was out of character for him. Cal was her right hand. He'd seen her through many a hairy deal and strange situation. Cal was the guy she used to meter out violence or clean up the messes. He was cool and even, no matter the task, and never once had she smelled a lick of coward on him. Until today.

Cal's sweat soaked the underarms of his standard black polo shirt, and he licked his lips over and over as his fingers picked at the skin around his thumbs.

"Who is it?" Del asked. Whoever it was had him spooked.

"Sorry, boss. It's just that... well... they ain't humans."

Del shrugged. "We ain't either. Do they got big guns or something?"

"No. No guns," Cal said. His hands shook, and he shoved them in the pockets of his jeans.

"Fuck this. Go piss in your pants elsewhere." Del shoved Cal out of her way and walked through the office door into the lobby. As soon as she sniffed the air, the hair on the back of her neck rose, her canine teeth elongated, and a deep rumbling growl issued from her throat. The air was thick with the stench of fish and Sulphur. Del had smelled a lot of nasty things. Dead things. Living things that stank. Living dead things that stank. The stench coming off the man standing in her lobby was the worst thing Del had ever smelled.

The tall man had salt and pepper hair and eyes so ice-blue that even if Del couldn't smell the supernatural on him, she would have thought he wasn't human because of his eyes. He was long and lanky and had the look of a negligent trust-fund kid, preppy and Ivy League, not just from his clothes, but from the bored entitlement she could sense coming from him. He looked around the room and a half-smile twitched at his lips. Del knew that smile. It was the smile rich kids smiled when they thought they would have fun at the expense of the corn-pone country kids. The smile they smiled when you didn't know who some MTV singer was or which fork to use or any of the other bullshit things they thought were signs of intelligence and culture. Del had been dealing with them all her life. Most of them she just shut down, but this one was all that entitlement mixed with a dark magic that she'd never sensed before and for a second, it froze her. Then his smell hit her again. Dead, rotting fish and rotten eggs, but he covered it with an expensive smelling cologne that didn't smell familiar or off the shelf. It choked even worse than his fish-egg stench, and Del wrinkled her nose and contained a gag.

He had an entourage with him. A tall rat-faced man—Del knew right away he was a vampire, a squatty man with a hairy face and skin that looked like cauliflower, a few more goons-they were bikers with the Red Hand on their leathers and they were also werewolves. Last was a tall brunette, slight, but impressive looking, dressed in a tailored black pantsuit. She smelled sort of human, but sort of not. She quirked an eyebrow at Del and gave her a closed-lipped smile. Del had seen that same smile before, long ago, and it simultaneously made her heart catch and made her angry.

The man grinned and nodded at Del as he strode across the room, coming disturbingly far into her personal space.

"Ms. Monroe. It is my distinct pleasure to meet you," he said. He had a flat accent, untraceable to anywhere, and he lingered over the word, pleasure, in such a way that it made Del's skin crawl.

"Well, I'm sure it is," Del said. She took the man's hand and tried to smile. The fishy-Sulphur odor almost made her gag, but she held it in. "And who might you be?"

"My name is Martin Price." He held Del's hand in both of his. "I received your message, and I wanted to come myself, to clear up any misunderstandings between us. Ms. Monroe,

I had hoped we could be... good friends." The man's eyes traveled up and down Del's body and he didn't disguise it.

Del knew how to play the game. She cocked her head and returned the evaluation. She gave the man a little smile and nodded. "I appreciate the personal call. You came a good long way for it. How's life in sunny California?"

"Oh, you know, work, work, work," Martin said. "Shall we talk?"

"Surely," Del said. She led him in to her office and offered him a seat on the leather sofa. "What can I get you all to drink?" The rest of the group had followed.

"Javier, Luis, out." The werewolves growled and slunk out. "This is Darius and Fernando," he said, pointing to the surly vampire, then to the cauliflower freak. "And this is Olivia." Martin smiled and gestured to the woman, who came forward and took Del's hand.

"Hello," she said. Her voice was deep and dark and smooth, like bourbon, and her face still held that funny smile.

"Hello yourself," Del said, shaking the woman's hand. She caught a whiff of ozone, slight fish, as a jolt of electricity passed between them. Del rubbed her hand on her jeans.

Del sat on the sofa next to Martin. She looked up at Cal. "Why don't you go make sure her boys is good. Show 'em to the bar." She smiled at Martin. "That all right with you?"

"That's more hospitality than they deserve, I'm sure," Martin said.

"I'll stay," the vampire said. He hadn't taken his eyes off

Del, and it wasn't love she saw in them. His face looked pinched and pained, and he scowled.

"Nobody said you had to go, Slim," Del said. "Cal, tell Janie to send in something for this feller too. I doubt bourbon will do for him." Del looked to Martin. "Bourbon good for you?"

"A woman after my own heart," Martin said, winking back. He leaned back into the sofa and relaxed.

"Boss, you sure—" Cal stuttered. He looked at the vampire, and Del knew what he was thinking. The bloodsucker was trouble.

"I'm sure." Del got up and poured three glasses of bourbon. "So I reckon my message got back to you."

"Yes, and I am deeply sorry that my people overstepped. I had no idea they cut through your valley," Martin said. His words dripped with insincere apology and lies.

"Well, you seem a little high up to know all them type of details," Del said.

"Yes. And no." Martin said. "I'm quite impressed by you, Delilah. May I call you Delilah?"

Del cringed at the name, but she smiled anyway. "Sure. But why is it you're so impressed?"

"You took a backwoods meth operation and turned it in to something spectacular," Olivia said, answering for him.

Del looked at Olivia, then she laughed. "You think so?"

"Oh I know so, Delilah," Olivia said, her gaze never leaving Del's face.

Martin sipped his drink and scooted closer to Del. "I'm a

man of vision, Delilah and one of my gifts is spotting others with vision. Anyone can cook meth in trailers in the forest. Anyone can run prostitutes. Anyone can manage gamblers and bookies, and other lowlife criminals. But you saw where the actual power was, and you seized it."

"I think you're giving me too much credit. I'm just swimmin' around in this little pond." Del fought the urge to get up and run out of the room. The man reeked—the stink of him choked her, and his presence made her feel like all the air had gone out of the room. She felt a burning sensation, not painful, more like a sunburnt spot, flare up in the middle of her back. She swallowed down her disgust and rippled her back muscles. The burn subsided and Del caught her breath and control.

"Modest. You're an enormous fish in an enormous pond, not just this Valley. We're aware that you control almost every level of government. That's useful."

"I have a few close friends that carry some weight, sure," Del said.

"US Senators? Judges, State Representatives, local law enforcement? Just a few friends?"

"They're just friends. I've helped them. Sometimes they help me," Del said.

"Let's talk about your distribution network. I'm told you can move anything anywhere."

"I doubt that," Del laughed. "I can move some things, sure, but anything I want? Anywhere I want? I ain't a miracle worker."

"Oh, but I've heard that you are. Information and Logistics. Your mastery is impressive. Your product, however, is not."

"My product?" Del asked. Anger boiled deep down inside her. It percolated in her gut and warmed her whole middle. He knew an awful lot, or thought he did, about Del's connections and protections. She kept all that low profile. Something had gone wrong if some demon from the West Coast had first-hand knowledge.

"Your methamphetamine is trash," Martin said. His voice was patronizing and sickly sweet, the way you'd talk to a small child if you were an asshole.

"All meth is trash," Del retorted. "It don't stop nobody from cramming it in 'em."

"Our product sells for five times what yours can. Production is not your core competency."

"So what is it you suggest?" Del asked.

"My product is excellent and varied. Your distribution network is vast, and you've never been caught. That, along with your information network, will make us an unstoppable team," Martin said.

"That's quite a proposal," Del said. She refilled his empty glass, handed it back, but didn't sit on the couch. "But what if I was to say I was content and doin' just fine on my own?"

"We say you're lying and stupid," the vampire said. He laughed and sneered.

"I don't recall asking you, Slim," Del said. He was a different vampire than Jerry. Jerry had been lazy and harmless. This one was all attitude and cliché, dressed in black with slicked back, greasy hair and the thin, pale look of Eurotrash.

The vampire hissed at her and took a step toward her. Del laughed out loud. "Did you just fucking hiss at me? Really?"

"Enough Darius. You're being rude. Go outside with the others," Martin said.

"I'm not leaving you here with this filthy wolf," Darius said. "She'll... she'll—" He didn't finish his sentence. He froze. His eyes widened and his mouth opened in a scream, but no noise came out. The blue veins on the side of his thin head enlarged and popped out against his stark white skin as he shook.

"I apologize for Darius," Martin said. He sipped his drink and smiled at Del. "He's rude and not bright, but you know, vampires."

Martin waved his hand. Darius snapped out of the trance and fell to the floor. He curled up and sobbed.

"I do know vampires," Del said. She stepped over Darius and sat back down on the couch.

"You'll quadruple your earnings if we partner. I can see many other ventures for us."

"Can you now?" Del asked. "That seems like a lot of money. Trouble is, I'd bear all the risk if the network gums up."

"But you never get caught. It's miraculous." Martin put his palms together and looked up at the ceiling in mocking reverence. He smiled at Del and sat forward. "Tell me your secret."

"Now, now, a girl's gotta keep a little mystery about her," Del said. "What's the benefit to me if I work with you?"

"You mean the split?" Olivia said. She'd been quiet, but Del hadn't forgotten her. Her lack of movement and talking told Del that Olivia was the smartest thug in the bunch.

"Yes. My end. What is it?" Del asked.

"Twenty percent," Olivia said.

"Try again," Del laughed.

"That's standard," Olivia said. Her face was an unreadable mask, stony, but there was a slight lilt in her voice that told Del it amused her, and that offer had been meant to feel Del out.

"Ain't nothing standard if the head honcho gotta carry himself all the way east to a backwoods shit stain holler and negotiate." Del winked at Martin. "I get that right, darlin'?"

Martin laughed long and loud. It wasn't a musical laugh; it was hard and heavy. It made Del want to growl, and the hair on the back of her neck stood on end.

"I knew I would not be disappointed in you, Delilah."

"Oh, well then, that ought to be worth forty-five. Risk is all mine and moving your product around in massive amounts ain't gonna be like trucking a few kilos to New Jersey. You know that or you wouldn't even be bothering with me." This was moving fast, and Del was flying blind. She needed a breath and more information.

"I'd like to consider your offer. I'd need to study on it a

bit and make sure I can deliver. How about we meet tomorrow and make a final decision?"

Martin nodded and smiled. "Of course."

"I'll be in touch," Del said. She exhaled through her nose and willed herself not to inhale as she led them out.

Olivia was the last to get in the vehicle. She stood by Del and watched the others.

"We both know you're taking the deal," Olivia said.

"Oh, we do?" Del asked. Her hackles were up, and she had a prickly feeling all over her skin.

"You're too smart not to realize you have no choice."

Del laughed. "Opinions on how smart I am vary."

"Mine's the only opinion I trust," Olivia said. "Martin likes a late meeting. Make it after ten tomorrow night." She got in the driver's side and they drove away.

Del growled long and low as she watched them go. "I wanna know where they're staying. Also, how many more of 'em are in town, and, most important," Del said as she grabbed Cal by his shirtfront and growled at him, "How in the fuck I didn't know they was here."

CHAPTER 5

THE STAFF at the airport was foggy and dazed when questioned. Del had Cal round up all the agents. There were only three, and none of them had clear memories of the past twenty-four hours.

"No planes came in," Shirley Ryder said. Her voice was far away and when she said the words, her eyes glazed over, milky white.

"The fuck no planes came in," Del said as she grabbed Shirley's face and sniffed. She smelled like White Diamonds perfume and Vagisil cream, but over top of that was the whiff of ozone that indicated a spell. "She's been bewitched."

"By who?" Cal asked.

"What are you, dumb? By somebody in their group. But they ain't very good at it, because of the eyes. A good witch can do that memory spell and you'd never know the poor bastard had their mind fucked." Del let go of Shirley and turned to Cal.

"Send Mickey over to the Holiday Inn. Send James over to the Best Western. We're going to the Hampton."

When Del got to the Hampton Inn, she did not find Mia, the usual clerk, behind the front desk. She'd known Mia and her family for many years, and the girl was one of the people in her network Del thought she could groom for a management position someday. Mia was observant and cool under pressure, two things that Del knew were hard to teach. She had Mia do odd jobs, errands, watch special guests at the hotel, and Mia had always done well. If the visitors were here, Mia should have alerted her. Why she didn't was the question Del needed answered.

A fat, pimply kid with thick glasses and a sparse mustache sat in Mia's chair. He stared at his phone and didn't look up when Del approached the counter. The twitchy, mean feeling she got sometimes tried to burble up, but she held her temper in check. She rapped on the counter to get his attention. He looked up slow, then wrinkled his face a few times to push his glasses up on his face. He didn't greet her, he just stared.

"Where's Mia?" Del asked.

"She ain't here," he said, then looked back down at his phone.

Del took the phone from him and crushed it in one hand. She dropped the mangled mess on the counter.

"I can see that. Why is she not here?"

"Lady, you messed up my phone," the kid said. His fat acne marked face reddened, and he slapped his pasty, sweaty palms on the counter.

Del grabbed his greasy hair and slammed his face into the surface.

"You got two seconds to tell me or we're gonna see how fast your face travels through countertop."

"Nobody knows. She was here yesterday but didn't come in today."

Del let him up. "Get me her address. Now."

"The manager got it. I ain't—"

Del quirked a brow at him and let out a long, low growl.

"I'll call him," he said.

MIA LIVED in a big Victorian house in a bad neighborhood. Overgrown lawns and uneven sidewalks prevailed and trash littered the ground-fast food drink cups, chip bags, and plastic sacks. The whole place looked like poor city. It differed from poor country in that the trash in the country was more mechanical and useful—empty wash tubs, busted up coolers. City poor was disposable and useless.

The house and neighborhood were quiet. Del wasn't sure what to make of that. She knew it was likely to get livelier after dark, but even now she expected some sort of hustle—somebody holding, pimps, look-outs, but there was nothing. Nobody was on the stoops or in the yards.

"Go on around back. Have a look. I'm going upstairs," Del said. She got out of the Jeep and waited a beat as she studied the house.

"You sure, Del? Maybe it ain't a good idea to go up there alone." Cal hesitated.

"I'll be fine. Go on." Del walked up to the third-floor apartment. She looked in the window and saw nobody, but she could hear the tv playing soap operas. She sniffed the door. It didn't smell like magic. It just smelled like composite wood and cat piss. She knocked and waited. After a minute with no response, she tried the door. The handle twisted in her hand, and she opened it.

"Mia? You in here?" Del closed the door behind her and looked around. The place was a pig sty. Clothes littered the floor, and the sink was full of dirty dishes. The whole place smelled like gym socks and spoiled milk.

She found Mia in the bathroom, huddled between the toilet and the vanity. The girl had vomit all over her front and she rocked and banged her head against the cheap panel of the cabinet.

"Mia, hey…" Del whispered. She bent to look in Mia's face. When Mia saw her, her eyes widened in terror, and she screamed. She flailed around and pointed at Del as if she saw a monster, then tried to stuff herself into the space between the wall and the toilet.

"Whoa, Mia… easy… it's okay, it's okay." Del tried to calm her, but the more Del talked, the louder Mia screamed.

Unable to get her to stop, Del punched her. The girl's

head snapped to the side, and she slumped against the toilet. She was out cold. Del picked her up and carried her into the bedroom. She laid her out on the bed and made a phone call.

"Lila. Come pick up this girl at 112 Beecher. She's in the upstairs apartment. No, she ain't dead. Passed out. Keep her that way til we can get somebody to look at her. No, she don't need the hospital. Not yet. Stop asking stupid questions and get the fuck over here."

Cal came running in. "What was all that noise?"

"Somebody fucked her up," Del said.

"Like that memory shit?" Cal asked.

Del shook her head. "Don't think so. This is something worse. Look, you stay here and go with her. Lila is sending a van. There's an empty trailer out there. Tie her up. I'll be there directly."

"Tie her up? She done something?"

"No. Something bad's been done to her."

CHAPTER 6

THE AFTERNOON LIGHT streamed through the windows, catching dust particles in the rays, and making them look so thick that Del believed she could cut through them with a knife. Her gran had supper cooking—squirrel gravy and there'd be big, fluffy dumplings, Del's favorite. She hoped she'd get to stay to supper. She probably would. Her mama was out and about. Del hadn't seen her in a day or two and had wandered down to her gran's house by the river.

She loved staying there. The yard was enormous, with ample shade trees to climb. The river bank was steep in most places, but they could walk down in one spot and fish. Every morning her gran would take her for a walk back up in the woods, pointing out plants and herbs. She showed Del how to find mushrooms and roots, what was poison, and what was safe. They'd forage for wild edibles too-dandelion greens, nettles, and onions. Del felt safe and *alive in those woods. She loved to dig in the dirt and grinned when she held up something her gran had tasked her to find.*

Gran whistled while she worked. It was an old song about a girl and pine trees that always gave Del the shivers, but fascinated her at the same time. It was one of her gran's favorites and she always sang or whistled it while drying herbs, making potions and tinctures, and putting together spell bundles. Despite the subject, it was soothing and pleasant as Del sat at her little table and colored. The coloring books were old—her mom's from the sixties. One was about Disneyland when it first opened. Del didn't care. She colored every page that her mom had left, and she corrected the ones her mom had colored, making sure the shading was just right and the lines were clean and smooth.

"Ready for tea time, Sissy?" Her gran called from her workbench.

"Yes ma'am," Del answered. She cleaned up her artwork and supplies, then wormed her way back behind her gran's ancient arm chair to get at the shelves behind. They housed all manners of cups and saucers, little sugar bowls, figurines, and glasses. None of them matched. Del's gran collected them, and the shelves were a favorite place of Del's to explore. She loved pretending to make potions and teas with the little chipped porcelain tea pot. She'd ask her gran what ailed her, then she'd brew up a pretend potion to cure the ailment. They played that game for hours on rainy days.

Del selected her favorite tea cup, a blue one, blue like a picture of the Caribbean Sea she'd seen once. She wanted to go there someday and see water that blue, swim in it, and make friends with all the sea creatures she'd read about. That would have to wait until she grew up and had grown-up money enough to do things. In the meantime, she had her cup. She found her gran's favorite. No matter which cup she picked, her gran would smile and tell Del it was her favorite.

Today the favorite would be the one with the little yellow roses on it and the delicate, swirled handle. Del took them over to her gran, who had just brewed up the tea. She smiled at Del's choice.

"Yellow rose of Texas," Gran said, smiling as she turned the cup in her hand and looked at the little flowers. "I love this one. Good choice, Sissy." She kissed Del on top of her head then set to work pouring the tea. She plopped two sugar cubes in Del's and stirred it well. Del sat at the worn wooden table. Her gran put down a plate of chocolate chip cookies, then slapped Del's hand away from them as she set the blue teacup down in front of her. She sat across from Del and sipped the tea.

Del sniffed the cup. The tea smelled awful, like the outhouse on a scorching day. "It smells like turds," she said.

"No dirty talk, sis."

"Well, it don't smell good," Del said. She wrinkled her nose a few times and gagged. "How come it always smells so bad?"

"It don't smell bad to everyone," her gran said.

"Does it stink to you?" Del asked.

"Nope. It don't."

"How come I think it does?"

Her gran smiled at her. "Cause you're special. Now drink it up."

Del steeled herself, then took a sip of the foul-smelling stuff. It tasted as bad as it smelled, like throw-up and dirt. Del gagged again. Her gran had doctored it up with a lot of sugar, but it wasn't enough to mask that taste of filth.

"Gran, it tastes so bad," Del whined.

"Drink it quick then. Get it down the hatch and you can have a cookie."

The cookies looked wonderful. They were big and round and full of gooey chips, just like Del liked. She wanted one, but the tea was so terrible. She shook her head.

"No thank you," Del said, remembering her manners. "I don't care for no cookies."

"Delilah. Drink that tea," her gran said. Her voice wasn't mean. It was slow and low and still had her gran's pleasant lilt, but she'd used Del's full name and that meant business.

"I can't, Gran," Del said. She sniffed the tea, and her stomach rolled.

"You can. You have to. It keeps you safe from harm, sis."

"Harm from what?"

"From things to come. It will keep terrible monsters away. Someday you'll understand, just now you gotta do like I say. Drink it."

Del loved and trusted her gran more than anyone else in the world. If she said it was to keep monsters away, then it was, even if it tasted like turds and made her sick at her stomach. Del picked up her blue cup and thought about giant sting rays in the Caribbean Sea. She took a deep breath and downed the tea in one gulp. The nasty stuff burned all the way down and Del screwed her face up and cried a little. Her gran pushed the plate of cookies closer, but Del shook her head.

"My stomach don't want one right now," she said. She doubled over as a cramp hit her. "Hurts."

Her gran pulled Del into her lap and held her. "I know it does, Darlin. Breathe. It'll pass and it will protect you." She hummed an old mountain tune as she rocked Del.

"What is it, Gran?" Del asked. She snuggled into her gran's body and clutched at her as the pain moved through her.

"Wolfsbane," her gran said. She kissed Del's forehead and went back to her song.

Del closed her eyes and concentrated on the tune, the good clean scent of her Gran's apron, and the dancing dust in the light rays. The cramps and nasty taste faded, but Del didn't move. She held tight, safe in her Gran's embrace.

CHAPTER 7

DEL CROSSED her arms and shook her head as she stared down at the girl thrashing on the bed. Mia pulled against the leather restraints. She hadn't stopped screaming since she'd woken up. She sat up as far as she could and sobbed and screamed, spittle and tears flying in every direction. It wasn't angry screaming. It was fearful screaming. Mia screamed as if the Devil himself stood before her.

"Jesus, she is fucked up," Lila said. Lila Robbins had gotten fat. She'd always been kind of pudgy, but since Del had promoted her to a management position over the girls and she no longer turned tricks on the regular, she had put on weight. Lila was now as round as she was tall. She still had bad skin and greasy thin hair but was one of those people that made the most of every meager opportunity, and she excelled at managing girls. She was one of Del's oldest employees, and she was loyal. She wouldn't let anything happen to Mia if Del ordered it.

"Yeah, she sure is," Del said. They had to shut Mia up. The constant screaming was freaking everyone out. Del didn't want to hit her again. "What do you have around?"

"Pretty much everything, but how are we gonna get it in her?"

"I don't wanna give her nothing from the street. Call that orderly you know from over at the state hospital. Get him to bring you some shit for schizos. That ought to help her til I figure out what the fuck is wrong with her."

"Yeah. I'll call him. He won't do it for free," Lila said.

"Give him credit or whatever. Less you wanna listen to her yell like that."

Lila nodded. "Alrighty, Del. How you gonna figure this out? She acts like a fucking demon is standing there."

"Yeah. She's afraid of something all right." Del turned to Cal. "Go back to that hotel. Get the security cameras. See who talked to her."

Cal nodded. "Where you gonna go?"

"I'm going to see somebody who might know how to fix her," Del said.

THE LITTLE WHITE house sat amidst overgrown grass and unruly trees next to the creek. Del made a mental note to have some words with the third cousin she paid to take care of her Aunt Jewel's place. He wasn't doing good work, but he was taking her money. That wouldn't stand.

She climbed out of the jeep and walked up the old home-poured sidewalk. It was uneven and cracked, making it hard to walk on. Aunt Jewel shouldn't be walking on it at her age. Ninety was too old to mess around with falling due to poor concrete sidewalks. Del'd have it fixed.

Everything on the front porch was peeling and worn. The clapboard floors, the porch swing that squeaked as it swayed in the breeze. Everything around needed attention. Del got angrier and angrier at the lazy relation who wasn't doing his job. He'd be a pleasure to wail on later.

Del knocked on the wooden screen door. She waited for a few minutes, but nobody came. She opened the screen door and knocked on the window of the inner door. It opened and her Aunt Jewel scowled at her as she shoved a shotgun in Del's face.

"Who are you come a knockin'?" The old woman yelled as she pressed the gun in Del's cheek.

"Jesus, Aunt Jewel. It's me, Del." Del held up her hands.

The old woman squinted and looked over her glasses at Del. She poked her twice with the barrel of the gun, then smiled.

"Oh, Delilah. So it is you. Why didn't you knock right so I'd knowed it was you?"

"What's the right knock?"

"Well, not that one you done," Aunt Jewel said. She put the gun down beside the door and motioned Del inside.

"Why are you answering with a shotgun? You could have blown my head off. Who's been bothering you?" Del asked.

"Huh? Oh, I forgot to load it today. I'd just have to whack somebody with it. And believe me, I will," Aunt Jewel said. She and Del walked back the hallway to the big white kitchen. It was sparkling clean and full of herbs drying. It smelled fresh and earthy, just like her gran's house had.

"An unloaded gun ain't no good," Del said. "And who are you planning on whacking?"

"Anybody who don't knock right," her aunt said. She said it with a grumpy finality, and Del didn't press it further.

An old man sat at the kitchen table, eating a pimento cheese spread sandwich. His dentures sat on a saucer beside the sandwich plate. He gummed the cheese spread and white bread and stared straight ahead.

"Who's that?" Del asked, thumbing at the old man.

"Oh, that's Dwight." Aunt Jewel began rummaging around in the refrigerator. "Sit down there Delilah and I'll make you a peanut butter."

"Dwight? Why is this old man here, Aunt Jewel?" Del waved a hand in front of the old geezer's face. He didn't pay any attention, just kept chewing the bread.

"I look after him. He pays. Gives me his whole check." Aunt Jewel set a peanut butter sandwich down in front of Del, then sat down at the table. She popped the top on a can of Old Milwaukee and took a long swallow. "How's Leona?"

"She's dead, Aunt Jewel. Been dead thirty years."

"Oh, yes, that's right. She is dead. Well, I wondered why she didn't call last week." The old woman took another swig of beer. She clapped at the old man. "Dwight! Go on in and watch the westerns on the satellite. Me and Del gotta talk."

The old man sat still. Aunt Jewel reached over and hit him on the head. "Dwight! Get out."

The blow shook the man out of his daydream. He rubbed his head. "By god, you didn't have to whack me. I heard you."

"Move or I'll whack you again," Aunt Jewel yelled.

The old man got up, then shuffled out of the kitchen, cursing under his breath.

"I'm going to find me another old man. He don't listen."

"None of em do," Del said. "Aunt Jewel. You ever seen anybody that screams like they seen something awful?"

"Sure have," Aunt Jewel said. She finished the beer, then belched.

"Why'd they scream?"

"Because they seen something awful," Aunt Jewel said. "You're gonna have to give me more to work with Delilah."

"I ain't got much, except some new people in town."

Aunt Jewel helped herself to another beer. "What manner of new people?"

"Just regular ones. Vampire. Some kind of goblin or something. Other ones? I don't know. They look human, but the one smells kinda fishy."

"Fishy like fish or fishy like shifty?" Aunt Jewel looked interested.

"Like somebody left a trout out to rot," Del said. "Like fish and Sulphur at the same time."

"Oh, well that's who done it. Demon. Bad one. Real old."

"Huh. A demon? Really?"

"Girl, demons is common as ticks on a dog's ass. They're all over if you look for 'em."

Del had never dealt with a demon, or at least she'd not known it. From the way Martin smelled, Del knew she'd have known if she'd ever crossed paths with one of his kind before.

"What do you mean by old?"

Aunt Jewel shrugged. "I mean, old. Some of 'em are only average. They got a few powers. Possess people. One of em smells like fish and hellfire means they're old and powerful. You best steer clear."

"Too late for that," Del said. "How do I handle him?"

Aunt Jewel laughed. "You don't. I'd have to see your girl what looks afeard, but I'd say that demon done it. Got up in her mind and done things to her."

"Can she be fixed?" Del asked.

"Ain't you gonna eat your peanut butter?" Aunt Jewel asked. She looked mad about the food waste and like she'd not heard Del's question.

Del picked up the sandwich and took a bite. "Can you help this girl? She's off her rocker and she won't quit screaming."

Aunt Jewel shook her head. "No. Can't nobody help that

girl. She's seen terrible things, and there ain't no fixing that. Best put her down."

Del stopped mid-chew and stared. "No. There's gotta be another way. Can't you mix her up a potion or something to ease her mind?"

"No, I sure can't. Ain't no potion I know that can erase that pain."

Del shook her head. "I don't wanna hurt her. She's a good kid."

"Only help you can be to her now is to put her out of her misery. She's suffering. You chuck her in the looney bin and she'll rot there."

"Well, can't you come look at her first?" Del asked. It was a long shot to get the old woman to leave the home place, but she felt like she had to try.

The old woman shook her head. "No. I can't leave. It ain't safe, and besides, I got that old man to deal with. Look here, Delilah, sometimes things can't be fixed."

"Don't nobody know that better than me, Aunt Jewel, but this is only a young girl. Ain't her fault. I gotta try."

Aunt Jewel nodded. She heaved her creaking ancient body up from the table and shuffled over to a huge old chifforobe. When she opened it, Del's nose crinkled at the variety of smells that escaped. Herbs, dirt, flowers, and death. Jewel rummaged around, bottles clinking and clacking against one another. She found what she was looking for and held it out to Del.

"You can try this."

Del took the jar. A decomposing rat's head floated around in the amber liquid. "What the hell is this?"

"No dirty talk!" Jewel said. She whacked Del across the back of her head. "It's a spell to cast out a demon, but it likely won't work on her if she got hexed by some powerful one. Open it up and put it under her bed."

"You got anything to knock her out or calm her down?" Del looked at the rat and shook her head. "I mean, I need options."

"I already gave you the best one. If that spell don't make her better, you'd best just shoot her, Delilah. It's a kindness. I said my piece." Aunt Jewel held up her hand and sat back down at the table. She would say no more about it.

"All right then," Del said. She got up and kissed Jewel on the cheek. "Thanks. Look, I'm going to send some people out here to mow the yard and fix up some things. That no account Bittle kid ain't doing his job."

"Oh, I told that boy to get out. I never liked that Morgan County crew. All degenerates. That father got a girl in trouble once, she wasn't but fourteen and him married. I wanted to curse off his pecker, but Leona wouldn't let me."

Del laughed. "No, she wouldn't have let you do that."

"Oh, Leona thought of something worse. She dried it all up." Aunt Jewel cackled and slapped her knee. "When Leona got through with him, his pecker looked like a dried up fishin' worm. Taught him."

"Well, I'm going to send some of my boys out here to fix

things up. Anything you want done, you tell 'em. And try not to shoot them with that gun."

"I can't promise that," Aunt Jewel said. "If they vex me, I might."

"I'll see that they don't." Del hugged the old woman one last time.

She tossed the rat jar in the seat beside her and took off for Lila's.

CHAPTER 8

WHEN DEL GOT BACK to Lila's, the orderly was there. He had just finished injecting Mia with something, and his face was all screwed up and red.

"She spit on me," he said, wiping his face.

"Don't that happen to you every day in the looney bin? And as I recall, you don't mind body fluids all over you. We won't charge you extra for it," Del said. She watched Mia. The girl had calmed down some, but she still thrashed and mumbled. Her eyes were wide. "What'd you shoot her with?"

"Ketamine. But it should have knocked her out by now," he said. "I gave her a lot."

Del sat on the bed beside the girl and stroked her hair. "She's been through a lot."

Del opened up the rat jar and put it under the bed. Everyone gagged at the rank odor, but that was nothing compared to the smell of feces when Mia sat up, screamed, and shit herself.

"No way! I gave her enough to tranq a Clydesdale," he said.

"Yeah, well, wasn't enough," Del said. Mia yanked and pulled at the leather wrist restraint and kicked at Del. She growled and began speaking in a language that sounded like a cross between Arabic and garbage disposal.

"The fuck is wrong with her?" Lila yelled.

"Uh, well, a lot," Del said. She stepped back from the bed as it shook. Mia screamed and ripped one restraint off the bedpost. Del grabbed her arm and held it down.

"What the hell is happening?" Lila yelled. She had backed up against the wall. The psyche ward guy was beside her, staring open-mouthed and Mia screamed and yelled in tongues at them.

"I guess whatever is messing with her don't like that rat jar much," Del said. She struggled to hold Mia's arm down and growled as she put her full effort in to tying it to the bed.

"How do we know if it's working?" Lila asked.

"It must be, or she wouldn't be so riled," Del said. She looked at Mia. "Mia, you're in there. It's okay. I promise."

Mia turned and looked at her. She smiled a hard, mean smile. "Like you promised Nina?"

Del's face flushed, and she got that terrible rage in her gut that she always got when she thought of Nina, a rage she hadn't been able to control for twenty years now. She drew back but stopped herself from punching Mia. It wasn't the kid. It was whatever was done to her. She couldn't have known anything about Nina.

Del smiled at the kid. "I think you got one foot out the door, fucko." She picked up the rat jar and held it close. Mia screamed long and loud, then convulsed. She shook and spit flew out of her mouth as she thrashed. Del didn't back away; she held the jar closer still. Mia sucked in a huge breath and let out a terrible yell that turned into a groan. She rose one last time, her eyes wide, then she collapsed back on the bed, still and silent.

Del capped the jar and set it aside. The liquid in it turned black, and it bubbled and boiled in the jar with no heat applied at all. The glass was hot to the touch as the liquid inside moved.

"Mia, hey. Kid, you there?" Del said as she shook the girl.

Mia's eyes fluttered open and when they found Del's, Mia didn't look confused. "That won't help for long. Del. Those people. That man. Don't... don't..." Mia tried to form words, but it was as if an invisible bubble was around her mouth, preventing the sound from escaping.

"Yeah, I get it, kid. They're bad news," Del said. "So am I."

Mia shook her head, then vomited all over Del's shirt. It was inky and black. "No, you ain't. Just leave them be," she said.

The rat jar steamed and shook. Mia's eyes went wide with terror. She looked at Del and pleaded. "You gotta kill me Del. Please. I-I can't go back to all that and they're coming back for me."

"Mia, I ain't gonna kill you. We'll keep them away. I won't let 'em—"

Mia grabbed her hand. "You can't. And it's awful. Please. Please kill me. Promise me."

"It ain't gonna come to that," Del said. She had a terrible sinking feeling that it would come to that, that Aunt Jewel had been right. The glass jar shattered, and the putrid black liquid pooled out over the floor. It steamed, and Del could hear whispers and shrieks coming from it.

Mia looked at Del. "You gotta do it. Please Del! Plea—" Mia's voice was cut off and the gargling raspy voice came back. Then Mia shrieked and wailed as the black liquid on the floor caught fire.

"Get out now!" Del yelled at Lila and the man. They didn't hesitate. They ran out of the room and house as fast as they could. Del stepped back from the flames and pulled the .38 out of her waistband. She closed her eyes and gritted her teeth as she came to grips with her lack of options. Her face was grim and determined as she aimed the gun at Mia's head and shot her. When Mia collapsed, the flames went out. The room was smoky and smelled like burnt hair and blood and Sulphur.

Del tucked the gun in the back of her jeans, then pulled out her phone. She made two phone calls. The first was to Bobby Ring.

"I need you to come get a girl at Lila's. Listen here. This ain't one you can eat. She gets some respect... yes, I'm serious. You fuck with her and I'll feed you to your own hogs. Hurry up and get over here."

She hung up, then paused. She pulled a business card from her pocket and dialed the number on it.

"Hello, Olivia. How's eleven o'clock tonight? Yeah. Good. Little place called Marv's here in town. It ain't fancy, but it'll do. Oh, yes, I very much look forward to seeing you all too."

Del ended the call, then threw the phone across the room, shattering it. She stalked out of the house, past Lila, and the man, got in the jeep, and spun dirt as she flew out of the hollow.

CHAPTER 9

DEL DOWNED a full shot of whiskey, then another as she
waited for Martin and his crew to arrive. Del had all her
guys on alert. Cal had twenty guys patrolling just inside the
tree line of the woods behind the building. They were to stay
hidden and quiet unless Del called them out. She had five of
her best guys waiting inside. All of them paced and panted as
they picked and harassed one another. The tension and
magic hung in the air and it hummed with the nervous
wolves.

Del came from behind the bar and whacked Mikey
Donnelly in the head. "Quit all your yammering. You all
sound like scared old ladies."

She sat at the big round table in the middle. She kept
Marv's Tavern open after the old man had passed. The place
was worn down and outdated, with nicotine-yellowed

American Flag wallpaper and dark wood paneling. She hadn't changed a thing, and she knew Marv appreciated that. She knew, because the old fella's ghost still stood behind the bar, polishing glasses. He never said anything to anyone but her and if there were other people around, he said nothing at all, but he watched and scowled if he didn't like the people Del brought in.

Cal came in from outside. "They're here," he said. He motioned for the five guys to get up and stand around the edge of the room.

"Alrighty," Del said, "Send 'em in." She relaxed and put her feet up on the table as she sipped her whiskey.

Olivia entered first. Del noted that the woman had a quick look around the room and inventoried the men. She even noted Marv behind the bar and gave Del an amused half-smile.

Martin came in next. He was intentionally over-dressed in a black tuxedo jacket and crisp white shirt. He sneered at the bar and gave a little laugh, then his eyes found Del and he grinned his fake smile. "Delilah! You look lovely. What a great place. Charming."

Del could barely contain her hatred and disgust as she got a good whiff of fish and Sulphur that came from Martin in heavy waves of odor. "Did you get all dressed up on my account? Looks like Oscar night up in here. We ain't been this fancy since the series finale of Hee Haw."

The thin vampire and the cauliflower man came in. The cauliflower man sniggered at the bar, and the vampire curled his lip and nose in disgust. He looked like he had some insult ready, but a look from Olivia made him contain it.

Del looked to Cal. "Cal, how about taking all the boys outside."

He looked confused. He'd wanted her to keep everyone inside, ready for a fight, but Del knew there'd be no fight, at least not one they could win. Cal opened his mouth to protest, but Del gave a little growl and he nodded, then signaled to the boys to leave.

"We'll be outside if you need something," he said.

"Roger that," Del said. She pulled out a chair for Martin. "What are you drinking?"

"Whatever you're having," Martin said. He sat down in the chair, looked around the room. Del noted wry smile sniggering at his lips. "I gotta say, I love the ambiance. Not something you find anywhere."

"I'm drinking rye. How's that suit you?"

"Perfecto," Martin said.

Del went behind the bar and grabbed two glasses and the bottle of rye. She set them on the table, then looked to Olivia and the rest. "Help yourselves to whatever you like." She pointed to the vampire. "Sorry, Slim, we're all out of O neg." She almost laughed at the pained look on his face. She could have stocked in a blood bag, but she wasn't feeling very hospitable, especially not to a bloodsucker and definitely not to that bloodsucker.

Del sat down next to Martin and poured two drinks. She

held one out to him and her own in the air. "To new friends," she said.

"To new friends," Martin said. He clinked the glass against Del's and held it there a second, then sipped the whiskey and grinned at Del. "So, my offer is, you exclusively distribute my products throughout North America, using your connections and miracle network. Your end is 40%."

"That seems pretty straight forward," Del said. "What happens if I have to dump a shipment?"

"You don't," the vampire growled. "Are you a pro or just some hillbilly madam playing at crank dealing?"

Del stood up. She walked over to the vampire and smiled. "What was your name again?"

"It's Darius," he said. His long ratty face annoyed Del and he stank of mothballs and something plastic and powdery, it was right in Del's brain what he smelled like, like toys, those scented dolls little girls liked, Strawberry Shortcake. Del knew why he'd smell of those, and she held back her disgust.

"Darius," Del repeated. "Yes, sorry, I couldn't recall it. This is the second time you've spoken out of turn and insulted me."

"He never does learn," Martin said. He nodded at Del. "He can be useful though." Martin shrugged. "As you will."

Del grabbed the vampire by his shirt front. He weighed nothing to her, and he was airborne when Del threw him through the old jukebox. He screamed as she yanked him out and rammed his face through the glass a couple more times. The ancient jukebox shuddered and flashed, then played an old Conway Twitty song. The first strains of "Hello Darlin'" sounded, then as Del bashed him some more, Conway's voice slowed down, then halted as the machine whined and sparked. Del pulled the vampire out and flung him against the wood paneling. His face was ripped to shreds and blood poured from it. Del stared at him a beat or two and watched his face start to heal as he howled in pain. He'd heal soon. She thought maybe she shouldn't have lost her temper, but the plastic smell hit her again and she buried her regrets. She'd deal with him more thoroughly later.

Del sat back down at the table and poured herself another drink, then slugged it back. "He ain't permanently damaged, but he does need to learn some manners." She smiled and put the glass down. "Now, where were we? Yes. What about a dumped shipment?"

"Well, of course, problems do arise, however, I expect you to deal with it and recover our assets."

"So it's all on me?" Del asked.

"Let's hope we never have to have that talk," Martin said.

"Yes. Let's hope," Del nodded. "Okay, well, I could say no, but that gets us nowhere, I suppose. So instead of going nowhere fast, let's all go somewheres," Del said. She poured two more drinks and held her glass up to Martin's. "To partnerships," Del said, clinking the glasses together.

"Partnerships," Martin purred. He winked at Del and smiled, and from that cold, fake smile, Del knew that he thought he had Del trapped. Del smiled her own fake smile back.

"I have a few stipulations," Martin said. He motioned toward Olivia. "I'm going to leave some of my people to help. Olivia, Darius, and Fernando and a few of the Red Hand will remain behind, at your disposal."

Del nodded. "Well, I don't really need any help, but I understand you wanting to look out for your interests and test the waters. You're all welcome here."

Darius the vampire dabbed at his ruined face with a bar towel as it healed. He stared at Del with an undisguised hatred. The cauliflower freak looked around the room. He reminded Del of a kid in little league, way out in the outfield that picked clover flowers and his nose instead of shagging fly balls. She also thought Martin was too smart to keep a useless freak in his employ. Whatever the cauliflower man was, he wasn't just a nose picker, but he was meant to look that way.

And Olivia. Olivia sipped a vodka tonic and smiled at Del. She held up the drink and saluted. Olivia was the most dangerous one of all. Del had known it the second she saw her, and if there was a trap to be sprung, Olivia was a big part of both the bait and the killing device. Del nodded back and held up her glass.

"Perfecto," Martin said. "Well, we're all agreed and settled. Tomorrow, I shall return home. Olivia will coordinate everything from us." He stood up and held out his hand for Del.

Del took a deep breath and held it so as not to smell him as she shook his hand.

"You must come visit me. We'll have a fabulous time."

Del knew that would be a one-way trip to California. The trap had been sprung.

Del had seemed trapped before, and every time, she'd made the person regret their snare. This creature—he sure as hell wasn't a man—this creature was powerful, but he'd find out the hard way that Delilah Monroe wasn't pleasant to trap.

CHAPTER 10

DEL SHOOK HER MOM, *but she wouldn't wake up. An empty Jack Daniels bottle and a full ashtray on the bedside table told Del her mom wouldn't stir for a bit, and when she did, Del knew she didn't want to be around.*

She'd like to leave and go back to their own trailer, but it was closer to town and the walk back from the Holler was long for anyone, let alone an eight-year-old. She'd do her best to disappear into the woods until her mom woke up and it was time to go. It was best to avoid Junior and every other denizen of the Holler, including her father. Most especially him.

Del tiptoed from the room and kept tight to the wood-paneled wall. She slid past the little room she slept in, then past Junior's. She could hear him inside, playing his video games. He yelled and cursed at the TV over the sounds of video game gunfire. Del's eye was swollen and black where he'd punched her the day before yesterday. He'd caught her looking at his PlayStation. She'd never even touched it, but he didn't like her anyway, so he decked her and then strangled her. Del was wiry, and she had wriggled away, then kicked him squarely in the nuts. He left her alone after that, but she thought it best to steer clear.

The other people around were dirty, wild-looking men and sad, beaten-up, broken-down women. They lived in shacks and trailers that lined the dirt road of the Holler and went all the way up the hill to the tree line. The men came out of the houses from time-to-time, and the women sort of sat around and waited for them. They weren't mean, but the men scared Del. They looked at her funny, like they were hungry, and she didn't like it. One tried to talk to her once, grabbed at her. She bit him and kicked him in the shin. Since then, she'd kept clear of everyone in the Holler, even the nice old lady in the trailer that smelled like her Gran's.

The main one she liked to keep clear of was Galen. Her mom said she should call him Daddy, because he was hers, but he didn't seem like it. He barely talked to her, or to anyone, and he hit her mom a lot. He never hit Del, he just stared at her hard. He didn't stare like the nasty men; he stared like he was waiting on her to do something. There was a tension and expectation that Del's eight-year-old brain couldn't identify, but knew was there.

Galen was a gigantic man, the biggest, broadest, strongest one Del had ever seen. His massive hands could grab a man by the throat easily and Del had seen him break a dog's neck once, one-handed. It was a mean old cur and Del had no fondness for it, but

Galen had gotten annoyed by its growling and reached out and snapped its neck like nothing, then gone back to skinning a possum. That's what he did when he wasn't giving quiet orders to the men or beating somebody—he skinned things. That upset Del the most. He skinned everything. Nothing was too big or too small for him—Deer, raccoons, possums, rats, cats, dogs, squirrels-everything. Del hated seeing them, hated the smell of the fat and untanned pelts, hated watching him work. He was calm, and deliberate, and cruel about it.

She moved into the living room, which was littered with beer bottles and cigarette ash, and past the kitchen. Galen was nowhere to be seen. Del slunk out the screen door, which was propped open in the brisk spring morning, and she was almost home free to run into the woods, but then she saw him and she knew he saw her. He looked right at her and she froze.

"Where you goin' Delilah?" Galen asked. He sat at the weathered picnic table, skinning a cat. A cigarette dangled from the side of his mouth, the ash long and gray.

"The woods," Del said. She kept her distance and made her way around him.

"No, you ain't going out in them woods. And you best steer clear of 'em the next few days," Galen said.

It was cold out. The light wasn't strong yet, and it always took it a long time to warm up the Holler in Spring. Del shivered in her little long sleeved t-shirt. Galen seemed unaffected. He wasn't wearing a shirt or shoes. His skin was scarred up all over with big scratch marks and hunks missing. If he was cold he didn't let on at all. He just kept smoking and skinning the cat.

She hated watching the cat. It wasn't her cat. She knew better than to get attached to any animals around Galen or Junior, but it looked sad, not like it was sleeping at all. Its eyes were open and Del imagined it was still afraid of Galen. As afraid as she was.

But Del was a determined little thing, and she had figured out at an early age showing fear just made things worse, so she bowed up a little and shrugged off the cat.

"I go in them woods a lot. There ain't nothing to be afraid of," Del said.

"I didn't say you ought to be afraid. I said don't go in the woods." He pointed his skinning knife at her. "Stay out of 'em."

"Well how come?" Del asked. It was dangerous territory. Galen didn't like questions. Del measured the distance between them and figured she could run fast up in the woods before he could hit her if he was so inclined.

Galen cocked his head at her and laughed. She'd never heard him laugh before, and the sound scared her more than if he'd yelled at her. The laugh was loud and full and not mirthful. It was hard-edged and cruel.

"You think you can run fast enough to get away from me?" he asked.

"I reckon I can. I'm quick," Del said. She dug her little Keds into the dirt and coiled her muscles, ready to run if he twitched.

Galen cocked his head and looked at her for a second or two. He put down the skinning knife and stood up. His huge muscles rippled, and he towered over Del.

"Tell you what, Delilah, you make it to them woods, you get away from me, and I'll let you go anywhere you want," Galen said.

Del took off for the woods, spraying dirt and gravel behind her little sneakered feet. She was lithe and fast. Usually nobody could catch her, not even the big boys on the school playground. She could outrun everyone. She'd make it to the woods, then she'd be free of her dad.

Except she didn't.

Del got two steps from the woods when Galen caught her. Galen yanked her up by her t-shirt and held her tight to the trunk of a slippery elm. The force of it knocked the wind out of her, and Del gasped and struggled to breathe. He held her at eye level, easy as you please, like she weighed nothing. She finally got her breath, kicked out at him, then bit him on the hand as hard as she could. Del shook her head like a dog, bit harder, and a little growl escaped her.

Galen didn't budge. He ignored Del's bite and stared at her.

"You done?" Galen asked.

Del let go. Her mouth was bloody, and she tasted the copper tang, then spit and scowled at him.

"You might not be as worthless as your brother. I guess we'll see. But you best remember one thing, Delilah. You can't never outrun me." Galen leaned in close, then let out a long, low growl. He showed his teeth and Del could see the two big ones on either side of his mouth get bigger.

The growl triggered something in her and she stared right back at him, bared her own teeth, and growled back.

He laughed that hard laugh and tossed her back toward the picnic table. He walked over calmly, sat back down and resumed skinning the cat.

"Stay out of them woods," he said.

Del hurt. She'd landed hard on her back, but she picked herself up, dusted herself off, and stared at the back of his head, her little fists balled up as the rage bubbled and boiled through her. She'd show him. Someday. She'd show him when she was bigger.

Until that day, she'd wait, and she'd be ready.

CHAPTER 11

DEL SAT at her desk and cleaned a pistol. The smell of metal and gun oil were heavy in the air. It was eight o'clock in the morning and she sipped a glass of beer mixed with tomato juice as she worked.

Olivia walked through the office door. She carried a white paper bag with transparent grease spots and two cups of coffee. She pulled one of the desk chairs closer, sat down, and pulled two Tudor's biscuits out of the bag. She placed one near Del, along with a coffee, then sat back and took a bite of one herself. She nodded at the beer and tomato juice.

"That's your idea of breakfast?"

Del didn't look up. She put the gun back together. "It's a healthier breakfast than that gut buster you're eating," she said.

Olivia nodded. "Probably so. I brought you one."

"So you are tryin' to kill me," Del said. She finished with the gun and took a big drink of her beer.

Darius and Fernando slunk through the door. Darius steamed a little and his face was red where the morning sunlight burned him. He huffed and cringed at the light that streamed through the window.

"Can you close that curtain?" he yelled at Del.

"No," Del said. She finished the beer, then went for the coffee.

Darius started cursing at her in some Russian sounding language and moved toward the window. He yanked the blinds shut, then whirled and stalked to the desk.

Del didn't get up. She sipped the coffee and looked at him.

"You done?" she asked.

He scowled down at her and balled his fists up, but he backed off. His face had healed from where Del had run him through the Jukebox, but his hatred for her remained, and he wore it like the scars he would never have.

Olivia waved him off. "Enough, Darius. You have work to do. I suggest you go do it." She nodded at Fernando. "Take him too."

Raul nodded. "Very well," he said. He pointed at Del. "This isn't over."

"Likely not," Del said. She winked at him. "Now get the fuck out."

Darius stomped out and Fernando followed.

"What work's he got to do?" Del asked. She nodded at Cal, who followed the duo outside.

"Side project," Olivia said. She finished the biscuit, wadded up the wrapper, and tossed it in the trash can. "So, what's the plan for today?"

"I don't make too many plans," Del said.

"I don't believe that," Olivia said. She leaned back in the chair and propped her feet up on Del's desk.

Del noted the expensive high-heeled shoes. The bottoms were red. She'd seen that once in a magazine. The shoes were expensive, just like everything about Olivia. She was beautiful. Her shining brown hair was chin length and hung over one blue eye. Del had the urge to push the strands back, but she thought it would be akin to touching a jungle cat. You might touch it, but more likely you'd get your arm ripped off. Olivia shook her head and brushed it back herself. Del finished her coffee and leaned away.

"Well, I got a meeting today with the County Commissioner. Then I need to check on some people. Pretty much what I do every day," Del said.

"And the network? We're scheduled to pick up the trial load next week. Are you sure you're ready for the test run?" Olivia asked.

"Well, you do a test run for a reason, so I reckon we'll find out."

Olivia sighed and shook her head. "You know what will happen if you screw this up?"

"Oh, I got a fairly good idea," Del said,

"Really? Because you don't seem at all concerned, and I'm not convinced you're ready."

"And how would you know how to judge that?" Del asked. "You people came to find me. You must think I know what the hell I'm doing, else you wouldn't have made a deal."

"Delilah, it's my job to look out for Martin's interests. I have to stay on top of things and make sure they run smoothly." Olivia got up and walked to the window. She opened it and let the morning light filter in. She crossed her arms and stared out the window.

Del joined her. "So when shit don't run smooth, you got a worry. Til then, just stay out of my way."

"Do you understand what he is?" Olivia didn't look at Del. She continued to stare out the window.

"Ah, yeah. I'd say he was a big-time drug dealer."

Olivia shook her head. "Why are you acting like you don't know? You're not stupid."

"I don't gotta say everything I know," Del said. "If you know I know, why you want me to say it?"

"Werewolves. Never in my dealings with werewolves have any of you ever acted in your own best interest," Olivia sighed.

"You had a lot of werewolves, have you?" Del asked.

"Enough to know you're going to do something stupid," Olivia said. "Martin is… old and powerful. And sometimes unpredictable."

"Why do you work for him then?" Del asked.

"No choice."

"Fucking demon bullshit," Del said. She plopped down on the leather sofa. "Look, I ain't interested in your weird-ass demon nonsense. I agreed to do a job. I'll do it. I fuck up, you do what you want with me."

"It won't be me doing what I want with you, Delilah."

"Oh yeah? And what do you want to do with me?" Del asked. She grinned at Olivia.

"Punch you, mostly," Olivia said.

"Yeah. I get that a lot," Del said. She eyed Olivia and tilted her head. "You're a demon too."

Olivia narrowed her eyes, then nodded. "Yes."

"And that body? You're possessing that lady?"

"Yes."

"And what happens if somebody makes you leave that body?" Del asked.

Olivia let out a long breath. "She'll die. I've been in this body for 178 years now. If I vacate, she'll rot."

"Does she know?" Del asked.

"No. She hasn't really been here for a very long time. After a while, they just sort of go quiet. She'll whisper every now and then, but nothing coherent."

Del shook her head. "Seems cruel."

Olivia laughed. "You... a murderer, a werewolf, the personification of rage, not to mention crime boss, who's made countless people suffer, wants to lecture me about morality and cruelty?"

"I never took away nobody's choice," Del said, bowing up. She stood up from the sofa and went to the desk. She found a bottle of whiskey in it and took a swig, letting the alcohol burn a path through the rage boiling in her gut, like a controlled burn to stop a wildfire.

"That's ridiculous. Of course you have," Olivia said. "How many vampires have you turned to cook your meth? How many people have you swindled and strong-armed? How many girls have you—"

"I'm gonna stop you right there, Liv. I have never forced anyone to do anything. They make a choice. Choice has consequences. Sometimes, I'm the consequences." Del got in Olivia's face and stared her down. "You stole somebody's body. Took their life and never even let 'em rest in peace. You don't got no moral high ground. Ever."

"I never said that I did, Delilah. I just said you didn't either." She didn't back away, and they sat in silence for a few seconds.

Del stepped back and composed herself. Anger and fear and something else she didn't want to admit burbled below her skin and she swigged the whiskey again. "I have a meeting in an hour. After that, I'm gonna go out to a few places and check progress," Del said.

"Progress? On what?" Olivia asked.

"On the shipping network."

"Do you have a project plan? Something you can share?"

"So, you mean, like, did I write down my big old plan to ship illegal drugs, weapons, and people all around North America? Yeah. Hold on, I got me a fucking Power Point presentation," Del said, rolling her eyes. "You'll see when you see."

"Yes. I'll see when I see," Olivia said. She grabbed the whiskey bottle from Del and took a long drink, never breaking eye contact. "It's difficult to keep from punching you."

Del nodded. "It ain't never gonna get no easier."

CHAPTER 12

"Jesus, Merle, I never said you had to give me all the road contracts. The deal was you give me that big one for 676. You give 'em all to me and looks like you're bid riggin'," Del said.

"Well, that was what Cal said. He said you said you wanted all of 'em. I had to tell him no."

Merle Whitehead, County Commissioner of Denton County, was a great fat man with a black head of curly hair. He had it dyed in a salon over in West Virginia. He thought nobody would know he had it colored if he crossed the river. Stupid thoughts like that were the least idiotic Merle had. Some of his dumber ones involved hookers and gambling and being beholden to Delilah Monroe. He was an idiot, but he was well connected, and nobody had bothered to vote him out of office in fifteen years, so he was useful to Del. She kept him indebted, and he kept her supplied with county improvement projects that allowed her construction company to look legitimate.

"He never said that, Merle. Look, cancel the township ones and give them to Ted Davis' crew," Del said. "I want you to give the water treatment consulting to Aqua Source. And keep Dobbins in as trash for the county roads."

It looked like Del was spreading work around, but she owned part of all those companies. Merle wouldn't know that, he'd just have to do what Del asked. His missing left pinky finger reminded him what would happen if he didn't.

Merle looked from Del to Olivia, who sat in the desk chair next to him and said nothing. She had an amused look on her face as she watched Del. Del sat on top of Merle's desk and threw pencils at the Styrofoam drop ceiling tiles. They stuck in precise groupings.

"I'll bring it all up in committee, but Del... that new guy, the one that moved here from Virginia, he's making a stink about contract review," Merle said. "And he's calling for us all to disclose financials."

"So? Disclose 'em," Del said. She threw the last pencil in the tile and sat crisscross on the desk top.

"Me? I can't," Merle said.

"Then you're bad at this," Del said. "You talking about that Tim Gray guy?"

Merle nodded. "Yes. He's a cowboy and I don't think he's gonna play ball."

Del laughed. "Oh he'll play. I'll take care of him. You make sure them contracts get divvied up right."

"What about the Sheriff?" Merle asked. "He's been asking around about things."

"How is that news?" Del asked. "Jacob will always sniff around. He sniffs exactly what I want him to sniff."

"Well, he's just talking around to everyone is all," Merle said. "Making folks nervous."

"Well chill 'em out, Merle. That's what you do best," Del said.

"Who's she?" Merle asked, pointing at Olivia. When they'd come in, Del hadn't bothered to introduce her. Olivia had sat down and never said a word.

"She's my new ass-istant," Del said, smiling at Olivia.

"Well, it makes me nervy that she's here," Merle said. "I don't like nobody hearin—"

Merle squawked as Del grabbed him by his shirtfront, picked him up, and slammed his entire 400-pound body up against the wall. She held him there.

"I don't give a fiddler's fart what you like, Merle. I'll bring the fucking Queen of England and the Rockettes in here if I feel like it. Shut the fuck up and do your job. That's all you need to worry about." She let Merle down and he slid down the wall.

Sweat poured down Merle's red face, and he shook, his blubber jiggling as he cowered on the floor.

"I'll take care of all your worries. You ain't got no worries.

Except me. You get me?" Del pulled him up and straightened his shirt and tie.

"Yes. Yes, Del, I do," Merle said.

"Excellent." She patted him on the shoulder. "I'll call Sherri and set up another meeting in a couple weeks." Del motioned for Olivia to get up and they walked out. When they got to Del's Jeep, Olivia climbed in and shook her head.

"You really think violence is the way to deal with that guy?" Olivia asked.

Del started the Jeep and laughed. "That guy? No. Violence ain't usually necessary. He loves a bribe, and he's a degenerate gambler. He couldn't afford his lifestyle without me, but sometimes, he needs reminded." Del turned the Jeep out on to Main Street and then got out onto the State Route, headed south.

"What's his worry with the Sheriff?"

Del shrugged. "Jake is the one person can't be bought, and I wouldn't even bother tryin'."

"Why haven't you eliminated him?" Olivia asked. "He's an elected official. Have him voted out or take him out. Put your guy in."

"No. Jacob couldn't catch me if I walked into his office and cuffed myself," Del said.

"So he's inept," Olivia said. "That's why you're not afraid of him?"

"Never said he was stupid. I just said he couldn't catch me. He can catch plenty of other people, and he cares about folks here," Del said.

"You make no sense at all, Delilah. Any cop you can't control is a threat," Olivia said.

Del stopped the Jeep in the middle of the highway. She turned and stared at Olivia. "I been operating for over twenty years. I know this Valley. I know these people, and I know my business. Since I ain't in jail, I reckon you're gonna have to trust me."

Olivia stared out the side window. "If this gets screwed up, it won't just be you who suffers. Everyone in your life, everyone you ever cared about will suffer."

Del nodded as she started the Jeep and got moving. "I know."

"Do you?" Olivia asked. "They won't just die. They will suffer. Martin can—"

"Yeah, I know what he can do. And even if he couldn't do it, he's head of a cartel. I knew it was a shit deal when I took it."

"But you had to take it," Olivia said. "You had to take it when you interrupted the chain."

Del laughed. "Look, Liv, neither one of us is dumb enough to think that me beating up some two-bit pedo was what caught you all's attention. I doubt you'll ever be inclined to tell me how you knew me, but it wasn't that dipshit Spider. We've been on a crash course for a while now."

Olivia nodded and gave a little laugh. "All of that is true." She turned in the seat and looked at Del. "I'm not your friend, Delilah."

"Oh, I know. I ain't yours neither," Del said. "but?"

Olivia shrugged. "But what? I represent Martin. What he wants done, I get done."

"Sure, but… if that's all you're trying to do, why are you warning me? Trying to get me to understand how serious my situation is? I mean, I fucking know it's serious. Most of my situations are serious. If I mess this shit up, you kill me and go back to drinking margaritas. What else are you playing at?"

"I just get the feeling you're thinking of playing a game. Like you can win it. You can't," Olivia said.

Del smiled. "Lady, I've been playing a game my whole life. I learned a long time ago I was never gonna win at it," Del said.

"Then why do you play?" Olivia asked.

Del looked at her and smiled. "'Cause it's the only game there is."

CHAPTER 13

THEY DROVE for about thirty minutes. The hills gave way to broad river bottoms, and the highway ran along next to a wide, winding river. The fields next to it were full of tall corn, bright green and lively in the summer heat. They came to a road that led down to the water and Del turned off on it. At the end was a huge dock with three coal barges tied off.

Del showed the security guard a badge, and he motioned them through.

"How in the hell did Homeland Security clear you for a TWIC badge?" Olivia asked.

"I know a guy," Del said.

She parked the jeep next to a white van that said, "Eckert Food Services." A tall skinny man stood outside it, smoking. His hand shook, and he jumped when he saw Del.

"Dennis. Everything ready?"

"Hey, hey Del. Um... yes, just waiting on the truck." His hands shook as he stubbed out the cigarette and eyed Olivia.

"Her? My new ass-istant," Del said with an amused smirk on her face. She liked that word. "You picked it up from my dealership in Shade?"

"The truck? Yes. Just like you said." Dennis lit another cigarette. His eyes darted around the yard. Workers finished loading coal and crates on the barges.

"Is the truck late? These fellas gotta go in an hour," Del said.

"A little," Dennis said. "We had some trouble at the warehouse."

Del scowled. "What kind of trouble and why didn't you call me?"

"Well, Del, I didn't think it was no big deal, it just took a little longer to load the trailer."

"What? That don't make no sense. Shouldn't have been no delay." Del narrowed her eyes and pulled out her phone. She dialed Cal.

"Why was there a delay loading the truck at the Millersburg warehouse? There wasn't one? You're sure? Okay. Thanks." She hung up the phone and smiled at Dennis. He shifted from foot to foot and held up his hands.

"Look that's just what I got told when I called—"

Dennis squawked when Del grabbed his ear. She hauled him away from the van and into a little trailer that served as an office. She motioned for the two men at desks inside to leave. "Take a break, fellas." She kept hold of Dennis, who cried. The two workers vacated, leaving Del, Dennis, and Olivia alone.

Del let go of Dennis. He fell on the floor.

"Start talking," She pulled a folding knife from her jeans pocket. "Or I start cutting."

Dennis held up his hands. "It's… it's fine… ah, we got it sorted out. We're just a little late. It's gonna be fine, I promise."

Del nodded. She reached out, grabbed his hand, and cut off the tip of his pinky finger so fast, Dennis didn't register she'd done it until the blood gushed. "You got plenty more to cut."

Dennis screamed and held his finger in his shirt to stop the bleeding. "I swear, just a delay.They had a forklift break."

Del grabbed Dennis by his hair and slammed his face against the side of the desk. She cut off his earlobe. "These ain't at all important parts, Dennis. What should I cut off next?" She flipped him over and grabbed his crotch. "I know…"

"Okay… Okay… Del, please. It was the Feds. They put a tracker on it." Dennis held up his hands. "I-I was gonna tell you first thing, but—"

"No, you wasn't. That's okay though." Del smiled. She let go of Dennis' balls and folded her knife up.

"How is it okay?" Olivia asked. "You've got the DEA involved now? This isn't a good start."

Del grabbed Dennis by his shirt collar and lifted him up.

"This idiot has been flipped for over a year. Didn't think anybody knew, Denny?"

"I-I ain't... You got it wrong Del." He blubbered and cried.

"No, I ain't got it wrong. You flipped after they caught you with all them pills down in Palmer. I told you not to get greedy." Del patted him on the shoulder. She sat down in one of the desk chairs, calm.

"Please Del. I didn't tell 'em nothing. I swear I didn't tell them anything for the case on you," Dennis said. He got on his knees in front of her.

"You're the dumbest liar in the world, Denny. You always was." Del picked him up and set him on his feet. "But it's okay. Let's all get going. No use waiting around now."

Dennis looked confused. "You don't want it loaded on the barge like normal?"

Del pushed him out the trailer door. He held his bloody finger stump close and the blood from his ear streamed down his neck into the collar of his polo shirt. "They can load it like always. It's fine." She smiled when she saw Cal waiting by the van.

"Denny, you've had a day. Cal's gonna take you to our doc and get you fixed up." She shoved Dennis at Cal. Dennis scrabbled around in the gravel and panicked.

"Please Del. I've known you since third grade. You know me, know my wife, my kids." Dennis looked at Cal, who stood stone-faced. "Please. Don't"

"Don't what? Come on, Denny. It's all okay. Cal is going to make sure you get where you're going. That's all." Del opened the passenger side door of the van. "Now come on. I got other shit to do today."

Dennis sighed. He wept, snot bubbled in his nose as he relented and got in the van. When Del shut the door, he put his face in his hands and cried.

Del walked around to the driver's side. Cal was already in and started the engine. "When you drop him off, next stop is over at Bealsville. Call me when you check on it."

Cal nodded. "Shouldn't take long." He rolled up the window and backed the van out, then took off back up the road to the highway. The van passed the box truck they had been waiting on. It also said "Eckert's Food Service." Del ignored it and got in her Jeep. She started the engine, and they followed the van out.

"So that's royally fucked up," Olivia said. "That was your plan and now DEA is on it? Not good, Delilah."

"Who said that was my plan?" Del asked.

"Isn't that why we're here?"

Del shook her head as she turned out on the main highway and headed for home. "No. Dennis needed dealt with."

"But what about the shipment? The DEA is going to seize that cargo for sure," Olivia said.

"That would be dumb. That shipment contains the food for them barge guys. Enough to get through til New Orleans."

Olivia squinted her eyes. "You knew he was a rat?"

"Of course I did," Del said.

"Why did you toy with him? Put yourself in that position?"

Del shook her head and looked confused. "What position?"

"To get caught. One of those Teamsters could have seen. More rats."

"Docks are always full of rats. That's why you bait 'em good. Everyone there just saw exactly what I wanted 'em to see. I ain't gonna get caught over Dennis."

"So that test shipment is screwed," Olivia said.

"That ain't the test shipment," Del said. "The test shipment left three days ago via railcar. And another one via truck."

"You lied to me?" Olivia said, her voice incredulous and scoffing, like she was hurt.

"No. I handled my business," Del said. "If everyone is looking at them barges, they ain't looking elsewhere."

"What if they're looking everywhere?" Olivia said.

"Well, you wasn't and you're smarter than cops," Del said. She winked at Olivia and grinned.

"You'd better hope all I ever do is punch you, Delilah," Olivia said.

"Time will tell," Del said. "Time will tell."

CHAPTER 14

WHEN CAL WALKED in the office, Del wrinkled her nose. He smelled of pig shit and sour milk.

"How are the Ring boys today?" Del asked. She didn't look up from the newspaper.

"They're filthy," Cal said.

"That they are," Del said. Billy and Bobby Ring had been covered in pig shit and rot since their mama had plurped them out. They lived on a filthy generational pig farm that could be smelled from five miles away even when there was no wind. Mix in the fact that they were ghouls and delighted in eating dead things, and the Ring Boys would turn anyone's stomach.

"Dennis is fine," Cal said. He started to sit down in one of the chairs and Del waived him off.

"Are you stupid? Don't sit in them chairs smelling like

that. They'll be fucked up." She ignored the comment about Dennis. She doubted very much that he was fine, but at least she'd never have to deal with him again.

"Alright, then I'm going on home. I'm gonna shower before the Turn," Cal said.

"I doubt you'd smell much worse when you woke up, that's for sure," Del said. "Hear anything from Davis?"

Cal nodded. "Shipments all made it for cross docking. No problem. They should be in Minneapolis tomorrow afternoon."

"Good. We'll meet at 2 at Kitty's," she said. She stood up and flexed. The Turn had her all wired and prickly feeling. All the sparring with Olivia hadn't helped that either. Del felt a pull at her stomach that she hadn't felt in a long time, not since she'd been a rookie at all this. It wasn't about the Turn, it was about Olivia. Del didn't like it. It was a complication, and it was something that threatened a memory that Del simultaneously hated and was terrified of forgetting.

She tried to banish it from her mind as she drove out to the Hollow. She was the last one through the gate and she parked, then closed it behind her. Del walked over to a small camper trailer and knocked on the aluminum door.

"Hey, Glenna, get out here and seal it up," Del yelled. She was shocked when Olivia came out of the trailer, smiling and leading Glenna, the little old witch Del had stationed, to put up the barrier. "What the fuck are you doing here?" Del asked. She'd begun to sweat and her stomach lurched and gurgled. The Turn was close.

"Nice night to be out here," Olivia said. She pointed to Glenna. "And I enjoyed meeting your pet witch."

"It's a dangerous night to be out here," Del said. A cramp hit her and she barely kept herself upright. "And she's an employee, not a pet. That ain't how we do things here."

"Dangerous? For me? Hardly. I'm not worried about a few werewolves," Olivia said.

"Oh really?" Del laughed and pointed to the dozen men stripping off their clothes and growling as they readied for their transformation. "They all feel different. They'll rip you apart. You best get gone."

"And you?" Olivia asked. She smirked at Del.

Del's face grew hot and next to the cramps, she felt a rage bubble in her guts. "I'd tear you to pieces and not think a thing about it."

"Except you would, Delilah. No need to worry. I just came to tell you I'm going back to California for a few days. I'll be back Friday."

Del doubled over as another cramp hit her. "What? You couldn't have left me a voicemail?"

"I like face-to-face communication," Olivia said. "Plus, I was curious to see how you managed all this. Quite impressive."

Del's teeth had already stared to elongate, and they ached as they grew. She snarled at Glenna. "Glenna! Get fucking busy. Get that barrier up and get on the other side!"

"Why do you care if you get loose? Isn't that part of the

fun?" Olivia knelt down and examined Del. Her voice was calm and gentle. "You're scared of what you are. Don't be."

"Scared? I ain't scared. But you should be," Del said through gritted teeth as a wave of pain and nausea hit her. She threw back her head and screamed as she felt the bones shift and break. She shook and looked to the witch. Glenna had just finished dumping a jar of white powder out along the gate. She murmured a few words, then climbed up and over the gate.

Del turned back to Olivia. "Get over that gate. Now."

Olivia laughed. She sat down in a rickety old lawn chair and crossed her legs. "No, I think I'll enjoy the beautiful summer evening and the fine view of the stars," she said.

They were just beginning to be visible against the blue hombre of the evening. The moon made its appearance from behind a cloud and as soon as the boys saw it, they all howled and screamed and transformed.

Del fell to her knees. She hadn't undressed and her clothes were drenched in sweat. They stretched and ripped as her body changed. She screamed. The white-fiery agony was relentless as every one of her muscles ripped apart and grew back bigger and meaner. Her clawed hands dug into the dirt and she looked up at Olivia, one last plea on her lips before everything went black. "Please, Liv, I don't want to hur—" but her word was cut off and the last thing she saw was Olivia's face just a few inches from hers, her hand cupping Del's face, unconcerned about the danger.

"You won't. I promise," Olivia said.

CHAPTER 15

AFTER THE LAST night of the Turn, Del stumbled out of the woods and made her way to her Jeep. Covered in blood and tufts of hair from the deer she'd mauled, she grumped down the pathway. Normally, she'd have clothes from the caches stashed at the edge of the woods, but nobody had stocked the bins the night before. Discovering that had made her grumpy and her foul mood was enhanced by the pain and ache she had as she healed. The last day was always the worst, after two other nights of physical trauma. When she'd been twenty-five, it had been a lot easier, the aftermath. A good sleep, a good feed, and a few chugs of whiskey and she'd have been fine. Now, it would take her three days and three times the whiskey to feel decent again.

As she limped down the path, naked and sore, the gravel cut deep into her feet, the chill of the morning bit just a little more than normal, and her mood degraded further. She stopped at the little trailer and banged hard on the door. "Glenna! You fucking forgot my clothes again!"

Glenna didn't answer, which was odd, she was supposed to be around of a morning to help everyone get moving. Normally, she'd be cooking something and have Del's morning concoction ready, but today, it was silent. The boys had returned earlier and were at their trucks, putting on clothes. Del called to Cal.

"Where's Glenna?"

Cal shrugged as he pulled on sweat pants. "Dunno. Didn't see her yet."

Del scowled and opened the door.

She didn't need her augmented sense of smell to know Glenna was dead. The coppery scent of blood was heavy in the air of the little trailer. Glenna's body lay on the linoleum floor of the galley kitchen, her wide, dead eyes stared up at the ceiling, a look of panic and fear still in them. It was hard to shock Del. She'd seen violence and death in so many forms that nothing really surprised her, so she wasn't shocked by what she saw so much as confused.

Glenna's body had been ripped open from crotch to sternum. All of her internal organs were missing—heart, lungs, liver, every inch of intestines. No blood remained. A little had splashed around on the linoleum, but it was smeared and looked to Del like somebody had licked it up. Waste not, want not, her gran used to say. The cuts on the torso were jagged, not smooth, so she knew no knife had done it. It

looked like somebody had field dressed Glenna with a dull
hook.

Del sat still for a second, closed her eyes, and inhaled
deeply. She filtered out the smell of Glenna's corpse—the
smell of shit and piss and blood and meat—and concentrated
on the other smells. One was gamey and wild, like the smell
of goats. She had smelled it a few times before and knew
where it came from. But there was something else too, a
more familiar smell, one she'd smelled every day for the past
month. It was human, but not, and it was distinctive.

Del opened her eyes and cracked her neck. Why Olivia
and that cauliflower freak, Fernando, had killed Glenna, she
didn't know, but they had. Del looked around the trailer.
Glenna kept a few potions, just random healing balms and a
few protection wards that might be useful in the hollow.
Nothing had been disturbed and nothing of note appeared
missing.

Del held her breath and opened the cabinet that she
normally avoided. She stepped back from it and bent down
to have a look inside. The last wolfsbane jar was still there.
She figured if they were after anything in the trailer, it must
have been that. It was powerful stuff, strong enough to keep
everyone in the hollow and off the road during a moon. Del
could think of several uses for it should anyone decide they
wanted to use it against her, but apparently, it hadn't been
what they'd been after.

She didn't bother closing the door. The trailer would be
gone by midday and the wolfsbane along with it. She

opened the little refrigerator and smiled when she saw a fresh batch of her morning shake. Glenna had stocked that. Del popped it open and went to drink, but stopped herself. She was thick headed and slow sometimes, but she had learned in the last thirty years never to trust anyone or anything. She put the bottle to her nose and smelled. She caught the delicious whiff of the shake, freshly ground meat, a few herbs, and something else. Dead blood and wolfsbane. Not much, but enough that if she drank that shake, she'd be sick for a week. She tossed the shake into the sink, then rummaged for some clothes. She found a t-shirt and jeans, the same that Glenna was supposed to stash but hadn't gotten to, and she pulled those on, then exited the trailer.

She motioned for Cal and Danny. They loped over and waited for instructions.

"You two, take the trailer over to the Ring boys. Feed Glenna to the pigs. Don't let the Rings eat her."

Cal looked green, and Danny puked.

"What? She's dead?" Cal asked.

"Yep. Nasty business. Look, I don't like them eating on people I didn't hate. Glenna was dumb sometimes, but she wasn't hateable," Del said. "Make sure them pigs get her. Better way to end up than for them boys."

Cal nodded. "Who killed her?"

"Well, that's easy. The hard part is the why," Del said, "And that I ain't for sure of right now." She motioned to Cal's truck. "You all hook up and take the whole trailer. After you get rid of Glenna, take that trailer to Harvey over at the crusher and see that it's cubed up."

She pointed at them and narrowed her eyes. "Crushed. You get it? Don't strip it. Don't fucking sell it. Crushed. Don't take nothing out of it except Glenna. You understand?"

Both men nodded but looked confused. "What's the big deal about the trailer, Del? Can't we keep it out here?"

"Just do like I tell you," Del said. She stretched and her back screamed at her as she did. Her head pounded, and she needed food and water soon. "When you get done, meet me at Kitty's."

Del got in her Jeep and checked her phone. She had five missed calls. None from Olivia. She'd expected her back today, but she had returned sooner. Olivia was too smart not to know that Del would have been able to smell them on Glenna. So they weren't trying to hide what they'd done. Why? That bothered Del much more than the poisoned shake or the dead witch. What was their angle? She let her brain spin on it as she drove, but could come to no conclusion. The mystery coupled with dehydration and the healing from her Turn made Del's head pound and her mood darker. What she saw when she pulled into her driveway did nothing to improve it.

Jacob Newsome, County Sheriff, and her oldest living acquaintance was parked in her drive. It wouldn't be the first time she'd rolled up on him outside her house, while she was covered in blood and gore. It wasn't going to be a big deal, but it was an inconvenience.

Del killed the engine and got out. Jacob got out of his truck, put on his Sheriff hat, and crossed his arms as he looked Del over.

"Why are you always covered in blood?"

"Why are you always bothering me?" Del asked. She stalked past him to the house. "You want coffee or what?"

He nodded and followed her inside.

DEL'S first stop was the kitchen. She rummaged in her refrigerator and found the pickle juice. Then she grabbed a bottle of whiskey. She chugged the whiskey first, then the pickle juice, then finished with more whiskey until she felt the pain and ache fade a little.

"I have never understood how you can do that," Jacob said. He sat down at her bar.

"It's for the best you don't," Del said. She put a pot of coffee on, then scrubbed her face clean in the kitchen sink. She drank another healthy slug of pickleback as they waited for the coffee.

"Nancy bought one of them single cup things. The Keurigs or something," Jacob said.

"That coffee tastes like shit," Del said. When the pot was done, she poured a cup for Jacob. "What do you want?"

Jacob sipped his coffee. "Been some interesting people in town of late."

"Yeah? Well ain't that something," Del said. She stretched and her back popped audibly.

"Jesus," Jacob said, wincing as he drank his coffee. "Maybe you ought to see a chiropractor."

"Wouldn't help. That's all you come here for at seven am? To tell me you seen some new folks in town?" Del switched to water and chugged a half-gallon.

"You ain't gonna help me at all, Delilah?" Jacob asked. "Because they don't seem like people, you'd care to let hang around."

"If you want 'em run out of town, do it your own self," Del said. "I ain't the damn Sheriff."

"I'm ignoring the fact that you're covered in blood and hair and you just drank a fifth of whiskey first thing in the morning. You can't give me a little help?" Jacob poured himself more coffee. Del opened up the whiskey and added a shot to his mug.

"It ain't illegal to be covered in blood," Del said. "And it sure as hell ain't illegal to have whiskey for breakfast."

"Well, now you're just bein' obstinate," Jacob said. He drank his spiked coffee.

"Jacob, best thing for you to do is steer clear of them people and stick to your regular shit."

"The Feds called me."

Del shrugged. "So? They can call all day long. What do you care anyway?"

"You really gotta ask me that? After all these years?" Jacob asked. His face looked pained and hurt. "I think maybe you're mixed up in something beyond you."

Del laughed out loud and shook her head. "You always was late to the party, Jake." She came around the bar and cupped his bearded cheek. His face was lined and worried, and his beard had grayed as he aged. "Stay away from 'em. I'll be fine. Or I won't. Either way, it's no worry of yours."

He grabbed her hand and held it. "We're the same age and you look the same as you did thirty years ago. Not a wrinkle or a bit of grey. You'll always be a worry for me. Not just because of all the shit you run in this county. You know it, Del."

"Everything is going to be fine," Del said. She squeezed his hand, then pulled away. He wouldn't give up. He hadn't given up in twenty years. Normally, it just annoyed her. This time, it worried her. She strode off toward the shower. "When you finish your coffee, put the mug in the dishwasher, Sheriff, then get the fuck out of my house." She waved at him but didn't look back.

CHAPTER 16

ONCE DEL SHOWERED AND ATE, she headed over to Kitty's. It was a county staple, one of the most famous places in the area and the only strip club for fifty miles. Del had taken it over years ago and, with the help of the girls who worked there, turned it into a thriving hub of cash and information. It sat at the edge of a steep hillside. Two giant boulders, one on each side, had crashed down years ago, but Kitty's remained in the middle. Defiant, as it waited to be crushed from above.

Del pulled into her normal parking spot. The music blared even at ten am on a weekday and there were ten men in there, all of them old and eating the free breakfast buffet. They downed powdered eggs and cheap bacon right along with morning beers as they watched a girl wind herself around the pole.

"Morning fellas," Del said as she walked through and back to her office. She knew all of them. They were old geezers with nobody to take care of them. The girls looked out for them and they returned the favor by tipping well.

"Morning, Del," they all echoed back. They didn't turn to look at Del, they kept their eyes on the stage and the girl as they gummed their eggs.

Del passed one of the regular girls, Tina. She wore a big red wig, an American flag bikini, and little white star pasties. She had tied a matching flag bandana on her neck. "Charity in the back?" Del asked.

"Yeah. She is. How are you Del? Ain't seen you in a minute," Tina said.

"Been busy." Del sniffed the girl and smelled something funny. She pulled the bandana down and noted the wound on her neck. "What the hell, Tina? No fucking vampires. You know the rules."

"Aww, come on Del. It wasn't here," Tina said. "And it ain't what you think."

"I'm sure it's exactly what I think," Del said. "Better not be here." She pointed at Tina and headed to the back. "Steer clear of vampires."

When she got to the office, Charity sat behind the desk, counting stacks of cash and working on a computer. Charity was an old friend. Her hair had faded to a brown-grey, but she still colored it bright red, and she had gained seventy pounds, but she was sharp as a tack, and Del trusted her above anyone else in her organization.

"Morning, Del," Charity said. She didn't look up from the money.

"Morning, Char." Del helped herself to a beer from the small refrigerator in the corner and plopped down on the sofa. "I seen Tina out front. That idiot has a big ole vampire bite on her."

"Yeah, she thinks she's foolin' me with that stupid bandana," Charity said. "I was gonna talk to her after I finish up."

"What vampires are dumb enough to hang around here?" Del asked. She took a long drink of the beer and winced as her back spasmed. She was healing more slowly than normal.

"The only one has been that foreign one. Your associate," Charity said. "Him and that squatty fella with the lumpy skin. They run up a tab too."

"Oh they did? You authorized it?" Del asked.

"I did. I figured I'd speak to you about it soon. Seems I was right." Charity finished with the money. She looked up at Del. "You look like shit, Delilah."

"Yeah, well, my time of the month," Del said. She finished the beer and tossed the can in the trash. "How often are those two coming in here?"

"Two, maybe three times a week," Charity said.

"And what tab are they running up? They don't drink."

"They do. The squatty one guzzles booze like it's his job." Charity heaved herself up and out of the desk chair, poured herself a cup of coffee from the machine, and sat in the chair opposite Del. "I don't like at all, but they come with that bunch of bikers you said to keep an eye on, so I figured better here than some other place."

"You missing any girls?" Del asked. Charity was right. If those two were here, at least Del would know their business. But vampires were bad in clubs. People ended up missing, and that brought unwanted attention.

"Two. Misty Dawn and Astrid."

Astrid was a big girl and friendly. She did well in the place where most of the clientele was after more than just tits in their face. Misty was a single mom with three kids and a meth problem. They worked hard to keep her square and her kids out of foster care, but Misty was tough to keep on the straight and narrow. Del had known her mom, Virginia, for a long time.

"You call Virginia?" Del asked.

Charity nodded. "Sure did. Misty left the kids with her. She ain't seen her in two days. That ain't unusual, Del."

"No, but it ain't good either," Del said. "Where's Astrid stay?"

"Little apartment over Beeman's Antiques," Charity said.

"You send anybody over there?"

"Not yet. I was gonna today."

"Don't bother. I'll check it out," Del said.

"Might be good if you let somebody else do that, Delilah."

"Nobody else will know what they're looking for," Del said. She got up, grabbed another beer, and chugged it.

"Lotta new people sniffing around. Jacob found you?"

"He did. This morning."

"Feds, Delilah." Charity sipped her coffee. "Might be best if you laid low and let somebody else go looking for trouble for once."

"I ain't afraid of Feds, Charity." Del sat back down on the couch. "They ain't got shit on me."

"They'll find them some, they sniff around long enough." Charity shook her head. "And besides that, you attract weird trouble of late. Them new pals of yours ain't exactly low profile."

"They ain't my friends," Del said.

"No, they ain't. But I am, and I think you should send Cal or Buster over to Astrid's." Charity sat back in the chair and crossed her arms. She scowled at Del. "But you won't. You'll go on over there yourself."

Del laughed as she got up and walked over to Charity. She kissed her. "Cal will be here in a bit. You can square up with him, and he'll make the runs for you. Tell him I want to meet him at my office at seven."

"Be careful, Del. I got a bad feeling about this," Charity said.

"I got nothing but bad feelings," Del said as she left out the back door.

CHAPTER 17

DEL'S first stop was at Misty Dawn's mom's place. Del had known Virginia Powell for forty years. They'd gone to school together since junior high. Virginia was a little churchy for Del's tastes, but she'd had big thick glasses and thicker thighs in eighth grade, which made her a prime target for boys on the bus. Del punched several of them for bothering Virginia, and they'd been friends since. Del found her sitting on the porch of her trailer, mending a child's pair of jeans. Misty Dawn's dirty little kids scratched around, playing in the sparse dirt and gravel in front of the trailer. When Del pulled up, all four of them ran to her Jeep and started climbing on it like a tiny zombie horde. Del stepped back from them. They were snotty and looked lousy as they yelled. She'd have preferred zombies to viruses and head lice.

"You'uns get off that vehicle right now!" Virginia yelled.

The kids ignored Virginia.

Del made her way up to the porch. She sat down on the rickety glider.

"Sorry about them kids, Del. I pray on it, but I can't do nothing with them," Virginia said.

"They're just kids is all," Del said. She winced as the little boy spit on her license plate.

"They might be demons straight from Hell," Virginia sighed, "But they're my cross to bear."

"Not technically," Del said. "Where's Misty Dawn?"

"Ain't seen her in three days," Virginia said.

"She didn't say where she was going?"

Virginia shook her head. "She don't never say. Just said she was gonna be working. Probably just laying out high somewhere." Virginia closed her eyes and muttered a prayer.

"She ain't working at the club," Del said. "What other job would she mean?"

"Oh, gosh, Del, I sure don't know. You don't know?"

"No, I don't. But I'll find her," Del said. She reached over and patted Virginia's knee. "You got enough to feed them kids?"

"Well, yes, Del. We're fine," Virginia said.

Del knew they weren't fine. Misty Dawn sold her grub stubs and Virginia still had to work at the Walmart. She was behind one month on the rent for the trailer, and Del doubted that they had much beyond some Sam's Choice mac and cheese in the kitchen. She pulled out a hundred-dollar bill and handed it to Virginia.

"I'm advancing you Misty's next paycheck."

Virginia shook her head. "No, no Del. I can't take that."

"It ain't charity, Ginny. It's owed. Better you get it than Misty Dawn." She put the money in Virginia's hand. "I'll send Charity out here with the rest," Del said. "If Misty turns up or calls you, you call me, alright?"

"Alrighty Del," Virginia sobbed as she pocketed the money. "You think she's in trouble?"

"Probably," Del said. "But when ain't she in trouble?" Del patted Virginia on the shoulder and started back to her Jeep. She growled at the dirty little kids and they scattered.

"I'll be praying for you, Del," Virginia said as she waved.

Del gave a little laugh. "I'll take all the help I can get," she said as she returned the wave and drove off.

ASTRID'S APARTMENT was a tiny little place downtown above one shops on Front Street. Del owned the leasing company that handled the apartment and most of the other apartments around town. She'd gone by the office and gotten a key from Lacy Gilbert, the old gal she'd put in charge of the company several years ago. Lacy hadn't blinked at giving Del the key. Del hoped she wouldn't need it; she hoped that when she knocked, Astrid would answer the door and be hungover or sick, or just an irresponsible idiot who hadn't bothered to call off work at a strip club, but Del doubted it. She'd need the key and she wouldn't like how she found Astrid, if she found her at all.

Del didn't bother being quiet or trying to sneak up the squeaky metal staircase that led to Astrid's apartment. She cop-knocked on the door and yelled. "Astrid! You home?" There was no answer, so Del repeated the loud knock twice more before she used her key to enter.

Astrid's place was neat and orderly. The carpets were fresh, and every surface was tidy. The only weird thing about it was it was decorated like an old lady lived there, with lace doilies and amateur pastoral oil paintings all over. Her book shelf held Amish romance books. The spiciest things on them were a few Danielle Steeles. It wasn't the apartment of a twenty-five-year-old stripper. Del would have laughed if she hadn't caught a whiff of dead things as soon as she walked into the living room.

The door to the bedroom was closed, but a good sniff at it told Del that something big and dead lay in that room. She growled and bared her teeth as she turned the door handle.

Astrid was dead, slit right up the middle, all jagged, just like Glenna had been. She sprawled on the bed, spread-eagled and naked, her mouth wide open and eyes staring straight up to the ceiling. The comforter on her bed had a little blood on it, but just like Glenna, hardly any blood remained, and all her innards were gone. From the smell, she'd been dead a few days. There were flies, not many, they had just come to the party, but they buzzed around. Del swatted at them and growled.

Misty Dawn hung from her ankles in the door frame of the bedroom closet. She was naked and there was a big jagged bite mark on her neck and her groin. A leather ball gag was strapped to her head and her body was littered with angry burns and welts. Del was no stranger to torture, and Misty had most definitely suffered until she'd finally bled to death. Her eyes, normally hazy with oxy, were clear. Del could tell that Misty had died screaming and afraid. She could see it in those clear eyes, and she could smell the remnants of fear that permeated the bedroom.

Her phone rang, and Del tamped down the disgust and rage as she looked at the caller ID. She swallowed once and cleared her throat before answering.

"Hello, Liv... yep... no. I'll be free in a bit. How about you meet me at Marv's? Great. Yeah, see you in an hour."

She cursed as she hung up the phone. Olivia. And her freak pets. That's who was responsible for all this destruction. Del's natural inclination was to track the vampire and burn him to death then to open up the cauliflower man and see what his guts held, but she recognized that neither of those things might be the smart move, not just yet. Del sighed, calmed, and collected herself, then she dialed Cal. "Get over to Astrid's. Another clean-up. Take 'em out to the Boys. Them pigs is eating good today. Then hang at my office until I call for you."

Del went to the kitchen and found a dishtowel. It had kittens on it. She used it to wipe off the door handles and took it with her when she locked up and left. She returned the key to Lacy, then headed to Marv's to deal with Olivia.

CHAPTER 18

IT WAS NOON, and Del helped herself to more whiskey at
Marv's. She walked to the jukebox and selected, "He Stopped
Loving Her Today." It was a new internet juke. She'd had it
installed a week ago to replace the old one she'd wrecked
with the face of the vampire.

Marv's ghost stared at it. "I don't like that thing, Leona."

"You'll get used to it, Marv," Del said as she sipped her
whiskey.

"I won't either. I liked the old one," the old man's spirit
groused. "I'm taking it out of your check."

Del nodded. "Fair." She sighed, rested her forehead
against the jukebox screen, and let the saddest words of the
saddest song ever written reverberate through her. "What
should I do, Marv? I can't let all this mess keep on."

The old man nodded. "When people cause trouble up in here, I throw 'em out. Bar 'em. Leona, wow, she would get so angry at them kids. I seen her grab one up by his ear, and he was a big feller too, and Leona wasn't no bigger than a minute, but by god, when she was mad, she breathed fire."

Del threw back her head and laughed. "Yes, she could get mad, that's for sure."

"She yanked that boy right over the bar and tossed him out." Marv nodded at Del. "That's what you do. You just toss 'em out."

"That won't be easy," Del said. "These things ain't gonna take kindly to a toss."

"Who does? You just gotta do it and show 'em who's boss."

"It's beyond that, Marv. I think I'll need an army."

"You take care of folks around here, Delilah. I think you got more firepower than you know."

Del shook her head, but she was thinking. She couldn't directly move on anyone. If she killed one of Martin's henchmen herself, and got caught, that would be bad, but maybe somebody else could. A plan formed in her mind. Del changed the jukebox over to Loretta Lynn and sipped her drink.

Annie, the ancient lady that cooked for Marv for years, brought out a cheeseburger and an order of fried mushrooms. She shuffled past Marv, ignoring his ghost as she had ignored him in life.

Marv hopped around, livid, and Del felt the temperature in the bar drop as he got agitated.

"She gave out a double order, and she didn't measure out that beef patty right!" he yelled.

"I paid extra," Del laughed. She sat down and attacked the food. She looked up at Annie with her mouth full. "Better bring me another sandwich, hon."

Annie patted Del on her shoulder. "You're too skinny. You need more meat," the old woman croaked as she headed back to the kitchen.

The little bell above the door tinkled when Olivia, Darius, and Fernando entered. Olivia pulled up a chair at Del's table. Darius and Fernando looked bored and settled in at the bar. The temperature in the room dropped again. Marv shook his fists at them, and the glasses behind the bar shattered.

Del swallowed her bite of mushroom and looked over at Marv. "Easy, Marv."

"I won't have it, Del. I won't have things like them in my place." He pointed at Darius. "That one... him, I don't want him in here at all."

Olivia looked over at the old man's ghost. "Your bar's haunted."

"It ain't my bar, it's his. I guess he can stick around if he wants," Del said.

"Hey, old man, calm down," Olivia stood up and held out her hands. "Nobody means you any harm."

Marv backed away from her. "This one... she's... she's...."

"I know Marv. Take it easy. Why don't you go supervise Annie? Make sure she's weighing out the meat right," Del said.

Marv nodded as he faded, his eyes still on Olivia. "All right, but you be careful Delilah." There was a little pop sound when he disappeared.

"You can get rid of him easily," Olivia said.

"Why would I care to do that?"

"Because he'll always hang around and cause you trouble."

"Yeah, well, I always hung around, and I caused him plenty of trouble, so I'd say we're just starting to get square with one another," Del said. "You're back from Cali."

"Yes, I am back from Cali, Delilah. How astute of you." Olivia sat back down at the table. She stole one of Del's mushrooms and popped it in her mouth. "Huh. That's not bad."

"Did you just want to set up a meeting to insult me?" Del asked. She finished her lunch and growled. She was still hungry, an awful gnawing hunger that seated deep down in her guts.

"Ah, well, that would be a noble reason for a meeting, but no. I called it to find out what the next step is."

Del wiped her mouth with her napkin. "The next step is to get me a load of stuff. In three days, they'll be six trucks in Laredo, ready for a border cross."

"They watch Laredo like hawks. How are you going to manage it?" Olivia asked.

Del leaned back in her chair and smiled. "Magic."

"Seriously. How are you going to manage it?"

"That fella over there, the one that looks like cauliflower. What the fuck is he?" Del pointed at Fernando.

Olivia sighed. "You're exhausting. Why do you care?"

"I like to learn something new every day," Del said.

"I doubt that. He's a Chupacabra."

"He's a Mexican goat sucker?"

Fernando growled and stood up from his bar stool.

Olivia held up a hand. "Basta."

Fernando continued growling and moved closer. Olivia stood up and flicked her wrist. He fell to his knees with his head in his hands and screamed.

"Basta," Olivia repeated. She looked to Darius. "Take him out of here."

Darius shot Del yet another dirty look, then he smiled and winked at her. He picked up Fernando and took him outside. It took every ounce of willpower that Del had not to rip him into pieces. He was taunting, baiting her.

"I guess he don't like being called a goat sucker," Del said.

"Would you?" Olivia asked.

"I been called a lot worse."

"Oh no doubt," Olivia said. "The Chupacabra are an old and a proud race."

"How did Martin end up collecting one then?" Del asked.

"It's easier to fall into his service than one might think. Sometimes there is no choice. You know all about it."

"I had a choice," Del said.

"You know you didn't," Olivia said. "Look, is your curiosity sated? He's a Chupacabra. Darius is a vampire. I'm a para-demon. There. You learned something new today. How are you going to get six truckloads of drugs across the most patrolled border in the country?"

"I told you already. Magic," Del said.

CHAPTER 19

THE SECOND TIME Del went out to her Aunt Jewel's place, the lawn was in good shape and they had repaired the sidewalk. She waved up at the guys as they cleaned out the gutters on the tiny house. She'd beaten up the Morgan county cousin herself for his poor work ethic. He'd sworn to shape up and get all the things done he'd promised, but Del was out of second chances for people, so she'd thumped him good and shot him in the knee.

"Well, now I reckon your disability check will be for real," Del'd told him after she shot him. She was glad to be shut of him. He didn't have the guts to come back at her, and he was at least smart enough not to report to the hospital who'd shot him. It was done and square.

The little house looked better than it had in years,

painted and fresh, neat, and clean. She figured Aunt Jewel would be pleased. She'd always liked to keep a tidy place, but when Del knocked on the screen door, Aunt Jewel shoved the shotgun in her face again.

"Who all is there?" the old woman croaked.

"Goddammit Aunt Jewel, it's me. Del." The shotgun barrel squished into her cheek and nose, making it difficult to speak.

The old woman squinted and looked over her glasses at Del. "Oh, Delilah. It is you. Why didn't you say it was you?" She pulled the gun barrel out of Del's face. "I could have shot you."

"Why do you keep answering the damn door with a shotgun? Who do you think is coming a knocking?" Del asked. She followed Jewel into the house. The old man snored in the ancient Lazy Boy. The strains of the Young and the Restless played on the old tube TV.

"You never know," Aunt Jewel said. She sat down in front of the TV. "Look, Delilah, there's twenty more minutes left of my stories, so you're just going to have to be quiet and wait."

Del rolled her eyes. The old woman was a fool for soaps, always had been. Del pointed to the old man. "He seems to enjoy them."

"Oh, I drug him good before my stories come on, otherwise he bitches. It's easier this way, so I don't have to shoot him."

"I don't see why that would bother you much," Del said.

Aunt Jewel had never minded shooting a man. She'd shot her first husband's eye out.

"I'd miss his check," Aunt Jewel said. "It's too much work to hunt up another old man. Now shut up, Delilah. My stories is back."

Del walked in the kitchen and checked her phone messages while Aunt Jewel watched The Young and the Restless. Del had a message from Olivia. They had plans to supervise a few shipments, and she wanted to go over travel details. The other message was from Virginia, Misty-Dawn's mom. She was frantic with worry. Del hadn't made it over there to deal with her yet. She knew she should do it, but she couldn't give Misty-Dawn back and that would be a hard conversation, so she'd avoided it and instead, sent Charity by with another check.

Once her stories were over, Aunt Jewel tottered into the kitchen and put on a kettle for tea.

"You want me to make you a cheese sandwich, Delilah?"

"No, Aunt Jewel. I need to know if you know anything about some umm… different types of people."

"I know a lot about a lot of different types of people. What are you wanting to know?" Aunt Jewel made herself some tea, then took out a tall glass. She poured some milk, added some Strawberry Quik to it and set it down in front of Del. "There's your Quik, like how you like."

Del hated Strawberry Quik. It tasted like plastic. But Aunt Jewel wouldn't be told, so she drank it. "I guess maybe they ain't people. More like, well, you ever heard of a Chupacabra?"

Aunt Jewel poured a shot of Old Grandad whiskey in her tea and sipped it. "Oh, you mean that Mexican goat sucker," she said.

Del nodded. "Yeah. You ever deal with one?"

"Delilah, you think I been to Mexico? I ain't ever even been to that Taco Bell over in Delphi." She added another shot to her tea.

"Well, you know what they are," Del said.

"Yes. I knew a girl one time, she come from Texas. I don't recall what brought her here, but she told me about them. Nasty things. I don't know why they call 'em goat suckers. They eat guts and drink up all the blood."

Del nodded. "Like a vampire."

"No, not. Didn't you hear me, Delilah? The eat insides." Jewel rapped her knuckles on the kitchen table. "Why are you asking? You find one?"

"Yes, and I want to know how to kill it," Del said.

"Well, the same way you kill most things, I imagine. Stab it good or burn it." Aunt Jewel shrugged at what she thought a stupid question.

"That's it? He looks knobby and kinda tough. I need to know if I just regular kill him or if I gotta do something special."

"For Pete's sake, Delilah, you could just check the Internets!"

"I don't... no, I ain't. Look, Aunt Jewel, do you know or not?" Del fidgeted and flushed, annoyed.

"Not for sure. But very few things in this world can't be killed. I ain't saying it's easy, but I reckon they can die, same as you."

"So I just stab him and see?" Del asked.

"Use a big knife. Shoot him too, burn him after. I don't know of anything that survives a burning, except a full demon," Aunt Jewel said.

"Any potions to help me out?" Del looked hopefully at Aunt Jewel's apothecary bench.

"Not that I know of, but I guess I ain't an expert on Mexican goat suckers." The old woman heaved herself up from the table and puttered around in her herb stores. She rummaged until she found an old Folger's coffee can. She opened it, sniffed, and grimaced, then closed it up and handed it to Del. "Throw that on him. That'll fell an elephant. It won't kill him, probably, but it might slow him down some." The old woman pointed at Del. "I don't like you messing around with no Chupacabra, Delilah. This sounds like you've gotten yourself in some trouble. I should call Leona and tell her."

"Well, she's dead, Aunt Jewel."

"So? That don't mean I can't call her and tell on you. She'll want to know." Jewel hit Del on the back of her head.

"Ow. I'm fine, Aunt Jewel. I ain't in no trouble." Del rubbed her head and scowled.

"Liar. You come up here knocking loud during my

stories, then you wanna know how to kill a goat sucker. You're in trouble. Like usual." Aunt Jewel put another shot in her tea cup, which was now empty of tea but full of Old Grandad.

"Aunt Jewel, you mentioned about killing demons," Del said.

"No, I didn't. I said demons was almost impossible to kill." Jewel sipped her whiskey.

"Well, how impossible?"

"You can't, really. They just find another body. You gotta bind them in the body and kill the human, but even then, that binding is hard, and you worry about them forever. They'll unbind eventually and girl, when they get loose, you'll wish you had steered clear." She pointed at Del and glared at her over her glasses. Her cheeks were flush with the whiskey. "Listen to me, Delilah, you keep shut of demons."

"Too late for that. I just need to know how to defend myself. Can you teach me how to bind them?" Del asked.

Aunt Jewel shook her head. "I doubt it. It takes concentration, good magic skills, and a whole lotta luck. You ain't got none of that."

"That is an understatement," Del said. "But could you get me the stuff? Just so I have a chance."

Aunt Jewel finished her whiskey. "I'll see what I can do, Delilah. But this ain't a good idea, and I will have to tell Leona."

"Well, go on and tell her then. I'll take the whuppin'. Do whatever you gotta do, but I need that spell." Del got up and kissed Jewel on the cheek. "You want me to send more boys out? You got a chore list?"

"No. Them two are good enough. I like that little one. I got a little plumbing he can work on too," Aunt Jewel winked at Del, then cackled at the look of horror on her face.

"I don't want to know nothing about that," Del said. "I guess use them how you see fit. How long for the spell?"

"Two weeks. Maybe. I don't know. I ain't as quick as I once was," Aunt Jewel said.

"None of us are," Del said.

"You know who you ought to get to help you? Them Boremans."

Del winced. "No. I don't deal with that clan. They're trouble."

"Yes, and they're dumb and crazy, but they are mean and numerous. Why, you can't throw a rock in the south of the county without hitting a Boreman."

"Aunt Jewel, they're nuts and dirty. And you can't trust them. Inbreds," Del said.

"You can trust 'em to be Boremans and if you know that, that's at least something. I bet they're crazy enough to go after that Mexican goat sucker, all right. And if he kills some? So What? There's a passel of 'em and they're just goblins."

"Yeah, that's true, but... Lord, Aunt Jewel. Boremans? Gran would die."

"Well, she's already dead and you need help," Jewel said. She crossed her arms and shoved Del out the door. "I said my piece. Two weeks."

Del waved and headed back to her Jeep. She winced as she heard Aunt Jewel call up to the boys on the roof and ask them if they wanted some lemonade and to do a little light work. She tried to put the image out of her mind as she drove away, but she'd need a whole fifth of Old Grandad to even begin, and she had other things to do.

CHAPTER 20

DEL WATCHED AS THE TALL, skinny woman finished crushing some herbs with her mortar and pestle. She was rail thin and the knobs in her spine stuck up through the threadbare white tank top she wore. Her arms were littered with bruises, old and fresh, and scabs. She looked sleepy and few times, Del had to clap at her and yell to keep her awake and on task.

"Hey! Damita! Keep after it. I ain't got all day."

Del checked her watch. This was the last stop of her three. Damita was the final witch to add her part of the spell to the paint. They'd already supervised batches in two other locations, one by a fat male witch over in Hillsboro that owed Del a bunch of money, and one by an old lady all the way on top of a hill in Skyview. She didn't owe Del anything; she was an old friend of Del's gran's, always there to help with a spell. She wasn't on Aunt Jewel's level—few were—but she was competent and could handle an easy glamour. That was all Del needed. Three easy glamours that combined into one and used to paint the right combination of runes on something would make it invisible to unfriendly eyes. She'd been running it on a small scale for a while, using her network of tractor-trailers, and barge shipments to move drugs, guns, alcohol, and whatever else she had that needed moving and not finding. Her operation with Martin required a scale-up, and that was the issue of late.

Del didn't trust anyone else with it, not even Cal. He was capable enough, but all of their lives depended on getting the spells and application right. In truth, it didn't require three spells, it only required one. Del added in the extra runes too, just so nobody could do the calculating and figure out the combination that made it all work. If anyone else knew, even Cal, it would put them and the whole operation at risk. Del couldn't chance it.

She liked to check in on each leg of the process once a week or so. It kept them all honest. Like today. Damita was an oxy whore. All Del had to do to get her to come was shake a pill bottle. It was easy to stock her with pills and kick her into gear a few times a month to keep the supply chain open. The pills made Damita sleepy and useless most of the time, but she feared Del and loved her oxy even more, so when Del said jump, Damita slowly asked how high.

She yawned and blinked a few times, then smiled at Del

as she finished up her work. "That oughta do it, Del," Damita said.

Cal picked up the buckets and loaded them into his truck. Del pulled a bag of prescription bottles out of her Jeep. She handed two bottles to Damita, who had perked up when she'd seen the bag. She hopped around, more animated than she'd been since Del had got there.

Del held on to the bottles for a minute. "Now, look, this is it for the month. You're getting out of control, Damita. I need you ready to work."

"I am ready, Del. I am!" Damita got agitated as Del held out. "Come on now. Pay what's owed."

"I always pay what's owed." Del grabbed Damita by her filthy shirt front and grimaced. "Take a shower and eat something. If I come back out here and you're still nasty, I promise you, you won't get nothing else. Handle your shit, Damita."

"Of course Del, of course. Now come on."

Del handed over the pills and Damita disappeared inside the shack she lived in. Del wouldn't see her again until next time.

"Cal, once you drop that shit off, go by the office Olivia set up. Tell her we'll be ready for that trip north next week," Del said.

"You can't call her?" Cal asked. He looked at his watch and scowled. "I had some shit to do."

"No, I can't call and leave a voicemail detailing our trip north to make sure our illegal drug smuggling operation runs smooth," Del said. "What the hell is the matter with you?"

He looked down at his feet and bowed his head. "Alright, Jesus, sorry. I'll go right after."

Del got in her Jeep. "Good. I'll see you in the morning."

"You ain't coming to the club tonight?"

"No. I got something I gotta do too," Del said. She took a deep breath. The thing she had to do had been the thing she'd been dreading for a few days, but she couldn't wait any longer and it had to be done.

"Well, what if Bob Reilly takes exception to you not showing up to his party?" Cal asked. Bob Reilly had a birthday party booked at Kitty's. He was on the City Council. He was a degenerate gambler and a serial philanderer which served Del's purposes nicely. She should drop in and maybe it would happen, but she doubted it.

"Tell him I had a problem I had to deal with, then buy him a bottle of that shit scotch he drinks, send one of the girls to blow him, and tell him happy fucking birthday from me. It ain't rocket science, bub," Del said. She started up the Jeep and left Cal standing there loading buckets of spell-spiked paint into his truck.

She drove slower than normal, hoping to prolong the trip, but in about thirty minutes, she was back at the trailer park. When she pulled into Virginia's driveway, the little kids scattered again. They were still filthy, and Del thought maybe they were wearing the same clothes she'd seen them in last time. They chittered and yelled at her, their grubby

131

faces brown-yellow and stained with what looked like powdered cheese. When she shut off the Jeep, they clamored off the porch steps and jumped on her vehicle.

"Listen, shits, if you scratch that Jeep, I'll get the switch myself," Del said. "Now you wanna make a dollar each, you all grab a rag and wash my windows."

The older girls conferred about that, then nodded and dragged their little brother off the bumper. They went to work washing the windows with the little boy's filthy shirt dipped in water from a bucket that hung under the hose outlet of the trailer. Del doubted the windows would get cleaner, but it might save her paint job. She walked up the steps and sat down on the old glider next to Virginia.

Virginia's hands shook as she smoked her cigarette. She fidgeted and fingered the gold cross hanging from her neck. She turned her red-rimmed eyes to Del.

"You found her, didn't you?"

Del nodded. "Yes. I'm sorry, Ginny. There ain't nothing to bring back to you."

Virginia dropped to her knees and sobbed as she prayed. Del sat still and watched the kids. They rubbed dirty water all over her Jeep as they yelled at each other. They were sad little things, skinny and dirty, but they had each other. Del figured having Misty-Dawn for a mother had made them all closer. It made sense as Misty was in and out of their lives so much that they naturally found stability in one another, even if they were dirty little shits.

When Virginia finished praying, she sniffed and got up, then sat back in her chair. "Tell me what happened."

"I know you think you wanna know that, Ginny, but you gotta trust me, you don't," Del said.

"She was mixed up in something bad," Virginia said.

"Yes. But that don't matter now. I done for her," Del said.

"She was always like this. Wild. Couldn't be a good mama. I tried, Del, I did, but no amount of church seemed to help her. I tried." Virginia collapsed, sobbing.

Del scooted over and held her. "You done the best you could, Ginny. This ain't your fault. Misty was Misty. Nobody could change that. Not you and not Jesus either." Del patted her back. "The cops ain't gonna help. I ask that you let me handle it."

Virginia nodded and sniffed. "Alright Del. You never been bad to me. But you promise you took care of her?"

"I swear it," Del said. She tried not to think about the pigs. "Someday, I'll take you where she is. It's a nice spot," Del said. "So grieve. It's alright. Report her missing, but don't give no details to the cops."

"I won't, Del. Jacob knows how Misty is. It won't surprise nobody none that she took off." At that Virginia erupted into tears again.

"Yes... I know. It's gonna be okay," Del said.

"What am I gonna do with these kids?" Virginia said as she sobbed.

"I'm gonna help out with that. We'll figure out something."

"You can't. That ain't right." Virginia shook her head.

"It's right," Del said. "It ain't your fault and it ain't these kids' fault. We'll work something out. You can work for me or something and I'll get Fred to cut you a deal on rent until you get things organized." She hugged Virginia and got up. "I gotta go. I'm gonna get with Char and send her this way. We'll fix things."

"You can't fix this, Del. Misty is gone."

"No, I can't fix that. But I can make sure nothing else happens," Del said. She felt the hate for Fernando and Martin's crew boil up in her. They took what they wanted with no regard for anyone else. They brought a shitstorm down on her Valley. It couldn't go on.

Del patted Virginia's back one last time in a one-armed hug, then she walked down the steps. The kids all lined up. They were soaking wet from their labor. Del pulled out a wad of cash. She handed each kid a twenty. "I ain't got any singles. You all be good and help your grandma. You don't and I'll be back out with a switch to whup you." She growled at them and they scattered, the money clutched in their filthy little hands.

As she drove away, Del let the rage fester and bubble. It would make it easier to do what had to be done next. Instead of going home, she went east and further up into the hills, to a place she'd rather not go if given the choice, but Del realized, she no longer had one.

CHAPTER 21

THE ROAD up the mountain was little more than a cow path, so narrow in places that her Jeep barely went through, and any other cars would have to stop and wait to pass. There wouldn't be any other vehicles. Nobody came up this way, because nobody in their right mind ever did business with Boremans.

Del shifted into low gear to get up the last long hill. At the top there wasn't a clearing, just more muddy road in disrepair. It wound around on top of the hill for a bit, then descended straight down into a wet hellscape, filled with rotting trailers, dogs beyond count, and Boremans.

Del steered the Jeep into the holler and pulled around until she was facing back toward the exit. She wanted to be able to get just as soon as she decided it was prudent and didn't want to chance getting blocked in. She noted the junk that lay near the entrance, an old cattle gate, rusty corrugated siding, some telephone timbers, and a barricade made of car fenders. Del knew these people, and she knew they were likely to box her in and cut her throat should one of them get a wild hair up their ass.

Dandy Boreman stood on top of an old picnic table. Like all Boremans, he was barely five feet tall and yet his pants were too short, riding clear up to his shins. He wore no shirt. His shoes were high polished black dress shoes. They stood in stark contrast with his translucent white skin and filthy dungarees. He pointed to the sky and yelled, "Hellfire and Brimstone!" then pointed at Del and began speaking in gibberish.

"Oh, Dandy's got the Holy Spirit in him," another Boreman yelled as he clapped. Del didn't know all their names. She doubted anyone did. There were at least twenty of them bee-bopping around, yelling back at Dandy and flopping about, apparently also filled with the Holy Ghost, or with plenty of meth and PCP. Dozens of dogs yelped and slunk around. They weaved in and out of the junk piles and peeked out from under the trailers.

"Pipe down there, Dandy. Where's Yella at?" Del asked. She tried to keep her distance from all the random Boremans who were now circling around her, singing, and speaking in tongues. She didn't trust that one of them didn't have a shank. One of the dogs got close to her and snarled. She growled back, and it yelped and ran off.

"And lo he has seen the degradation and the wanton...

hubris from which you have descended and I sayeth unto you... you will know the fear and might of the Lord and the wrath of Jay-sus!" Dandy screamed, then began dancing on the table. His shoes had taps on them and they made an unbalanced rhythm that matched his frantic ranting.

Del rolled her eyes. They were all out of their gourds on Angel Dust. It would be a fruitless trip unless she could find Yella. Del grabbed up one of the nameless Boremans. His shirt was greasy and his skin and hair so white they glowed even in the daylight. All the Boremans were near albino and most of them were blind as bats, with thick, Coke-bottle glasses when they could afford glasses. "I need to talk to Yella. Go fetch her," Del said. She gave the Boreman a good hard shake and his eyes met hers. He nodded, then scampered off among the trailers.

Del stood in the middle of the mess, shoving away Boremans if they got too close. They all smelled like taco meat and nightcrawler worms. She doubted if they had running water to bathe. Little white-haired kids came peeking out from under the trailer underpinning, like skittish rats in the corncrib. They'd be fearful at first, but they had a sly mean look about them and Del figured just like mean barn rats, they'd all bite when they got emboldened.

The Boreman she'd tasked with finding Yella came sprinting back through the mess. He didn't stop and ran right past Del and up into the woods.

"All you all out here, shut up all this gottdamned racket!"

Yella Boreman stood about four feet tall. A long Virginia

Slim hung from her mouth and she wore a turquoise crop-top t-shirt, adorned with plastic beads and fringe that had the iron-on message of "Bad to Tha Bone" in shiny silver cursive. Her gut hung out over the top of her frosted denim miniskirt, and she was barefoot. Yella fired her shotgun once straight up into the air, scattering the mess of her kinfolk. Dandy refused to stop dancing, so Yella aimed the shotgun at her brother and blew a chunk out of the table. Dandy yelped, slipped, and landed on his ass on top of the picnic table. He seemed back to himself and no longer quite so filled with the Holy Ghost.

"Dammit, Yella, you almost got me that time!" Dandy screamed. He beat his fists on the table.

Yella reloaded her shotgun, then shot another chunk out of the table. "Well then shut up about it and quit a ruckus when I say," she said. She loaded again and turned her barrel on Del. "Del. Who said you could come out here and order us around?"

Del held up her hands and held her growl. "I ain't ordering nobody around. I told that other one there to see if you was around is all," Del said. "I got a job for you."

"I'm Yella Boreman and I'm the meanest and the baddest Boreman there is, and I say who does the whats around here." She shot the gun toward Del. It missed about five feet away and tore up a hunk of dirt, spraying Del a little. Yella said that same line every time Del had ever met her. She was actually the meanest and the badest, and also the smartest, but considering Boremans, that didn't go very far.

"Goddamit, Yella. I didn't come out here to fight!"

"Well what do you want? You want to buy a dog?" Yella asked. She finally put the shotgun down and walked up to Del. She stared up at her and grinned. "Member that time we dated, Delilah?"

"Ah, we never did, Yella. I'm sure I woulda recalled," Del said.

Yella looked her up and down and winked. "Well... we still could, even if it is against what Jesus says. Dandy will keep mostly quiet about it if he can watch."

Del gagged. She swallowed down the bile and cleared her throat. "Ah, well, I can't Yella. I'm off the market. Look, I need you all to snatch somebody and hold 'em out here till I come get 'em."

"Snatch a person? Why, that's easy enough. Why can't you just grab 'em yourself?" Yella asked. She wrinkled her nose up at Del and squinted through her thick glasses.

"Because I don't want nobody to know I grabbed them," Del said. "I'll give you five to grab him and five to hold him."

"Well, what kind of feller is he?" Yella asked. "That's a lot just to snatch somebody."

"He's strong. Little guy, but muscular. Face looks like cauliflower covered in hair. Mexican guy," Del said. "You gotta be quick and quiet about it though."

"We're always quick and quiet!" Yella screamed. "Who said we wasn't?" She pointed the gun at Del again.

"Nobody said shit about you, Yella. For fuck's sake, stop pointing that gun at me." Del had enough of shotguns pointing at her for a while. She growled low, reminding the little goblin clan who she was.

"Alright, Del, jeez, you ain't got to get surly about it," Yella said. She put the gun down, wise to heed Del's growled warning. "We want seven to snatch him and ten to hold him and you gotta buy three dogs."

"I don't want no dogs. Just grab the guy," Del said.

"I said three dogs!" Yella screamed. She fired off both barrels into the air and everyone else scattered. All the dogs howled and barked.

"Alright, Jesus fucking Christ. Three goddamn dogs!" Del yelled.

"Praise the Lord!" Dandy yelled. He got back up on his table and danced.

Yella laughed and clapped. "Don't nobody dance like Dandy when the Pentecost comes upon him," she said, admiring her brother's dance steps.

"That's an understatement," Del said. "Watch the man for a bit. He likes Kitty's. You can probably grab him there of a night." She tossed the Folger's can of tranquilizer to Yella. "That should knock him out."

"You ain't got to tell a Boreman the Snatching Bidness," Yella said. "We know how to snatch people and we'll say how to do it."

"Alright, fair enough, but I ain't paying if you all make a mess of it," Del said.

"We won't make no mess of it and ain't nobody ever

gonna see us get him. We're professionals," Yella said. She spit a big green wad in her hand and held it out to Del.

Del grimaced, then spit into her own palm and slapped it into Yella's sealing the deal.

"He'll be here in two weeks," Yella said. "We'll hold him a week. But we ain't gonna feed him. So if you don't come get him and them dogs, he'll die."

"Alright. Two weeks. See you then," Del said.

The little white goblins started coming out from every nook and cranny in the mess of trash, and the dogs howled and growled. It was time for Del to get moving. She kicked a few dogs aside and slammed the fingers of one little Boreman who hissed at her as she got in the Jeep. The engine roared to life, and she gunned it, spinning out in the muddy clay before her tires finally got traction. She sped out of the holler just as the riled-up clan of goblins picked up the bumper barricade in an attempt to trap her.

Del wiped her hand on her jeans, disgusted that she had to stoop so low as to enlist the Boremans, and wondered if she'd ever get the stank of goblin spit off her.

CHAPTER 22

"I DON'T WANT *to go out there," Del said. She crossed her arms and thumped her back into the bench seat of the Oldsmobile Cutlass. The car had big rust spots and Del could see the road going by through a big hole in the passenger side door. Her mom lit another cigarette and blew the smoke at Del.*

"Too damn bad. Your daddy wants you out there," her mom said.

"I don't give a shit what he wants. I don't want to be around him. Ever," Del yelled. She punched the door and the whole car shook. All day she'd been feeling funny. Angry and twitchy. Deep down inside her, it felt like something was gnawing at her insides, biting and pulling at them. She'd had cramps and bouts of sweats all day. The school nurse thought she had a fever, but when she'd taken Del's temperature, everything had been normal, so she'd sent

her back to class, dripping with sweat and dealing with muscle spasms, but otherwise healthy.

It wasn't just the pain that Del felt. The itchy, twitchy restless feeling pricked and prodded at her all day. She'd snapped at Jerry when he'd asked her if he could copy her history questions and she'd blacked his eye. She'd fought with Jacob too, screamed at him to leave her be. The hurt on his face upset her, she didn't want to do that to him, but she hadn't been able to control the rage that built inside her. It had all come tumbling out in flying fists and hateful words.

When Del got home from school her mom handed her a peanut butter sandwich and told her to get in the car. She hadn't told Del that she was taking her out to the Holler until she'd gotten moving too fast for Del to jump out. Galen wanted Delilah out there tonight and Galen got what Galen wanted. Always.

"He's your daddy. You'll do as he says. That's in the Bible," her mom said around the cigarette.

Del laughed meanly. "Oh you know all about the Bible now. You skip over that part about fucking without marrying somebody?"

Del's mom reached over and slapped Del hard across the face. "You watch your mouth, Delilah. You ain't too big for me to beat the shit out of you and wash your dirty mouth out with soap."

Del punched the car door again and left a fist-sized crack in the plastic of the door. "Yes, I am." She kept her fist balled up and she thought for a second about punching her mom right in the nose. She'd love to see it gush blood and hear her mom scream. Del remembered back to beatings with belts and hard-soled shoes. Her mom had doled those out for minor infractions or none at all. She'd beaten Del bloody with a belt once for putting the roll of toilet paper on backwards. Just then, Del would love to return the favor.

"You just keep civil or I'll... I'll tell your gran!" her mom screamed. She smiled at the look of panic on Del's face.

If Del's grandma caught wind of her being hateful, punching people, or saying the F-word, well, that wasn't something Del ever wanted to happen. She took a deep breath, three of them, and calmed herself. Her gran didn't know her mom was taking her to Galen. If she had known, she wouldn't have allowed it. Gran hated Galen and she'd done everything she could to keep Del from him. Galen couldn't come near her place. She'd put a protection spell up. Unfortunately, her daughter didn't share the same feelings and if Del was with her, she took her out to the Holler if Galen said to do it. They'd lived out there briefly, but Galen had gotten mad at her mom for something and kicked them out. He'd largely ignored Del for a few years, then when she'd turned thirteen, he'd started to get interested again. That enraged her Gran. She'd whispered with Aunt Jewel about it, but in the end, she couldn't be everywhere at once and Del had to go.

"Fine!" Del screamed. A wave of nausea hit her and she doubled over. When it passed, she sat up. The sun had dipped low behind the horizon. It gave off its last light, purples and blues that matched the chill of the late fall air. She sweat through her ratty sweater and jeans and Del shivered, shaking as her teeth rattled. She'd ask to turn on the heater, but it didn't work.

They finally reached the Holler just as the sun set. Her mom didn't stop the engine or even get out of the car. Galen opened the car door and yanked Del out of the Cutlass. He wore only a pair of old jeans. He leaned in and yelled at Del's mom.

"Get out," was all he said. He still had a hold of Del's sweater and didn't seem to even notice that she yelled and wriggled around, trying to get free.

Del bit his hand and he let her go, but shoved her. She flew ten feet across the yard and hit a pine tree. Del slid down to the ground and coughed.

"Do that again and I'll knock your teeth out," he said. He grabbed Del again by the scruff of her neck and shoved her ahead of him. He walked away, off toward the clearing in the center of the hollow, past all the chained up dogs, and miserable trailers and shacks.

Del walked, doubled over in pain as cramps and sickness hit her. When they reached the clearing, she puked.

Junior and some other older boys were there. They were shirtless and barefoot, like Galen, and they laughed. "What a fuckin pussy," Junior said as he laughed and pointed at her.

Del felt a hot ball of rage boil up her gullet and she growled and launched herself at Junior. Somebody grabbed her before she could get there. Galen's meaty fist held her sweater.

"Get on up in them woods," he said to Junior.

"I wanna watch her break," Junior said. "I bet she can't take it."

"Get in them woods or she won't be the only one gets broke," Galen said.

Junior didn't argue further. He spat at Del, laughed, then took off into the underbrush.

Del thought of following him and beating him with a solid

branch, but any other thoughts were erased from her brain when the cramps and pain intensified. Del fell down on her knees and screamed as every muscle in her body began to stretch and pulse. Del felt like all her skin was stretching thin and the pain was agony, white and hot as she heard her bones crack and break.

Galen paused before he headed off into the woods. "You can't stop it. You'll survive it, or you won't." That was all he said before he disappeared into the woods, leaving Del writhing in pain and misery.

She panted and her chest heaved as she started to hyperventilate. She'd never done that before and her inability to get a good breath scared her and she sobbed. Del felt her heart beating erratically in her chest and a heavy feeling came over her. She flipped over on her back and gasped for air as her head pounded. She vomited all over herself and choked on it. She convulsed and her eyes rolled back in her head as everything felt huge and far away all at the same time. Del sucked in one last big breath and then she just lay still. She didn't think she was breathing at all and there was no sound except a great whooshing in her ears. She thought maybe she was dead, it was so still and quiet, but then the pain hit her again and she screamed.

Del wasn't dead, but she wished she was as her bones grew. He teeth elongated and pushed out from her gums. Del tasted blood in her mouth and when she spat, great globs of blood came out. She was on her hands and knees in the dirt and she watched in confusion and terror as her hands elongated into claws. Her regular nails flaked off and black claws erupted in their place.

The whooshing sound filled her ears and the pain was replaced *by that boiling rage and the urge to rip and tear. Del smelled blood and she growled and snarled, then there was one last terrible wave of pain. She screamed and everything went dark.*

*W*HEN *D*EL *woke up*, *it was morning and the ground was hard with a frost. The ice crystals and dirt bit into her bare skin and she shifted around to see where she was. She smelled dog shit and something else, something metallic. She tasted it too and when she opened her eyes, she realized that she was laying among the dog houses. Normally, the dogs would snarl and lunge at her; they were all mean and violent, but they were silent. All fifteen dogs were dead, ripped open, their guts and organs strewn about the place like a tornado hit it. The dog houses were smashed and ruined. Del stood slowly and was dizzy. She wobbled a bit, then steadied herself. Why were the dogs all dead? What could have done that? Gotten close enough to the vicious animals and ripped them apart?*

She felt sticky and like her skin wouldn't stretch right and when she moved, her muscles ached and she yelped in pain. Del was so sore she could barely move. She looked down at her hands and screamed when she realized they were covered in brown, dried blood. She screamed louder when she realized she was naked.

Del heard laughing and hooting and looked up to see Junior and his buddies emerge from the woods. They pointed and whistled at her. Del flattened herself to the ground and tried to hold back tears as they approached. She tapped into the anger she felt and hoped it would keep her from crying in front of them.

"Holy shit, look, she fucking killed all Dad's dogs! He's gonna beat you good, Delilah!" Junior said, laughing. All the boys wore old sweat pants and t-shirts. They were barefoot and filthy. Some were bloody. Junior's face and chest were bloody. He kicked Del hard in the ribs. "Too bad you survived it. Bet you won't make it through the next two. They hurt worse," he said. One of the boys picked up a dog turd and threw it on Del. Then they all started. They hit her with mud, sticks, dog shit, dog parts, whatever was around, laughing and jeering at her as they pelted her.

Del kept her head down and cried. She cried tears of rage and confusion and embarrassment at being naked. Their taunts faded, and they scattered when Galen came out of the woods. He was naked and covered in blood. He carried a huge buck across his shoulders, and he stopped when he got to Del. She looked up at him, her eyes full of terror and tears. He looked around at the carnage surrounding her, then smiled down at her.

"Go find something to wear. One of them whores got clothes."

"I-I wanna go home," Del sobbed.

"You ain't going nowhere Delilah."

He walked off with the deer and left her there in the frozen mud, crying and sore, and confused.

CHAPTER 23

"ARE YOU SURE ABOUT THIS?" Olivia fidgeted with the seatbelt in the Jeep.

"What do you reckon's gonna happen? You think they slap you in jail?" Del asked. It was the first time she'd seen Olivia even remotely sweat, and she found it funny.

"Yes, that's precisely what I think, Delilah," Olivia said. "You're reckless."

"I ain't reckless, and they ain't gonna do shit to us. How many shipments have cleared the border?"

Olivia knew to the penny how much cargo Del had moved. It was a massive amount of drugs, worth hundreds of millions of dollars. Martin was so pleased with the results that he'd asked to expand the smuggling operation to other goods. The truck in front of them as they crossed the Ambassador bridge and drove into Canada was full of guns and explosives. She'd bring the trailer back full of something else. Everyone was winning, yet Olivia still wanted to see it firsthand. Del drove her to the Canadian border to watch a cross and exchange. Olivia would see how the system worked, and Del hoped it would be the end of it. It was a stupid hope. They were determined to find out how she managed the routes and crossings, both north and south.

"Many," Olivia said.

"You mean all," Del said. The Jeep crept closer to the border checkpoint.

"This is the busiest border crossing in to Canada. Why would you choose it?" Olivia asked.

"We're nothing here. That truck is one of hundreds. Nobody cares about it."

"But they will. And they'll care about us. How are we going to waltz into Canada without passports? Canadians are laid back, but even they have limits," Olivia said.

"Open the glove box."

Olivia scowled, but she pulled out two blue Canadian passports. She looked inside, shook her head, then held them up. "And what good will the passports of two men from Quebec do us?"

"They'll work just fine," Del said. She grinned and took them from Olivia. When they pulled up to the border agent's booth, Del handed the passports to him and smiled. He looked through them, then smiled at Del.

"Heading home, Monsieur?"

Del grinned back at him, then at Olivia. "We sure are. Can't wait to get back to good old Quebec."

"What was your business in the US?"

"I bought a bunch of handguns. She sold some moose knuckles and is importing a shitload of bananas."

He nodded and smiled. "That sounds like a pleasant trip." He stamped the passports and handed them back. "Welcome home."

"Thanks," Del said as she tossed the passports in Olivia's lap and drove through the checkpoint.

"You bewitched them," Olivia said. "How?"

"Who cares? It worked," Del said. She drove about an hour across the border and pulled in to a warehouse. The truck they'd followed was waiting in one of the docks.

Del got out and stretched. This was the part that made her nervous, the exchange. A lot could go wrong at this point. All things she couldn't control, like people's emotions and reaction to giving up money. In her experience, there was a tendency to want to keep the money and yet still get the goods, no matter the size of the transaction, but these big ones were fraught with double-crosses. Cal's team normally handled this, and still would. It was important for Del to remain as behind the scenes as possible. The less it exposed her to the network, the harder it was to find her and trace it.

"You couldn't have done a spell that fast," Olivia said. "How did you do it?"

Del shook her head and stared at Olivia. "You really expect me to tell you?"

"No, I don't suppose I do," Olivia said. "He will find out, eventually."

"Maybe," Del said. "I'll be ready if he does."

"I sincerely doubt that you will be, Delilah."

They hung back and let Cal's team handle the offloading and exchange. Half of the load was ear-marked for Toronto and the other half for Montreal. They broke it out in two shipments and loaded it on trucks marked for carrying Canadian chips and snacks.

The buyer was a French-Canadian named Marcel. A quick sniff of the air told Del he was also a para-demon. He smelled like Olivia. Human, with an underlying odor. Marcel yelled at Cal's guy, Jack, in French. He waved his hands all over and in Jack's face. Jack somehow stayed calm and waited. Del crossed her arms and listened.

"This shipment is late. You were supposed to be here at 6 and it is now 6:30. I want a discount."

Jack looked over at Del. Del laughed. Jack looked back to Marcel. "You got a problem, you talk to your contact."

"My contact? My contact? Non. Non. I want a discount now. I am not paying. Je ne paie pas!" Marcel stamped his feet and waved his hands over his head.

"Well, then you ain't getting the shipment," Jack said.

"Not get the shipment? Not get the shipment? You are an idiot! Of course I am getting the shipment! I am not paying full because you are late."

"Truck pulled in here at a quarter til five. We started unloading at six. Nobody was late," Jack said.

"Idiot! It is six-thirty!" Marcel screamed.

Del poked Olivia. "Ain't he kind of flighty?"

"He hasn't been in that body very long. He can't keep everything in line yet. It can take a bit of time," she said. "He'll twitch and fly off the handle a bit until he gets the vessel under control."

"Who sent a flaky demon to make a deal?" Del asked. Marcel's agitation grew until finally, he screamed and started speaking gibberish to Jack. Jack howled in pain and dropped to his knees. Del had enough. She growled and was on Marcel in a few seconds. She threw him against a set of racks.

He screamed at her in French, then pointed and resumed his gibberish, directing it at her. Del could hear something, none of it was discernable, just wispy fragments of words, but they had no effect at all, not like they had on Jack. She felt a slight burning between her shoulder blades. She shrugged it off, grabbed Marcel by his hair, lifted him up, then slapped him.

"Stop that nonsense right now. That truck wasn't late and you're gonna pay what you owe." Del looked over at Jack. He was on his feet and out of breath. His face was white, and he looked like he was going to vomit, but he was otherwise fine. "Jack. Does he have the cash?"

Jack shook his head. "He's missing fifty."

Del looked back to Marcel. "You came with a short load? I think you're the idiot."

Marcel tried to hex her again. Del punched him in the

mouth. "Knock that shit off or you're going back to Quebec without a tongue." She dropped him on his ass. He held his bleeding mouth and cried. Del looked to Olivia. "It's your money. You better handle this."

"Which you are responsible for," Olivia said. She pulled out her phone and dialed. She spoke in perfect French and nodded several times, then hung up. "He left with all of it."

"Oh, really?" Del looked down at Marcel and snatched him up. He yelped and spit blood everywhere as she dragged him over to a stretch wrap machine. She grabbed an end of the plastic wrap and pulled it around Marcel's face. He panicked and squirmed, and the plastic wrap bulged around his mouth as he tried to breathe. "Where is that money?"

Marcel flailed around. Del ripped the wrap off him, and he coughed and sputtered. "I-I do not have it."

"Bullshit. You left with it. You stashed it between here and Montreal. Tell me where it's at." She wrapped him up again and waited. After a few seconds, he looked ready to talk or die, so she pulled the plastic away.

"Kill me, what do I care?" Marcel laughed. He lay on the concrete floor of the warehouse and flipped Del off. "I will find a new body."

Olivia began to chant. She made a few hand motions toward Marcel, and he pleaded with her. She ignored him and finished her spell, then she smiled. "He'll tell you now," she said.

"You bound him there," Del said. "But what happens? He still can't die."

"No, but he'll linger in that corpse, rotting until he frees himself." Olivia said. "It's highly unpleasant."

"Sound like it." Del grinned and went to wrap Marcel up again, but he held up his hands and relented.

"A house in town. Not far."

"Address," Del said. She snapped her fingers at him. "Let's go."

"368 Nelson," he said. "It is ten minutes away."

"Jack, go see," Del said.

Jack ran out, and they waited. Del grabbed Marcel and wrapped his entire body, except for his face in the stretch wrap machine. He struggled against the plastic, but the clear cocoon held him tight. After about twenty minutes, Jack returned.

"I found it. It's all there."

Del smiled. "All that for fifty-grand?" She looked to Olivia. "Something ain't right here. New body, stupid brain. I smell a rat."

Olivia shrugged. "He's low level and on his own. I called Montreal and they know nothing."

"Bad news for you then, buddy," Del said. She wrapped the rest of Marcel's face in the stretch wrap, then dropped him to floor to let him suffocate. They ignored his thrashings and muffled cries. "Send off the shipments, Jack. Go on with the rest of it like normal. You got all the couriers ready?"

"Yep. Everything's good, De—" He stopped himself before he told her name. "I'll get them headed back that way."

Del patted him on the shoulder. "You done good. You couldn't know he'd be some dumbass half-demon."

"Yeah, thanks. I don't know what he did to me. Hurt like hell though. How come it didn't hurt you?" Jack asked.

"Don't know. Maybe he run out of juice," she said. "Well, we're heading out. Don't freeze your nuts off up here. I'll send somebody else to help next time. You won't need to worry about no demons again." She shook Jack's hand, then they left.

"I hope you don't think we knew anything about that. Why would we short ourselves?" Olivia said as she strapped in the Jeep.

"I didn't say you did," Del said. She pulled the Jeep out on to the highway and headed back to the border crossing.

"But you think it," Olivia said. "You'd be stupid not to, I suppose."

"I don't know that I do," Del said. She said nothing else as they crossed the border into Michigan with no more issues. They checked in to a fancy hotel in Detroit for the night, then had a couple of drinks in the hotel bar.

"Can demons even get drunk?" Del asked.

"It takes too much alcohol," Olivia said. "It would kill this body. Can a werewolf get drunk?" She smiled and clinked her glass against Del's.

"Not nearly drunk enough," Del said. She clinked back and slugged the entire thing down. Del let her eyes wander up and down Olivia's body. "Where'd you get that body?"

"Melbourne, Australia, January 23rd, 1875."

"Shit, that's an old gal," Del said. She clinked glasses again. "To finely aged women and scotch."

"You don't trust me, do you?"

Del shook her head. "Sure don't. It don't pay to trust anybody, especially not demons that been slinking around since 1875."

"Oh, I've been slinking around a lot longer than that."

"Yeah? How long?" Del signaled for the bartender to bring two more drinks.

"So long you cannot fathom," Olivia said. She had a sad, far-off look in her eyes.

"I can fathom a good long while," Del said.

Olivia looked at Del, cocked her head and pursed her lips. She said nothing for a while, then exhaled a lengthy breath. "Why didn't Marcel's hex effect you? You should have been writhing in pain."

"He couldn't get it up, I guess," Del said. She gulped down the scotch and asked for another.

"No, he was fine," Olivia said. "It's you."

"How do you know he was fine?"

Olivia grabbed Del's chin and held it fast. She looked into Del's eyes, and got closer, a few inches away. Del held still. She broke eye contact and looked at Olivia's lips. That didn't help. Her face got feverish and tingly and she knew if she didn't stop herself and get away, she would do something idiotic. The skin on her back prickled and burned again. She hesitated one more long, painful second, then she shook free of Olivia's grasp and leaned back.

"Because I just tried to do it to you and couldn't," Olivia said.

"You just tried to whammy me?" Del asked. The hot flush changed emotions, from want to hate, and she fought back the rage ball that always lurked beneath the surface.

"I did. And it didn't work. That's curious," Olivia said.

Del grabbed the receipt and signed for the bill, then stuffed it in her pocket. She slammed the pen down on the bar.

"Curiosity killed the fucking cat," she said. "We'll leave at six. Long drive." She stalked out of the bar and left Olivia siting there, staring after her with an amused smile on her face. Del mashed the up button on the elevator panel. She let the anger boil as the elevator carried her higher. When she got to her room, she poured herself another drink from the minibar and called Cal.

"Get them girls working on some binding spells first thing in the morning... no, don't worry about that. We got enough. I need a reliable bind, something simple and easy that your guys can handle... yeah, I'll call you in the morning when we get moving."

She hung up the phone and looked out over the nighttime Detroit skyline. It wasn't so fancy as some she'd seen, but she hadn't seen many, and it was beautiful to her. She liked the way the lights twinkled, and she loved the energy of a city, but the noise and smells, all layered and mashing together in a rippling, pulsating din, were too much for her. Del had always wanted out, and she thought the city was the place to be, any city, but whenever she got near one—didn't matter which, Indianapolis, Columbus, Cincinnati—the noise and smell overwhelmed her enhanced senses and made her nauseous.

It would never be a place for her or her kind. She knew that now, but that had been a hard pill for her to swallow at twenty-five. Still, she could shut off the noise and stink for brief times and enjoy the lights and energy while she could. She sipped her drink and imagined a different life as the rage ball retreated.

She wasn't surprised by the knock at her door. Olivia leaned in the doorframe with a full bottle of Scotch and two glasses. She cocked her head at Del, raised an eyebrow, and smirked.

Del stepped to the side and let her in.

There wasn't any need for talking.

CHAPTER 24

"Seems like we could have used a trailer over by Norma's."

Del pulled Nina's body closer and kissed the back of her neck before answering. "Somebody would see. Norma wouldn't mean to rat us out, but Galen got a way of finding out shit, and I ain't aiming for him to have no power here."

Nina reversed position in Del's arms, so they were face to face. She reached out a hand and smoothed Del's hair back, then kissed her. "He's already got the power, darlin.' We're sneaking around and laying in the back of a truck on an air mattress."

Del snuggled closer and kissed her. They were warm underneath the flannel sleeping bags and it wasn't snowing or raining. She figured it was the best she could do under the circumstances. "He ain't gonna have the power forever. I promise." She dipped her head and kissed along Nina's collar bone as she traced slow circles on Nina's bare stomach with her hands.

"You can't promise that. He's always gonna have power and he'll kill—"

Del cut Nina off with more kisses. She didn't want to hear any more about Galen and what Galen would do. When she thought about him, a rumbling rage percolated in her guts, and she envisioned smashing his head until it was pulp, then burning him until he was nothing but smoking ash. Sometimes those visions made her smile, but right at the moment all she wanted to concentrate on was the feel of Nina's silky skin and the salty taste of her.

When their mouths separated, Nina was short of breath and she gasped. "That wasn't fair at all, Delilah," she said.

"You're right. Wasn't fair at all. Reckon I'll stop and let you tell me—" she grinned as Nina growled, grabbed her head, and pulled her back to her lips.

The sun was low in the sky casting orange and red shadows on the falling leaves and the late October chill had crept in as they lay in the back of the truck, tangled up in each other and unwilling to move.

"Damn mattress got a leak," Del growled. Nina was sprawled on top of her, and Del's back dipped down through the leaky air mattress, contacting the rapidly chilling metal of the truck bed.

Del felt Nina chuckle against her skin. "My mattress is just fine." She looked up into Del's eyes. "Not sure I ever want to move."

"If you could go anywhere in the world right now, where would you go?" Del asked.

Nina cocked her head and exhaled. "I-I don't know. Best not to wonder on those things." She shifted around and started to get up, but Del grabbed her and held her close.

"I'm serious. Where would you go?"

"I lived for a while in a little beach town, outside of Boston. I waited tables and couldn't hardly afford to live, but it was beautiful until..."

Del watched the sadness roll into Nina's eyes. She kissed her and touched their foreheads together.

"I never seen the ocean. I heard the water's clear blue, and you can see all the way down."

Nina laughed. "Some places maybe. But some places the water's black and some places brown. Doesn't matter much. It's beautiful just the same."

"I want us to go where it's warm and the water's clear and blue. Mexico. How about we just go?"

"It ain't like that all over Mexico."

"Well, we're goin' to the part that is. Me and you."

Nina buried her face in Del's neck and tightened her grip on Del's body. "I'd love that. I'd go anywhere with you, if we could."

"We can. I'm workin' on some stuff and soon as I finish, we're leavin' this shitstain valley."

Nina raised her head and when her eyes met Del's, Del saw the terrible sadness in them again. "He'll find me wherever I go. He ain't one to set nothing free."

Del sat the up and wrapped her arms around Nina and hugged her tight, desperate. "Then I'll kill him. I swear I will." There was a fierceness in her voice that surprised even her and when the last word was out, she gave a rumbling growl that reverberated through both their bodies.

Nina pulled back and cupped Del's face. She searched Del's

eyes, and Del saw Nina's cloud over again. "I think he'd let me go before he'd let you go. And I don't think you can kill him. He's the strongest I've ever seen."

"Fuck him. He's an old man and I'll get him, eventually. And he fucking knows it too." Del smiled at the thought, and the rage ball in her guts flipped and fluttered pleasantly as it got hot.

"He's old, but he's no man and he will see you coming, Delilah. He always sees it coming. He'll take what you love and destroy you with it."

Del smiled at her and kissed Nina's nose, then lips. "Nah. He can't take that from me. Can he?" She kissed Nina again.

Nina exhaled and pulled Del in for a tight hug. "He'll do what he does. You should just leave."

"It will be a cold day in Hell before I ever leave you."

"What if I want you to?" Nina asked.

Del pulled back and searched Nina's eyes. "Do you?"

"Some days, yes, because I know it will save you. But most days, I think I'd die if you did."

Del smiled at her. "I never will. Never. I want your face to be the last one I ever see."

Nina shivered and Del saw a look of fear pass over her face. In a flash it was gone, and Nina said nothing, she hugged Del to her. "You're so young. You don't know what's going to happen in life."

"I'm only five years younger than you, old girl. And I know some things, don't you worry." She kissed Nina and smiled when she pulled back. "I know we best get home because it's fucking cold and my ass in numb from laying' on this truck bed. Last time I buy a cheap ass Walmart mattress."

"It doesn't matter the brand. Air mattresses are always leaky. Some things ain't meant to last forever," Nina said as she found her clothes and dressed, shivering against the chill of the setting sun.

"Yeah, well some things are." Del grinned and kissed Nina again before she jumped down out of the truck bed then lifted Nina down. She cranked up the heater on the old truck, but they cuddled the whole way back to the Holler, neither willing to let the other one go until they absolutely had to.

DEL SAT STRAIGHT up in bed and gasped. She dripped with sweat and the sheets beneath her bare body were soaked. Her heart thundered in her chest and she closed her eyes, squeezing them tightly as if that would banish the image of Nina from her brain. She didn't want any image in her brain. Not the way Nina looked when she slept, or when she worked at her apothecary table making potions and spells, her dark brown hair all messy as she hummed and puttered. And Del certainly didn't want the image of the last time she saw Nina, in the bunker, a torn bloody mess that hardly resembled a human at all.

Olivia slept beside her, her dark hair cascading over the pillow, a peaceful look on her permanently unlined face. Del slid out of bed and pulled on a pair of jeans and a t-shirt. She padded over to the big picture window that looked out over her Valley and rested her head against the glass. It was an old nightmare, one she'd been having for thirty years and it had never gotten easier to stomach. Never. Olivia gave a little grumble in her sleep and Del saw her roll over and reach for Del. Her eyes opened, grumpy and confused when her grasp was empty. She propped her head up on one hand and stared at Del.

"Why are you all the way over there and why are you dressed?"

"Couldn't sleep." Del never slept all night and she never ever slept all night with someone else in her bed. Most everyone who was invited knew better than to stay. Olivia was hard-headed.

"Come back to bed," Olivia said.

"The sheets are all sweated up," Del replied. She stayed where she was.

"They're going to get sweatier. Come back to bed."

Olivia sat up and let the sheet fall away. The moonlight streamed in and her skin glistened in it. Del swallowed hard and held herself still. She simultaneously wanted to throw herself in the bed and throw herself off the cliff in the front yard.

"If I was to ask you to go somewhere with me, would you go?"

"If you come back over here and lose the clothes, sure," Olivia said.

Del walked over and sat on the edge of the bed. "I'm serious. What if I asked you? To go with me and not come back."

Olivia tugged at the hem of Del's t-shirt. "You know that I can't." She pulled Del's shirt off, then moved to the waistband of her jeans, searching for the button in the dark.

Del grabbed Olivia's hands and held them tight, then drew them to her mouth and kissed them. "You could."

"Delilah. You know I can't. I'm bound to Martin."

"Fuck him. We'll figure out something. Don't you just wanna go? Leave all this horseshit behind and go?"

"Sometimes, but it's just not possible for me."

Del gave a short sigh, more of an exhale, then closed her eyes. She got up and went back to the window. She'd had this very conversation before, and the sense of déjà vu was dizzying. "It ain't possible for anyone, I guess. Once you're in this, you're in it."

She heard Olivia get out of bed and come behind her. Olivia spun her around and pushed her against the window. Del's bare back got goose pimples where the cool glass touched her and more from Olivia's fingers on her skin.

"Yes. Once you're in it, you're in it. It doesn't have to be terrible though." She kissed Del's neck, then nipped her. "Is this terrible?"

"It ain't terrible, no," Del said.

Olivia unbuttoned Del's pants and slid them to the floor. "Is this terrible?"

Del bit her lip and shook her head. "I reckon not," she said.

Later, Del extricated herself from Olivia's possessive grasp. She dressed again and walked outside into the warm summer pre-dawn. The sky was blue and black, and the light blue just peeked up over the hills to the east. Despite Olivia's attentions, Del still had another brunette on her mind and the remembrance of so many promises broken that her heart tightened in her chest, and she fought back a scream. There was only one thing to stop it, and Del took off running through the wet grass. She didn't stop when her bare feet hit the twigs and leaf litter of the woods. She ran until she couldn't anymore, breathless, dirty, and wet with sweat.

She found Olivia gone. No note or sign that she'd been there except the lingering smell of her and the rumpled bed. Del poured herself a morning whiskey. She watched the sun rise above the hill and drank, hoping to mute the memory of both brunettes, but knew that was always going to be the one truly impossible thing in her life of impossibilities.

CHAPTER 25

THE SUN SCORCHED the yellow-brown scrub brush and concrete of the Laredo dockyard. Heat waves rippled and shimmered up from the bleached earth and burned everything they contacted. Del dripped with sweat. She huffed out air that seemed chilled compared to what she was breathing in and looked at her watch. Olivia was forty minutes late. Del despised tardiness, and she abhorred the oppressive heat of the border town. She wasn't afraid of the characters that ran it. They fit the definition of the wild, wild, west—and at any rate, she was used to handling characters, but everyone here was unpredictable. What worked with them on Tuesday didn't work on Wednesday. Del liked to know what was going to happen. She liked to think two or three moves ahead, but here on the southern border, it was impossible. If you thought you were playing chess, the others were playing

Yahtzee. You weren't even close. The sooner she got business done here, the better, but she had to wait on Olivia and that posed another problem.

A healthy bead of sweat ran down the side of her face and dripped off her chin. Another followed it. Del wiped her face with her hand, then rubbed it on her jeans. Everything stuck to her—her shirt, the denim, and an overwhelming sense of dread. The first two would unstick when she left god-forsaken Laredo. The last wouldn't unstick at all. It hadn't in forty years, and Del didn't expect it to ever. There was a lot to worry over. The southern border wasn't as easy to move things across as the northern. US Border Patrol and the Mexican Federales operated fast and loose, just like the criminals, and while they weren't smarter than the northern-ers, it was harder to control them. Del had a system and as yet, no shipments had been stopped, but it took more effort, more magic, and more focus.

Fuck Olivia for making her wait. Del blew out a stream of air and wiped her face again. She looked at her watch. An hour late. She checked her phone. No messages. She jammed the phone into her back pocket and crossed her arms. After another half-hour and two more complete sweat throughs of clothes, a black Chevy Tahoe pulled into the drive and parked next to Del's Jeep. Olivia got out, accom-panied by a man so short he had to jump down from the truck. The man was Hispanic, and he wore high-heeled cowboy boots with long, pointy toes. Feathers of every kind hung from his cowboy hat and he wore rings on each finger and turquoise bangles and bracelets all up and down his arms. His vest was made of skin and a sniff told Del it was human. When Del looked closer, she thought he was wearing eyeliner, and he colored his hair and long mustache unnatural black.

"You're late," Del said, scowling. She ignored the fancy midget.

"We had a delay at the border," Olivia said. She pointed to the little man. "This is Lalo."

Del sniffed the air. The man was just that, a man, but Del smelled a strong whiff of ozone. Lalo was human, but he was a magic user. It put her even more on edge.

"I don't care. He important enough to be late over? We're on a schedule," Del growled.

"Yes, he is," Olivia said. "You know how the border is. I got across as quickly as I could. Stop being such a grump."

"You think I enjoy sweating my ass off?" Del looked Lalo up and down. Mexican. Magic User. There was only one reason for him to be there. They were trying to detect her spell. Del smiled despite the heat and the sweat. They'd never figure it out.

Lalo walked all around both trailers. He picked up some stray gravel from the driveway and tossed it around the trucks while he jabbered away. He wasn't speaking Spanish, Del could tell that. The language hissed and slithered from his mouth. He pulled a set of rattles from his belt and shook them. Del's skin prickled, and the scent of magic tickled her nose like ammonia.

One of the warehouse guys came out and motioned to Del.

"All done, ma'am," he said. He kept his eyes on the ground, but occasionally, he'd glance over at Lalo. The warehouse guy looked nervous. He bit his lip as he watched Lalo, and he crossed himself.

Del nodded to the little Mexican. "He make you nervous?"

The kid nodded. "You don't wanna mess with that guy."

"You know him?" Del asked.

"I know a brujo when I see one. Nasty business. Be careful, ma'am." He went back inside the warehouse, keeping an eye on Lalo as he walked.

Lalo yelled something, then nodded and swaggered over to them.

"Ya entendi," he said. He jutted out his hips and smiled at Olivia.

Del didn't speak Spanish, but from his cocky look, she knew what he said.

"Oh, you think you got it, huh?" She smiled and looked at Olivia. "I gotta give you some credit for not even trying to disguise what you're doing here."

Olivia sighed. "It's not me."

Del rolled her eyes. "Of course not. You're just doing as you're told."

"Commanded, actually," Olivia said. "You think I have a choice?"

"Everyone got a choice, Liv," Del said. "But whatever.

Your fancy midget there thinks he's got it? Great. Hope it works out."

"You're playing a dangerous game, Delilah," Olivia said. She got closer and Del could feel the heat between them.

Olivia was just an inch away, and Del licked her lips. She simultaneously wanted to kiss her and punch her. The look in Olivia's eyes and the way she bit her lower lip signaled to Del that Olivia felt the same. Del resisted both urges. "There ain't no other kind," she said.

The big Kenworth started its engine, and the driver released his airbrake, then honked his horn. He pulled away and waved at Del as he headed east. "That shipment will be in New Orleans on Thursday. Headed up the Mississippi on a barge Friday. We'll offload in Huntington next week. And I been doing it for a month now, no issues. That ain't good enough for his highness?"

"Apparently not," Olivia said. "Although I doubt he would be so perturbed if you would have just showed us how you're doing it."

"That's the only thing keeping me alive," Del said.

"It's not the only thing," Olivia said. "He was always going to find out. You don't know him like I do."

"Bullshit. I know him. Wants to run everyone and everything. Don't care how. I've known plenty like him."

"You think you run everyone and everything," Olivia said. "And you think you're too slick with this spell to get caught, but I've known Lalo a long time. He's going to get it."

"Maybe," Del said. She got back in her Jeep and cranked

the air conditioner. The scorching air blasted from the vents and made her feel worse. Olivia walked up to the window.

"Meet me in Dallas. For the weekend." She put a hand on Del's arm and left it there. She rubbed her thumb on Del's skin in a slow circle.

"I gotta get home," Del said. She didn't move and the heat from Olivia's hand and the motion of her thumb made her flush redder.

"Please?" Olivia whispered.

Del glanced at the brujo. He was going to be trouble. She didn't have the magical firepower she needed to fight him. She'd have to consult with Aunt Jewel. But what really upset her was the blatant disrespect shown by bringing him there. She knew it was Martin, but Olivia was in front of her and Olivia made her vulnerable.

"You don't shit where you eat," Del said, spitting the hot words out as hatefully as she could, hoping it would hurt Olivia.

"That hasn't seemed to be a problem until now," Olivia said. Del was impressed that the woman didn't take the bait. "Don't act like a child. We're past that."

"Now who's playing a game?" Del said. She ripped her arm away, threw the Jeep into reverse, and spun out of the driveway. She shook her head to clear it and headed north, hoping the midget wasn't as good as he claimed.

CHAPTER 26

THE TALL MAN stood next to Del's booth and blocked the morning sun streaming through the diner window with his lean body. He smelled of knock-off Calvin Klein cologne, hair gel, and cheap leather. As he slid into the other side of the booth, his smooth, baby-face lit up in a fake smile. It was the eyes, Del thought, a genuine smile is smiled in the eyes. There was none in his. He wore a standard blue suit with a plain blue tie. He couldn't look like more of a Fed if he tried.

"Hello, Mrs. Monroe."

Del tilted her head and regarded him. "I ain't married."

He held up his hands and placed them flat on the table. "Sorry, slip of the tongue."

A woman, dressed almost identically in a blue pantsuit and cheap black pumps, stood next to the table. Her hair was pulled back in a bun so severe that it stretched her skin tight all over her face. The woman didn't smile. She stared at Del with cool detachment and crossed her hands in front of her.

"Hold on. I gotta call my lawyer and tell her the Federal Government is harassing me," Del said. She sipped her coffee and relaxed back against the booth.

"How is this harassment?" the woman asked.

"You weren't invited to sit. I'm minding my business, enjoying some coffee in this fine establishment." Del waived her hand around the diner and smiled. "You should wait to sit until after you've been asked. Even a dog knows how to do that. I guess they don't train you feds right, to do what a dog can do."

The man smiled. The woman looked pained, as if she wanted to say something or punch Del. Del winked at her.

"My name is Agent Chase. This is Agent Crane. We'd like to talk to you," the man said.

"Let me see your badge," Del said. She examined both and tossed them back. "I reckon I have nothing to say to the FBI."

"We think you do, Delilah," Crane said. She sat down next to her partner. "We think you have a lot to say."

"Everything I got to say to you ends in fuck and off," Del said. "You wanna haul me in for something, best get on with it. I got other things to do today besides sue the FBI."

"We just want to talk," Chase said.

"So you've said."

Chase leaned back and loosened his tie. "You have a huge problem, Del."

Del bristled at the familiarity. The irony wasn't lost on her. "I doubt you'd be of help with any problem."

"Martin Price. He's a tremendous problem," Agent Crane said.

"I don't know who you're talking about, Scully." Del held her coffee cup out for the waitress.

Crane squinted and scowled. "Be cute all you want. It's going to get you killed."

"Aww, you think I'm cute. Gosh, ain't that nice?" Del said. "I don't know nothing about nobody named Martin. I'm sorry I can't be of more help to you all. Now fuck off."

"We know he's been here. We know he has associates in the area," Crane said.

"It's a free country. Anybody can be anywhere. Even tables they was rude enough to sit at uninvited," Del said.

"We can help you, Del," Chase said. He leaned forward in the booth and across the table. His face had a fake look of concern. It was too much. He didn't know how to lie at all. He'd go nowhere in the Government.

"I don't require no assistance," Del said. "What I require is for you both to fuck right off." Del finished her coffee and stood up. She pulled a twenty from her pocket and threw it down on the table.

"Martin is dangerous. Help us catch him and we'll make sure everything works out for you. If you don't... well then we can't make any promises." Chase sat back and smiled at her.

"If you wanna make deals, call my attorney. Fuck off and

have a pleasant day," Del said. She left them there at the booth.

When she got to her Jeep, she made a phone call.

"Liz? What's up with the FBI? You catch wind they wanted me? No? Well, get Frank on it. They want information for a deal and so far as I know, they ain't got shit on me. You know different, I need to know now."

CHAPTER 27

IT HAD RAINED SO MUCH in the last two weeks that the dirt
cow path to Boreman holler was washed out in places. Big
ruts ran through the clay where the runoff cut paths through
it. The Jeep's tires and the four-wheel drive were the only
things saving Del from an uncontrolled slide down in to the
holler. She concentrated hard on keeping control. Beads of
sweat formed on her lip and ran down her face as she shifted
and steered through the mire of clay and debris. When Del
made it over the rickety plywood bridge, she wiped her face
on the sleeve of her shirt. She pulled the Jeep around facing
out of the holler, just like last time, but she pulled it up
across the choke point where they stored their garbage
barricades. They'd try to box her in again, she was sure, but
with the Jeep blocking it, they'd have to think around it, and
no Boreman had enough brain cells for that kind of work.

When she got out of the Jeep, a dozen tow-headed kids stuck their heads out from under the trailers and up out of the tall weeds. Del counted at least twenty dogs barking and growling around. The adults came wandering out of the trailers too, but they kept their distance as they whispered among themselves. Del checked her pistol and tucked it in the back of her jeans. She pulled out her big Bowie knife and belted it on, then grabbed the duffle bag of cash and headed toward the trailer.

The evening wasn't much cooler than the day. The late summer air hung heavy and still, and the humidity from all the rain made the smells of dog shit and garbage and Boremans worse. Del wrinkled her nose as she squelched through the mud and up to Yella's trailer.

Three goblins blocked her path. The biggest one, maybe three and a half feet tall, stepped to the front and held up a stubby arm.

"You ain't got no business up in there," he said. He had a terrible lisp and was missing some teeth, so the word business came out a spitting mess.

"I got business with Yella. Ain't that her trailer?"

"Can't just nobody knock on Yella's trailer like that."

"Why not?"

The little man looked up at the sky and squinted one eye. Del could tell he was doing his best to think and failing. He got a pained look, then nodded.

"Ah, because she said."

Del rolled her eyes. She didn't have time for any Boreman

idiocy, but she couldn't just shoot a bunch of them. She didn't have enough bullets. "All right then. One of you all go tell her I'm here," Del said.

He looked confused again. "We ain't allowed to knock either."

"For fuck's sake," Del said. She grabbed him by his shirt and tossed him aside. He yelped when he hit the mud. The other two hissed at her, but she growled at them, and they scattered. She climbed the steps to the trailer and banged on the door.

Del dove to the side just as the shotgun fired. A few fragments caught her in the shoulder, and she yelped as they bit and burned. Tiny wounds bled into her shirt in a spatter pattern. Yella Boreman stuck her head out the door. When she saw Del, she smiled.

"Oh. Sorry about that, Del. I told these 'uns not to knock." When Yella saw Del was bleeding, she laughed. "Ha. I got you."

Del got up and winced at the burning pain in her shoulder. She'd heal just fine at the Turn in a few days, but it would be annoying and make her change hurt more.

"Goddammit, Yella." Del got to her feet and grabbed the shotgun. She growled and squeezed the barrel, crushing it. She tossed it over the edge of the porch and into the weeds.

"Hey! That was my good shotgun!"

"You're lucky that's where I put it and not up your ass," Del said. She tossed the bag of money at Yella's feet. "Where's the guy?"

"What's your rush? You wanna come in and get a drink? I got a margarita machine," Yella said. She unzipped the duffle bag and rooted through the money.

"No. I wanna see him," Del said. She kicked the bag and made Yella look up. "Now."

"This deal ain't done. You gotta take a dog," Yella screamed.

"Take me to him or I swear to Christ, Yella…"

"All right, fine," Yella said. She tottered down the steps on her short legs and started off through the mud.

They walked about a quarter mile back up into the woods. A rusted shack, made of salvaged corrugated sheet metal, wood, and tarps sat on top of a little rise, close to a spring. The water burbled up through the ground, trickling down an ancient black rock and feeding into the creek. The side of the building was black and charred. Del knew it for what it was, a failed moonshine still. There was little chance all the Boremans put together had enough brainpower not to blow themselves sky high with a still, and the burnt-up structure confirmed it.

"We was extra cautious on the binds," Yella said. "Matter of fact, Del, I reckon we need you to pay extry, 'cause Dandy got bit, and we had to use the log chains on this feller."

When Yella opened the door, the rusted hinges squeaked and groaned, and Del coughed at the rancid odor that flowed out of the opening.

Fernando sat on the bare dirt. A heavy log chain circled his waist, and another attached a cuff around his neck to the wall. His hands were also chained. He was naked and the hair all over his body matted in filth and dirt. The white lumps of his skin were even more prominent in places where his hair had fallen out. When he saw Del, he gave a scream, like a big cat, and strained at the thick chains.

"Stinks, don't he?" Yella said.

"Any reason you took his clothes?" Del asked. She was no prude and well used to nudity, but the sight of his lumpy, hairy dick and balls made her ill.

"We always do that. They don't go nowhere, you take their clothes," Yella said. "Plus I wanted to see what his pecker looked like."

"Pinche puta. You better get me out of this. And you better hope my people don't think you had anything to do with it," Fernando hissed. He lunged at them and screamed again.

Del said nothing. She pulled out her gun and shot him in the knee. Green, foul smelling blood erupted from the wound, but it healed over in just a few seconds.

Del bent down as he writhed in pain and looked him in the eye. "Who said you could go around killing my people?"

"Chupame la verga!"

Fernando sat up and spat at her. She jumped back, and the spit sizzled and burned at the ground as white vapor wafted up and away. Del's nose burned at the tart smell of acid. She took a step back and thought for a moment. "Yella, you got a sock, a garbage bag, and some duct tape?"

Yella screamed for a cousin to go get the things. As Del

waited, she pondered her options. He healed, so stabbing him wouldn't work. She could behead him and that might be a start, but she wasn't certain it would kill him.

When the random Boreman came back, he had a dirty pair of underpants, a plastic Walmart bag, and a roll of pink camo duct tape. Fernando spit great wads of acid at them, each white glob sizzled and smoked. Del sidestepped all the gobs, aimed her pistol, and shot him three times in the chest. While he was distracted and healing, she shoved the dirty underwear in his mouth, covered it with the plastic bag, then wrapped the duct tape around it.

"Ha. I guess he won't spit now," Yella laughed. "He burned off Delmar's good arm. Oh, by the by, Del, we're gonna have to charge you extry for that too. Delmar wants him a fancy hook."

Del ignored her and focused on Fernando. "I guess you can't tell me anything now, but that's all right. You ain't gonna be killing anybody else."

The gag muffled Fernando's laugh, but it was hearty. He stared at Del and motioned with his head to come closer. Del smiled and shook hers.

"Oh, no, I don't think so," she said. She raised the gun and plugged him three times in the head. He slumped over and twitched. Del approached cautiously. His head gushed the green blood, but it was healing. She shot him again, blowing a good part of his head away, but the knobby flesh rippled, and fresh cauliflower nubs grew up out of the charred, ruined skull. Del watched it heal and shook her head. "Well, this ain't gonna be easy."

Fernando's eyes flew open, distracting Del for a second. A curved black claw burst from between his middle and ring fingers, and he swiped it at her. The claw caught her stomach and tore into it as he raked it across her body. Del jumped back and growled. The jagged gash in her midsection had hit no organs, but her muscles were ripped, and blood seeped out.

Yella whistled and winced. "Oh that ain't good, Del. He's got him some kind of poison. He clawed Dandy, and he's been sick for a week."

"Seems like you mighta mentioned to me he could do that," Del growled.

"Oh. Yeah. Del, he got him a big claw," Yella said. "I forgot till just now." She pulled up an old rusted folding chair and sat down, watching the scene as if she were at a movie theater. "How you gonna kill him? He seems hardy to me."

Del doubled over and took a few deep breaths. The intense pain made her nauseous and her guts burned. She ripped the bottom of her shirt off and held it over the wound, then wrapped the duct tape around herself. White hot waves of pain pulsed through her as the poison burned. Del leaned over and threw up. She spit a few times to clear her mouth of the bile taste. She felt a little woozy, but she'd been poisoned before and while she might get sick, like she was now, her quick healing dealt with it.

Fernando smiled at her, laughing behind his gag as he

flashed the claw. Del aimed and shot him, blasting the claw off his hand. He screamed and held up the ruined stump. Del plugged him in the head again. Before he could heal, she pulled out the Bowie knife and slashed until his head came off. She watched for a minute as the flesh around his neck shimmered and contorted. The nubs multiplied and got bigger, and Del realized his head was growing back.

"Son of a Bitch," she muttered. She tossed his head aside, then looked back to Yella. "I need some gasoline and a lighter."

"That might could work," Yella said, nodding her head, "But Del, I'm gonna have to charge you extry for that."

"Yella, go get me a goddamned gas can," Del yelled.

She poured the gas on him, then lit the match and tossed it. Fernando thrashed around as the flames caught him. Del pulled her shirt up over her nose, gagging at the smell of burning hair. He convulsed and strained against the chains. As he burned, his head stopped growing back, and he lay still.

It took a while to burn him, but when he was smoldering, Del kicked at him and busted him up until there was nothing left but a black pile of ash. Aunt Jewel had been right. Most things got dead real quick when you lit them on fire. Del turned to Yella.

"Take these ashes and get rid of 'em."

"Sure, but that's—"

Del held up a hand. "It's extry. I get it. I'm good for it."

They walked down the hill and back to Del's Jeep.

"Just keep it quiet. You think you wanna flap your gums about, you think twice. His people won't be kind to you."

"We know our business, and Boremans ain't dirty rats," Yella said. "Pleasure doing business with you, Del. You sure you don't want to marry me? We ain't got to stay married. We could just do it."

"I ain't the marrying kind," Del said.

The pack of Boremans was fit to be tied as they struggled to figure out how to block Del's Jeep in. Two of them were screaming in gibberish as they banged a piece of house siding against Del's Jeep. She scowled, pulled out her pistol, and shot one of them in the ass.

Yella squinted, then laughed as the little goblin man rolled around and cried. "Ha! Doral! She sure got you good!" Yella looked at Del. "I won't charge you for shooting Doral. I was fixing to shoot him tomorrow, so you saved me a bullet. Now which dogs do you want?" Yella waved her hand at the pack of mangy curs that growled and circled them.

Del climbed in the Jeep, started it up, and spun out of the hollow. In the rearview mirror, she saw Yella jumping up and down in rage with a dog by the scruff of its neck. Del ignored her and decided if she never saw another Boreman again, it would be too soon.

CHAPTER 28

DEL GROANED *and when she moved around, she smushed her face into something soft and sticky. Strange smells assaulted her sensitive nose: fish, garbage, and metallic somethings. She coughed. It was overwhelming. Her gran warned her about it, said she'd have to learn to control it, to filter it out, but Del hadn't figured out how to do that yet. In the year since she'd started Turning, she'd learned many things—not to panic when the change started, how to manage the pain, and how to find her way home if she wandered, but so far, she hadn't learned to control her superhuman senses. Sometimes light was so bright to her she got migraines. Her hearing was so acute that it was a distraction in crowded places, all the voices and sounds coming at her at once. But by far, the worst thing for her was the constant barrage of scents that were magnified to her. Sometimes she couldn't breathe, and she choked on the*

smells. The fishy garbage smell was familiar to her. That, coupled with the squishy feeling under her face and limbs, and the sound of running water suggested to her she was near the river. She opened her eyes and saw that her guess was correct.

Del lay face down in the sandy-muck of the riverbank. She'd gone quite a ways from the holler. Each Turn, she roamed further and further. Last month, she woke up three hills over, well over ten miles from Galen's. The river was ten miles in the other direction. She supposed she was just getting bigger and running faster when she changed. She had no idea, really. When it started, everything went black to her. One minute she was writhing in pain and misery as her body cracked and broke, the next she'd wake up, naked and unable to recall anything from the night before.

She pushed herself up with her palms and got to her knees, then cracked her neck and stretched. Everything hurt. It always did. Galen and Junior acted like nothing was wrong when they came walking back after a turn, but Del was in pain for days after. There was also a little butterfly in the stomach feeling, not unpleasant, and a hum of energy. It had been more prevalent the first few times she'd changed, but now it mostly just hurt. Nobody could tell her anything about it, and she didn't want to ask her gran. Gran acted mad when she talked to Del about the Turn, and it scared Del. Her gran had never said a cross word to her in her life, but discussions of Del's problem made her gran turn dark and broody and worried. Del could see it on her face, that worry. Gran would purse up her lips and get all tight-looking around the eyes, and Del could smell it too. Her gran smelled different when she talked to her about it. Nobody had to tell her what fear smelled *like, it smelled like nothing else in the world, repellent and delicious all at the same time. Even at thirteen she knew it for what it was the first time her nose had been sensitive enough to discern it, a little bit sour and prickly to the nose and at the same time, like a juicy steak on the grill. That's what Del smelled on her gran when she'd talk about the Turn in relation to Del. Fear.*

It was a cool summer morning, and a breeze swirled around the riverbank, chilling Del's bare skin and raising big goosebumps. Her sore muscles protested, and she grimaced but got to her feet. She swayed a bit but dug her toes deep in the sandy riverbank and shook her head. Her eyes finally focused and cleared. Del's hands felt funny—sticky and taught when she flexed her fingers. When she looked down at them she screamed. They were covered in thick, dried blood. She whirled and looked around but saw nothing. She took a few steps backward into the tall marsh grass, then tripped on something and fell on her butt. When she saw what it was she tripped over, she screamed again.

The fat man stared backward at Del with his mouth wide open in a silent scream. His eyes bulged and flies buzzed around him, thick already on the summer morning. The bloody metallic smell mixed in with the smells of death, hitting Del so hard that she got dizzy. She scooted backward away from him, then noticed she was scooting through something slippery. When Del looked down, she saw more blood and innards. She yelped, then flipped over on her hands and knees and scrambled to her feet. She went four steps, then tripped over something else and sprawled face down into the mud. When she raised her head, she saw that she was in the middle of a ruined fish camp. Another man lay on his back with his throat and stomach torn open. Del had been slipping around in his guts. She found two more dead men, their arms and legs ripped from their bodies, and one's head was gone. Their limbs lay about, mixed in with ripped up, overturned beer coolers and ruined fishing tackle.

For the briefest of seconds, she wondered what could have done it, caused this much carnage and destruction, then she looked down at her hands and the rest of her body, and she cried. Del had a strange sinking feeling in her stomach and her hearing cut out, replaced with a static hum. Her chest tightened, and a pressure built around her heart, as if someone were squeezing it. Del couldn't breathe. She clutched at her chest with her blood-crusted fingers and struggled to catch her breath. A hot wave of odor hit her again, putrid and dank, and Del lost all control. She vomited black tar and hunks of meat all over herself. She couldn't have said how long she lay there and puked. It came in wave after wave, an impossible amount of vomit. When it turned to dry heaves, she was spent, sobbing and spitting bile and blood onto the ground.

Murderers went to jail, she thought. They went to jail, and they went to the electric chair. In the electric chair they sizzled and crisped until they were black. She was a murderer and just because she was only fifteen, she wouldn't get out of it. She'd fry.

What could she do? Somebody would miss them. Lots of people spent the summer nights on the riverbank, fishing for big old catfish. They likely had a regular thing. Del sniffed and stopped her tears. She wiped her eyes on the back of her bloody arm and stood up. She didn't want to go to jail and fry in the chair. The four men were dead and nothing was going to bring them back, not even if Del confessed and burned.

She steeled herself to do what had to be done. The thought of touching them made her sick all over again, but she didn't have a choice. Del looked at the headless one. He was small and nicotine skinny. She grabbed him by the one arm he had left and pulled. He weighed almost nothing, and it was easy to drag him into the river. Del watched him slowly sink beneath the brown water and she felt prickly and amped, like somebody had run a little shock through her. It gave her energy and she drug the others over and shoved them into the river too. The last one, the big man, was harder. He was further from the water's edge and his massive bulk was three times Del's size. She geared herself to strain when she tugged on his corpse, but fell backward when she pulled and he flew at her. She screamed when he landed on top of her, then scrambled to get out from underneath him. Del scooted away and hugged herself. Was he alive? His dead eyes and open chest cavity suggested he wasn't. Del kicked at him and he jiggled, but didn't react. He was dead, no doubt about it. She shook herself out of the freakout, grabbed his arms, and pulled, gentler this time. Despite his size, she still moved him as easily as if he were a small child and she barely had to flex to do it.

To be safe, Del drug him out to the deeper water and shoved him under. He stared up at her from just below the surface for a second, then slowly disappeared into the murky brown Muskingum.

Del cleaned up the rest of the kill as best she could. She tossed all their gear into the river. She couldn't do anything about the *blood, but she scooped up every other part of them she could and fed it to the current and the snapping turtles. She roamed a bit and found two old pickups. The backs were full of beer cans and trash. She pushed them into the river and let the water claim them too. When she was done with her tidying, she waded out into the river and washed the blood and gore off herself as best she could. She scrubbed at her bloody hands, but she couldn't get them all the way clean. The blood stuck all the round her nails. She couldn't stop looking at it. She pushed down the image of their faces and mouths open in terror, those images were becoming fainter as she walked home, but when she looked down at her fingers, she was reminded of what she'd done and Del cried. They were silent tears; she didn't sob or wail, but they burned and they hurt and Del didn't think she'd ever get that brown crusted blood off herself, no matter how strong a soap and brush she used.*

She didn't go to Galen's. She followed the river and ended up at her gran's place. She stood in the doorway and burst into tears. When the old woman saw her, naked, filthy, with an uncharacteristically tear-stained face, she burst into tears herself and held Del tight.

"I didn't mean to do it, Gran. I swear, I didn't know."

They stayed like that for a while, until all of it was gone. When it was, her gran wiped Del's face with her apron and led her inside. She washed Del's hands herself with a stiff horsehair scrub brush and the homemade lye soap. When she was done, they were red, but they were clean. She said nothing to Del, she only whistled the soothing tunes that Del loved. She sent Del in for a proper bath and when Del came out, clean and dressed, her gran made her break-

fast. Del ate all of it and drank the tea her gran made that cured aches. Her gran watched her devour the meal. When Del finished, her gran stood up and kissed the top of her head.

"I'll show you how to stop it from happening again, sis. I promise."

CHAPTER 29

"THAT'LL BE ENOUGH. Take it out to Boreman Holler tomorrow."

"Del, you're out of your fucking mind if you think I'm going anywhere near a Boreman. I would rather eat glass and shit fire." Charity shook her head and shoved the stacks of cash into a duffle bag.

Normally, if an employee told her they would not do something, they didn't remain employed, and they rarely remained alive, but Charity was the exception and Del would have told somebody to go to hell too if they tried to make her go out to that holler again.

After the incident with Fernando and her refusal to take dogs, the Boremans had snuck into town and slashed her tires. One of them had scratched 'cunt' on the side of her Jeep, only the n was backward. Getting into a war with a passel of dirty goblins wasn't worth the hassle, and Del had plenty of hassle at the moment.

She had Jacob calling her every day, wanting to talk. She had the two FBI agents, Chase, and Crane, sniffing around, and she Olivia and her pet brujo skulking about, trying to decode her shipping system. Del had a lot of balls to juggle and adding in the Boremans just wasn't something she needed to deal with at the moment, so she had the scratches buffed out of her Jeep and calculated up what she owed Yella for all the extry. Once the Boreman's got their money, they'd crawl back up in their filthy holler and leave her in peace.

"Well, I guess I'll do it," Del said.

"I could send Kenny," Charity said.

Del thought about that a moment. Kenny was a vampire and he wouldn't be missed by anyone, that was for sure. He'd blown up two meth labs and currently, Del had him doing janitor work at Kitty's until she decided what to do with him. He was just as inept at unclogging toilets and mopping floors as he was at cooking, but Del hadn't given up hope that he could be useful for something. Kenny could be erased after he delivered the money, if he should he survive the encounter with the Boremans. But even to Del, who had no love for vampires, that seemed a little harsh. "Nah. I'll run it out there and toss it at them." Del picked up the bag and grabbed her keys. "I'm gonna go check on Virginia. You got a package for her?"

Charity nodded and handed Del an envelope. "How long you gonna keep this up?"

"What's the problem?"

"Del. I'm just saying, you ain't responsible for Misty Dawn."

Del tucked the envelope in her back pocket. She was responsible. The vampire and the cauliflower goat fuck were there because of her. "It ain't Ginny's or them kids' fault either."

"Suit yourself. Ginny has never been good at resource management. You can give her a million dollars and she won't know what to do."

"Maybe you should manage it for her," Del said. She grinned. "Yeah. That's it. You do it."

"I can, but you're still gonna go out there. You gotta let it go, Del."

"Charity. I trust you, but stop telling me what I gotta do."

"Somebody has to sometimes. You're in a bad position and this is a distraction. There's Feds in the parking lot. Jake is sniffing around. Some envelopes been light lately too, from your pack. I got a lot of cash to get cleaned and I need help, but you're too worried about Ginny Jesusfreak to help me. Get your head out of your ass, Delilah. I'm gonna pay her rent for a year and give her twenty-five grand. We got bigger fish to fry."

"Whoa, what do you mean, envelopes been light?" Del held up a hand. "From who?"

"All your guys. Last week. I told Cal to handle it, because I knew you was working them others."

"Charity, that's the sort of thing that requires my immediate attention." Light envelopes across the board were bad. Cal should have been the one to tell her, and he'd said nothing.

"So quit fucking around with Virginia and attend to it."

Del grumbled and growled under her breath, but she knew Charity was right. She had too many irons in the fire and all of them were ready to burn her if she didn't quit screwing around with people who wouldn't ever be able to take care of themselves. She grabbed the bag and kicked the back door open.

WHEN SHE ARRIVED at Virginia's trailer, the first thing Del noticed was that only the little boy was in the driveway. The three little girls were nowhere to be seen. When Del walked up, Virginia didn't look at her. She pulled long drags on a menthol cigarette and stared off into space.

Del knelt in front of Virginia. The woman's eyes were cloudy, and Del smelled that whiff of ozone that told her Virginia had been hack glamoured.

"Ginny. Where are the girls?"

"What girls?"

"Misty's girls. Where are they?"

Virginia looked around and then up at the sky. "Around here someplace, I suppose," she said.

For a second, Del was tempted to slap the glamour off her, but that didn't always work, and she didn't want to hurt

Virginia. She'd have to hit her hard. Del stood up and called Cal.

"Send Donny over to the trailer park. Lot 887. I need him to watch out for somebody over here. He don't need to go inside or nothing. Just watch in the driveway. Make sure nobody else comes here. Tell him to hurry the fuck up about it."

Del took Virginia by the arm. "Come on now, Ginny. You look tired. Let's rest a bit."

"Thanks, Del, I do feel kinda tuckered out," Virginia said. She allowed Del to lead her inside and settled in on the threadbare sofa.

Del looked around the trailer. There were pictures of Jesus everywhere. Jesus with kids, Jesus with angels, that disco Jesus picture with the rainbow coming from his hands. What was missing, and Del only noticed because of the dust outlines on the walls, were the crosses. Each one had been removed.

Del growled. She stood in the middle of the tiny living room and breathed in deep, sifting through all the scents until she found one that stood out. It ignited a rage and worry deep down inside her. She growled again and focused on it, shutting out everything else. The scent was faint in the living room, but Del followed it back the hallway to a bedroom. Discarded clothes hung from the rickety bunk bed and a few busted up toys littered the floor. The room reeked of the kids, but it also smelled of decay and cheap cologne.

Del punched several holes through the wood paneling

and ripped great hunks out of the wall, growling and screaming until she had punched the anger out. She took a few deep breaths and calmed herself. She needed to focus. There might still be time to find the girls.

Del knelt down next to Virginia. The woman stared ahead at the blank TV, but acted as if she was watching the Wheel of Fortune, remote control in hand.

"Ginny, was there a man here? Tall and skinny, black hair?"

Virginia didn't look away from the TV. "I can't recall, Del."

Del grabbed Virginia's chin and hauled back to slap her, but stopped. It wouldn't help to hurt Virginia, and it might be best if she stayed glamoured. "Okay, it's gonna be fine, Ginny. I'm going to go find your girls." Del stood up.

"What girls?" Virginia asked.

Del patted her on the shoulder. They'd have to de-glamour her. It wasn't hard, but Del didn't have the time to wait. She found the little boy.

"Bub, was there a man here? Tall and Skinny?"

The little boy nodded and picked his snot-crusted nose.

"He was? When?"

"This morning," the little boy said.

"He took your sisters?"

"I wanted to go too. They said they was going to the Dollar Tree for candy."

Del patted him on the back. "Well, I'm gonna go get 'em. You go on inside and sit with your grandma for a while." She deposited the little boy on the porch and shoved him toward the door.

Del pulled out her phone and found the number for one of her witches to come help Virginia, but thought for a second, then put the phone away. Virginia could wait. The little girls couldn't.

CHAPTER 30

DEL DROVE FAST as she could to the Hampton Inn. Olivia rented a house on Main, but everyone else, the goatfucker, the werewolves, and the bloodsucker were all staying at the Hampton.

Del got out of her Jeep and sniffed. The dead smell was strongest around the black Chevy Malibu with the dark-tinted windows. Del growled as she circled it. She ran her fist through the driver's side window, ignored the blood dripping from her hand, and stuck her nose up to the hole. She smelled the little girls.

The rage and fear rolled in her guts. Del stalked across the lot and into the lobby. She didn't bother with the desk clerk; she didn't need him to tell her what floor or room. Her nose led her there as the reek of the vampire and the girls' scents intensified. It stopped in front of room 345.

Del flexed her hand, growled, then rammed her fist through the door lock. She yanked it out, leaving a jagged hole, and tossed it behind her. Del grabbed the hole and yanked, pulling the door free. A few steps inside the room and her heart sank.

Two of the three girls were dead. Their little bodies were limp, thrown together in a pile on one bed, like discarded dolls that no longer held any fascination. In the movies, vampire bites were two neat little holes made by fangs that resembled hypodermic needles. That couldn't be further from the truth. Vampire bites were jagged, with chunks ripped out. They left gaping holes, not prim pricks.

Darius stood over the other girl, his face covered in blood from his nose to his chin. He sucked his fingers slowly, savoring the blood and pain. The little girl was dying; she choked and convulsed as blood pumped from the massive hole in her tiny neck. Darius smirked at Del and laughed.

She was too late before it even began. It was her problem, the deal with Martin, and it was a runaway train that Del couldn't control, couldn't stop, and couldn't even jump from.

The impotent rage inside Del boiled over, and she threw back her head and screamed. It ended in a long, hateful growl. Del clenched and unclench her fists. The bones in her hands and fingers popped and creaked as they grew and the muscles stretched, tore, and healed. Del welcomed the pain. She let it flow into the hate and rage. When the black claws shoved their way through her nails, Del growled again and she smiled at Darius, her long canine teeth showing as they erupted from her gums.

Darius backed up against the window. "Fucking werewolf whore," he said. "If you do anything to me, Martin will—"

His words ended in a gurgle as Del swiped her claws across his neck. Black, putrid blood poured from the slash and Darius put his hands to his throat and gagged. Blood swelled and bubbled from between his fingers, and before he could heal, Del let out another growl. She grabbed the sides of his head, sunk her claws in deep, then twisted and pulled. Darius's head popped off his neck like a grape from the vine. His body crumpled to the floor in a black, bloody heap.

The muscles in Del's claws spasmed, and she screamed. She dropped the vampire's head as the cramps worsened. The black nails pushed all the way out and fell to the floor, leaving bloody spaces that burned as her human nails grew back. She felt her teeth loosen, and she spit the big canines out in a bloody mass. Her normal canines pushed down through her gums. Del's hands twisted and cracked as they returned to their human form. They throbbed and shook. She kept hold of the pain and the rage and let them help her heal.

She couldn't give the little girls to the Rings or their hogs. She just couldn't. For the first time in many years, Del looked at a body, three of them, and she had to hold back a sob. Senseless. Waste. Ultimately, it was her fault and her responsibility. She understood both, and she didn't shy away from either.

Del pulled out her phone.

"Jake. Come on over to the Hampton. Room 345. When you see it, you'll know that I didn't do it, but you'll still have to come for me, and I'll understand. I can't say more now. Just come and help."

Del pocketed the phone. She picked up Darius's head. The magic that kept him alive had run out, and he was decaying. Soon he would be a black-green putrid mess. She pulled a pillowcase free, stuffed the head in it, and walked out of the hotel to her Jeep.

On the drive to Olivia's, the rage was still there with her, burbling just below her navel, in that place it liked to live, but it didn't feel bad; it felt like a trusted friend.

When Olivia saw her, she smiled and stood up at her desk. Del smiled back, then dumped Darius's rotting head out on the desk. Olivia looked down at it, then she looked up at Del and she shook her head.

"Del, this will not go—"

"Shut the fuck up. You got one hour to gather up whatever pieces of shit you got slinking around this town. In one hour, I hunt, and I will kill every last motherfucker I find."

"You can't win this," Olivia said.

Del turned and walked to the door. She pointed to the clock on the wall. "You're wasting time."

CHAPTER 31

"YOU TRAILED ALL OF 'EM? Every single one?" Del asked. Cal and three of his boys stood at attention in her office. The hour was up, and she was determined to hunt, but Olivia had cleared out of the Valley as Del demanded.

"Yes. All of them. We tracked them all the way to '77. Looks like they headed to Columbus," Cal said.

"Yeah and looks can be deceiving." Del loaded shells into her shotgun, then checked the clip in in her pistol. "Would you leave a billion-dollar operation in one hour just 'cause I told you to?"

"I reckon not."

"And neither would I. They ain't gone, leastways not all of 'em." She pointed at Joe and Frank. "You two, I want you to start at Olivia's house. Make sure all the trails lead out. Cal, go check at that office."

"Where are you gonna go, Del?"

"I'm going to Kitty's."

Cal looked confused. "Kitty's? Why?"

"Because if they're looking to set a trap for me, that's where it'll be." She tucked the pistol in her jeans, then grabbed the shotgun.

"You're just gonna walk into a trap?" Cal asked. "Let me go to Kitty's."

"It's only a trap if they catch you," Del said. "I ain't playing with them. You find a single one, you kill 'em. We don't need nobody for questioning. I don't give a shit if they beg. You see any of that crew, you put bullets in them until you ain't got no more bullets. You understand?"

WHEN DEL GOT to Kitty's, she sat in the Jeep for a moment and watched. The parking lot was full of cars, and music blared from the open doors. It was a perfect place to ambush her. The music, the thumping bass, all the smells of so many people assaulted Del's keen senses and made it impossible for her to discern any one sound or scent. Even the flashing lights and strobes from inside hurt her eyes. If she went in there, she'd be deaf, blind, and vulnerable. But that was where they would be, so Del would oblige them.

She shouldered the shotgun and checked her pistol, then walked a few steps away from the Jeep and took a couple long slow breaths in through her nose. She closed her eyes and concentrated, then smiled when the wind changed direction and she picked up a familiar scent—the earthy, wild aroma of other werewolves.

And stupid werewolves at that, Del thought. They were upwind of her, and the gentle night breeze carried their scent right to Del's nose. The pistol wouldn't be much use. You could shoot a werewolf just about anywhere except right between the eyes with a small caliber weapon, and it wouldn't do much except make them mad. The shotgun would work, but it would be noisy. She left it in the Jeep and took her Bowie knife instead.

Del kept low and made sure the wind was blowing in her face as she crept through the lot. The smell of him got stronger, and she saw him—one of the Red Hand Wolves, camped next to one boulder, guarding the side exit. She watched him a bit. He looked bored and paid no attention to the wind as he scrolled on his phone. Del smiled and held back the happy growl that meant business, then she clamped her hand over his mouth, pulled back his head, and ran the knife across his throat. He gurgled and choked as the blood sprayed out and over the boulder. She let him bleed a few more seconds, then she made another deep cut and didn't stop until she hit his vertebrae. She notched it, then snapped his head back. It hung on his body by the flap of skin in the back. He wouldn't heal from that. Del dropped the body behind the boulder, then crept to the side of the building. She crouched and sniffed the air. The other idiot stood by the back door. He looked more alert, at least he wasn't on his phone, but he yawned and stretched as if he needed a nap. He was no more difficult to deal with than his partner. Del lopped off his head and tossed it into the woods behind her. She threw his body in the dumpster.

There were more of them inside. The back door led right into the club office and she figured they'd be waiting for her there. She ran back to her Jeep and grabbed the shotgun. Loud was bad, but a shotgun in a tight place could be handy and her customers didn't get upset at a gunshot. It was worth the risk.

Del growled that happy violent growl and let the hate and rage percolate in her guts. It made her strong. She went to grab the door handle, then had a thought. She stopped and smelled the door. It was faint; whoever cast the spell was good, but it was tough to hide the smell of magic from a werewolf. She couldn't tell what spell was on the door, but Del was certain it wouldn't be a friendly one. She backed away and contemplated.

It would take too long to clean the door up, and she didn't want to be seen walking in through the front entrance. She needed whoever was inside to come out. Del ran back to the first body and grabbed his phone. She got the other one's phone as well and looked for a text or recent call they'd both been on. When she found it, she called the number from both phones and waited. When they answered, she said nothing, figuring a lengthy silence would do the trick. It did. The voice got agitated and Del grinned. She put the phones down, chambered a shell in her gun, and waited for the door to open.

When it did, she blasted him in the guts, felling him as soon as he stepped clear of the door. He cursed at her and growled as he crawled toward her. Del kicked him in the face, then blew his head off with the shotgun. She dragged him to the dumpster and chucked him in with his friend, then checked the door.

Once he'd come out, whatever spell they put on it was gone. She poked the door open and went inside. Nothing was amiss, but the place reeked of the California were-wolves. She growled. She'd have Charity repaint.

Satisfied that was the end of them, Del left out the back door. She tossed the first wolf's body into the dumpster, then walked back to her Jeep. The music and lights still blared from Kitty's. Nobody had heard the gun, and even if they had, it wasn't uncommon for rednecks to blast shotguns.

Del needed a drink. She left Kitty's and headed over to Marv's. She'd wait a few days before going home and she could bunk in the room above the bar until she made sure everything was clear. Marv was a great security system.

When she got to the bar, she put the shotgun down on the table and poured herself a large whiskey. She downed it and looked around. Marv wasn't there. Del scowled. He almost never left from behind the bar unless she asked him to pop off to an elsewhere. She took a sniff of the air, but all she could detect was the ancient cigarette stench of the place and a slight odor of fish.

Del poured one more shot, downed it, then picked up the shotgun and walked to the kitchen. She eased the door open and scanned.

She found Marv. He was screaming, but silently, stuck inside a salt circle that bound him to the spot. He yelled and pointed behind her, mouthing something. She smelled the fish more strongly, and something else, the rotten taco smell of Boremans.

A passel of them launched at her, at least three. Two of them went for her legs. One of them sunk his nasty goblin teeth into her thigh. She bashed him in the head with the butt of the gun, then blasted him. The other one bit her calf. He shook his head like a dog and Del shot him too, then kicked him away.

One jumped on her from behind. She rammed her back into the wall as hard as she could, and he dropped off. She pulled out her pistol and plugged him until he twitched. Del heard a noise behind her and whirled. When she did, white powder hit her in the face. Del coughed and choked. She dropped the gun and fell to her knees. Her vision blurred and she couldn't breathe, but she let the rage flow and caught her breath. She blinked a few times to clear her view and saw Yella Boreman standing in front of her with the Folger's can. The tranquilizer Aunt Jewel mixed up really could fell an elephant, most definitely a werewolf. It slowed her down long enough for Yella to jam a hypodermic full of Wolfsbane into Del's neck.

Yella stood over her and waited for her to pass out. "Sorry about it, Del, but they paid us extry. No hard feelings."

Del tried to tap into the rage and fought to stay awake, but the Wolfsbane was concentrated and it did its job. The last thing she saw before she lost consciousness was Yella clapping and Dandy Boreman dancing a jig as he called upon the Holy Spirit.

CHAPTER 32

WHEN DEL WOKE UP, she had all of her clothes on, a splitting headache, and she thought she was going to puke. It was the clothing that worried her. When Del woke up naked, she'd Turned, and she understood what she would deal with when she opened her eyes. Waking up clothed and groggy meant something terrible happened to her, and it wasn't something she could blame on the Turn.

She lay on her stomach on carpet that was sopping wet with blood. Del's priority was that it wasn't her blood. After examining herself, she surmised that it wasn't, but she wished that it was. It would be better than whatever came next.

She was hungover from the Wolfsbane. It dulled her senses and she couldn't detect anything. It also left her with a headache, nausea, and weakness. She pushed up and could barely raise herself to a sitting position.

"Sonofabitch."

Jesus in every iteration possible stared down at her from the walls. Virginia's body sprawled next to her on the carpet. She'd been gashed open all the way up the middle, and her throat was a wide red river where somebody slashed it. Del sniffed and tried to get a bead on who did it, but the Wolfsbane prevented her from detecting anything other than what a human could, which was blood and death.

Del strained and pushed herself to her feet. She was weak and dizzy, but she had to get moving. Movement would push the poison out of her faster, but it was also critical to avoiding the trap they'd laid for her. She knew the thing for what it was, a set-up. If she was lucky, she had a few minutes to get out and get gone before the cops showed up.

She looked down at Virginia. Poor Ginny with her thick thighs and Bible bookmarks. The boys in school had made her miserable. Del had always hated that, and she'd done her best to help. Now Ginny and her entire family were dead, and it was Del's fault. A part of her wanted to roll over—sit right back down on the blood-soaked carpet next to Ginny's corpse and wait until Jacob showed up with every deputy he employed. She deserved it. She deserved worse. But that wouldn't help anything. It wouldn't stop the monsters that did it from doing it again. It wouldn't bring back Ginny, or Misty-Dawn, or those three little girls.

As she thought about the family, Del realized, she was

missing one. The little boy's body wasn't in the living room. He could be dead somewhere in the trailer and Del debated if she wanted to find another kid's body, but she had to know. Del limped down the hall and checked the bathroom. He wasn't in the shower. She checked Virginia's bedroom. He wasn't under the bed or in the closet. Del swayed as she walked to the end of the hall to the kids' room, stopped, and listened. The whooshing sound in her ears was clearing out, and she heard a few little sniffs. She found him wedged back up under the bunk bed.

"Hey," Del said. "You wanna come out from under there?"

The little boy shook his head. "They killed my mammaw."

Del nodded. "Somebody did, yep. They're gone now."

"I know. I seen them leave you. They didn't see me because I hid."

"Good job, bub," Del said. "Why don't you come on out?" If the kid had seen them dump her, he'd be the key to her getting out of the mess.

"Okay, but if they come back, I'm going back under there." He squeezed out from under the bed and looked at Del as he picked his nose. "You figure they'll come back?"

"Naw. They ain't coming back." Del got to her feet. She lost her balance and caught herself on the bunk bed frame. She took a second to rest, sucked in a big breath, then held out a hand to the little boy. "Come on, let's go."

He shook his head and cried. "I don't wanna. I don't wanna look at Mammaw no more."

"Close your eyes. I'll tell you when to open 'em."

"We can't just stay back here?"

"No, that ain't a good idea."

"Why?" he asked. "Is it dangerous? You said they wasn't coming back."

"They ain't, but we should get gone." Del looked around the room and found a cheap fleece blanket with a puppy on it. She wrapped it around him and made a blinder. "Pull that over your head, bub. I'll carry you."

Del wasn't sure she could carry him. She could barely carry herself, but it would be the only way to get him to go, and she couldn't leave him in a trailer with a corpse.

He nodded and held out his arms. "Okay. I won't look."

Del took a deep breath and steadied herself, then she picked him up. He put his arms around her neck and buried his face in it.

"You ready, bub? Remember, no looking until I say."

"Yep," he said, muffled in the blanket and her skin.

Her arms could barely hold him. They shook with the effort of supporting his weight, but Del somehow got out of the trailer with him. She had just come down the steps when she saw the flashing lights of the patrol cars.

Jacob was calm, but the deputies all fumbled out of their cars and drew on her. Del's senses were returning, and she smelled the fear on them. It didn't smell delicious to her, as it once did.

"Put the kid down and get on the ground, Delilah," Jacob said. His voice was calm, and even, and sad.

"Tell them to put them guns away. I ain't gonna hurt this boy," Del said as she set the kid down.

"Get down on the ground, Delilah. Face down." Jacob wasn't playing.

The little boy peeked out from under the blanket. "Uh oh. Cops," he said.

Del got on her knees. "Listen, bub, you walk over there, real slow, to that big one. The one that looks like a bear. You see him?"

The kid nodded. "Yeah, but he's a cop. Mama said—"

"He is, and he's a nice one. He'll help you out." Del nodded toward Jacob. "Go on now."

She gave him a little push. He looked at her and paused, but then went to Jacob. Del lowered herself flat on the ground and waited. The deputies swarmed around her. They yanked her arms back and cuffed her. She growled as they kicked her a little. The anger helped her clear her head, and she felt her strength coming back. They hauled her to her feet and slammed her against one cruiser. Jacob put the boy in the patrol car, then walked over to Del. He looked at her blood-soaked clothes, lowered his head, and looked sick.

"Ginny in there?"

Del nodded. "Yep. I didn't do it, Jake."

"I know it."

"Let me go. I'll find the ones who did."

Jacob shook his head. "Not this time, Del."

"I reckon you gotta do what you gotta do," Del said. She

didn't struggle as they bashed her head into the door jamb and shoved her in the back of the cruiser.

She ignored all the shit talk and threats from the deputies. They'd been the crew that had found the little girls, and that carnage was still angry and fresh in their minds. Likely it would never leave them, it certainly would never leave her, so she let them cuss and spit at her and didn't even fight back when one of them hit her a good solid lick with a nightstick. She stayed calm and silent. After they booked her and chucked her in the holding cell, Jacob came by.

"This is bad, Del. I don't think you're getting clear of it this time."

Del didn't comment. She sat down on the bare metal bench in the holding cell and folded her hands. She cleared her throat and looked up at Jacob. "I'd like to speak to my attorney."

CHAPTER 33

IN THE YEARS that Elizabeth Barton-Carr had been Del's attorney, she had never once failed Del in any task. She'd made countless charges disappear, handled financial transactions, set up strange accounts, found people that didn't care to be found, and so many other things that Del couldn't have kept track of them if she'd tried.

And further, in all those instances, never once had Del seen Elizabeth rattled or uncertain of the outcome, but there was a first time for everything. Elizabeth fidgeted with her pen and kept taking her glasses off and cleaning them. She was over seventy, but still one of the sharpest women Del had ever met. She hadn't slowed down a second since she'd gotten Del out of her very first murder investigation thirty years ago, but now she looked tired and old, despite her tailored suit and expensive make-up and hair.

"So, they have you at a murder scene covered in the victim's blood. You called in a homicide of three small girls, and you were fleeing the scene with a five-year-old boy. Really, Delilah?"

Del was shackled to the table and unable to move much, but she still managed a shrug. "That's all circumstantial."

"Don't tell me what it is and what it isn't." Elizabeth put her pen down and folded her hands. Del noticed they shook a little. "I'm going to go for procedural problems. Did they Mirandize you properly?"

"This time? They sure did. Jacob has learnt his lesson there."

"Great. Well, they'll mess up evidence handling. Don't worry."

"I ain't. Except what about bond?"

Elizabeth sighed. "It will be tough. That's a lot of dead bodies, plus, the FBI is involved. They jumped on you and that boy. Why didn't you just leave him? He wasn't in any danger."

Del narrowed her eyes. "His entire family is dead. He was under a bed in an old trailer with his dead grandma. I ain't leaving a kid to that."

"It was stupid. Now they want you on kidnapping, which is Federal. That will make the bond impossible."

"It ain't impossible. Who's the judge gonna be? Dub Taylor?"

Dub Taylor was the likely Common Pleas judge, and he was also on Del's payroll. He liked whores and cocaine. It would be simple enough to get the bond if he was the one setting it.

Elizabeth nodded. "Yes, it will be him. But even though he's ours, his hands might be tied by the FBI."

"Well, he best see that they ain't," Del said. She rattled the chains that held her to the table. "You got forty-eight hours to get me out of here."

"You don't go before him until tomorrow."

"Well, then you got less than that," Del snarled.

"Don't give me any shit, Delilah. This is beyond fucked up. We talked about you putting yourself in these kinds of positions."

"Couldn't be helped," Del said. She said it with an angry finality and an ominous look.

"We need to be ready if an alternate plan is required," Elizabeth said. "Everything is in place for that. Are you prepared?"

"Always," Del said. She lied. She wasn't. Del had worked the Valley and beyond for so long now that the idea of disappearing into another life didn't seem like it could be a thing. She wasn't like normal people who could just go anywhere. Her needs were specific.

Elizabeth looked skeptical. She eyed Del over her glasses and raised an eyebrow. "I do not understand how you're such a good criminal yet such a terrible liar."

"Liz, I'm sitting in the pokey up on four charges of homicide and one of kidnapping. How good a criminal can I be?" Del laughed at it once she'd said it out loud.

Elizabeth cracked a smile, then laughed too. "We're not licked yet, as you would say."

The saying sounded funny coming from Elizabeth in her New York accent, and Del laughed harder. "No, we ain't. That little boy might could help. He saw who killed Virginia, and he seen them dump me in the trailer."

"A traumatized five-year-old boy is our star witness? We're fucked," Elizabeth said.

"Almost always," Del said, "but he's what we got. Nobody glamoured him. He wasn't scared of me."

"I'll look into it. We can't afford to leave any stone unturned." Elizabeth gathered her things, then buzzed for the deputy to let her out. "I'll get busy. We're on for tomorrow at ten. I'll try to get to the judge before then."

"I think you'd better do more than try, Liz."

The old woman nodded. "This will be one to quit on Delilah. No doubt." The deputy opened the door and Elizabeth left Del there, chained and uncertain.

"No fucking doubt," Del said as she watched her leave.

THEY WOULDN'T LET Del change out of the County Orange for the hearing. She stood before Judge Avery "Dub" Taylor in pants too short for her and a tight orange top. They had shackled every inch of her. Her feet were double chained together and she could barely shuffle walk. It was annoying, but it made them feel safe. They didn't really know what she was, but Jacob did, and he used every trick he had to secure her. It wouldn't have even been close to enough if Del decided she wanted free. She could pop those chains and cuffs as if they were crepe paper streamers. It wasn't time for that yet.

She shuffled in next to Elizabeth at the table.

Dub Taylor scribbled on a notepad. He looked up from his papers at Del, then he read all the charges to her, and asked her if she understood them.

"I understand," Del said.

"And how do you plead?"

"Not guilty," Del said. She squinted and looked at Dub. His eyes looked cloudy, but she couldn't tell from that far away.

"Defendant has entered a plea of not guilty," the judge said. "Pretrial Hearing is set for August 17th."

"Your honor, that is two months away. That's not acceptable," Elizabeth countered.

"That's when it's scheduled," Dub said.

"An Appellate court will love this," Elizabeth said to Del. She looked to the judge. He was about to set bond.

"Based on the extreme nature of this case, bond is denied."

Del sniffed the air. She caught a whiff of ozone. She busted the chains holding her feet and got to the bench before Jacob or his deputies could stop her. Dub's eyes were cloudy and when she got close, he reeked of magic.

The deputies tackled her and shoved her to the ground. Del didn't resist, and when they hauled her upright, they dragged her back toward the jail. Del looked over at Elizabeth and shook her head.

"Gonna have to go to Plan B."

CHAPTER 34

"LET'S GO, MONROE." The pimple-faced deputy whacked the bars with his nightstick and chomped his gum. He adjusted his crotch, then banged on the bars again. "Somebody wants to see you."

"Fuck off, Kyle. Why can't you just send 'em in here? I ain't in the mood for all them chains and shit."

"FBI."

"I don't need to talk to them."

"You don't get a choice."

"The fuck I don't," Del said. "I talk to my lawyer."

The door buzzed and opened. The two FBI agents sauntered through.

"Thanks, deputy," Chase said as he patted the deputy on the shoulder. "We'll take it from here. Hello, Del. Can we speak?" Chase smiled at her.

"Speak all you like." Del reclined on the bunk and put her hands behind her head.

"You're in a pickle," Chase said. He whistled a long missile sound. "A real jam. We think we can help. And you can help us."

Del snorted. "Oh yeah? You want me to help you catch a serial killer? Fuck off."

Agent Crane crossed her arms and cleared her throat. "You're going to prison for life. You may get the death penalty. We'll ensure that doesn't happen if you help us catch Martin Price." She had no bedside manner at all. Del respected that.

Del closed her eyes. She didn't need their deal, and she wouldn't be in jail for life. She might die, but it wouldn't be in the State Pen by lethal injection.

"Help us, Del. We'll help you. That kidnapping charge is a problem. We'll fold that into a RICO," Chase said.

Del hated him, with his slicked-over, earnest hair and fake concern. At least the woman was all business, even if you could likely freeze ice in her pussy.

"If I'm going to the chair, why the fuck would I care about a RICO? Call my lawyer. I got nothing to say to you."

"You will die, Delilah," Crane said. "This way, you live."

"I don't know how much clearer I can be. Fuck the fuck off," Del said. She rolled over on the cot and gave them her back.

"Mistake, Delilah. Huge mistake," Chase said. He sighed. "We'll see how it plays out."

"Yeah, I reckon we will," Del said. She closed her eyes and ignored them until they went away.

An hour later, Elizabeth stormed through the door.

"Somebody has more pull than you, because they won't budge on the bond. I suggested a ridiculous amount, and he still didn't bite."

Del sat up. "Not more pull, just more magic."

"There's no coming back from this."

"There was never gonna be any coming back from this," Del said. "I can't stay here tonight."

The Turn was coming. She could already feel the tingles and cramps. In the back of her mind was always the thought of losing control, and the incident with the vampire had only added to that anxiety. Her hands still ached from that partial transformation, and the rage ball lurked, popping up from time to time and threatening to erupt. She'd sweat through her county orange twice already and everything pointed toward a violent and unpredictable Turn that night. There was no chance of Del remaining in the jail for that. It wouldn't hold her, and everyone in the building would die. Del didn't want that, not at all.

Elizabeth nodded. "All right. Everything is ready. You'll be in touch?"

"Yes. Look. Lizzy, get clear of it. Soon as you can."

Elizabeth nodded. "I have enjoyed you, Delilah. Until we meet again."

Del stood up and went to the bars. "I appreciate all your help. Take care of yourself."

Elizabeth nodded again. She opened her mouth to speak, but couldn't seem to make any words come out. A first. Del watched her face. The old woman who had been a raging ball-buster for as long as Del had known her seemed to be holding back emotion.

"It'll all work out, Lizzy," Del said. She sat back down on the bunk and winked at the old woman. "Best leave it to me."

DEL LAY still on the cot as she listened and took deep breaths. She needed to be strong, yet focused. She couldn't afford for the rage ball to take over if things got heated.

Through the metal door, she heard the desk clerk finishing up and the deputies jawing at each other as they passed through at shift change. She waited another twenty minutes until the second shift was on by themselves. Del got up from the bunk. She yawned and stretched, then she grabbed hold of the bars and pulled. The metal hinges screeched and popped as she ripped the door free. Del tossed it aside, then pulled the outer door open. The magnetic plate at the top ripped out of the wall, and she walked calmly through the door to the office.

The night clerk's mouth dropped open. He stared at her for a second, then fumbled at his gun. Del vaulted over the counter, hoisted him up, and took the weapon.

"Please, don't shoot me," he blubbered, closing his eyes as he waited for the shot.

"I ain't gonna kill you," Del said. She set him on his feet. "Give me your car keys."

He unhooked his key ring. His hands shook, and the keys jingled as he held them out to her.

"Not to your fucking personal vehicle. I want your patrol car."

"I-I don't have one. I'm just the desk—"

"Fucking find me a set," Del growled. She was cutting it close. The deep rumble had started in her guts and little beads of sweat formed on her upper lip as her body recognized the Turn was near.

He went to a cabinet on the wall and unlocked it, then pulled out all the keys and handed them over. Del took them, then pointed toward the jail. Once inside, she cuffed him to the metal bunk.

"Keep quiet, Stu. I know where you live. You get it?"

He nodded and cried. "I swear I won't yell. Don't hurt me."

Del rolled her eyes. If she was gonna kill him, she would have just shot him and left. Jacob hired stupid cops these days.

She left through the back door and found two patrol vehicles, an old Crown Vic cruiser and a new SUV. Del figured Jacob could afford to replace the old Crown Vic. She was about to open the door and get in when she heard somebody behind her.

"Where you going, Del?" Jacob loomed, his arms crossed on his massive chest.

"Can't stay, Jake."

He shook his head. "I can't let you go."

"You can, and you're going to," Del said. She opened the car door, and he drew his gun. Del looked at it and smiled. "You ain't gonna sh—". She screamed when he shot her in the leg. "Goddammit!"

"The next one goes in your shoulder," Jacob said. "Come on back inside now."

The pain in Del's leg was white hot, but she had a high tolerance for it. She growled, pulled her gun, and shot Jacob in his right shoulder. He grunted and fell to the ground. Del limped over and kicked his gun away. Del took off the orange sweatshirt, balled it up and held it to his shoulder.

"You big, dumb, fuck. I didn't want to shoot you."

He nodded. "Well, at least now your escape looks legit."

"I didn't kill Ginny or those little girls," Del said. She pressed harder on his shoulder. "You gotta do it tight to stop the bleeding 'til the squad comes."

"I know you didn't. You couldn't. But you can't just leave jail."

"I have to. It ain't safe." A cramp hit her guts and she bit back a yell. Del got up and limped to the car. "Don't mess with these people. I'll take care of it. You gotta trust me."

"I do, but—" Jacob got to his feet.

"Goodbye, Jake." She felt a lump form in her throat. He had been a soothing presence in her life for the entirety of it. Even when they were at odds, he was there, loving her, whether or not she wanted him to. She'd never feel that again, him occupying that comforting space. Del left him there in the parking lot, bleeding, as she sped off in the stolen Crown Vic.

She ditched it back up an old log trail and ran the rest of the way to the Hollow. Her leg was screaming at her, but she'd be fine once she turned. It wasn't the first time she'd been shot.

The boys stared and whispered, shocked to see her there.

"Dang, Del, what did you do, bust out?" Donny Belvin asked.

Del rolled her eyes. "Nah, they let me out for good behavior. Where's Cal?"

Cal was supposed to be there, coordinating the Turn for everyone, and making sure somebody sealed the Hollow.

"Ain't seen him all day," Donny said.

Del didn't like it. With Glenna gone, they had nobody to seal them in. Cal should have seen to a new witch.

"You all get as far back up in them woods as you can," she yelled. "Go now, before you start."

They all grumbled. They liked to strut around and jaw before the Turn. This cut in on their fun.

Del let out a hateful scream that ended in a loud growl. "I fucking said get up in them woods, now!"

They all scattered and headed off into the trees, looking back at her as they did. She was testy of a Turn; they had all seen what she could and would do when pushed. Some of them had scars as reminders.

Del ran back up in the woods too. She needed to get

farther back up in there than anyone else. She would be the most dangerous if she went out on the roads and couldn't guarantee she wouldn't, not without a barrier up.

She limped as far back as she could and shucked off the orange pants and t-shirt before the cramps hit her hard, and she had to stop. Del dropped to her knees and panted as the pain gripped her. She focused on that and let the heat and agony take her. That was all she needed to worry about. Not jail breaks, or demons, or murder charges. Surviving the moment was all there was, at least until the morning.

CHAPTER 35

WHEN DEL WOKE UP, she didn't head back to the Hollow. Instead of walking back down the mountain, she went further up, to the peak where the old phone tower stood. The rusted top spier had collapsed, but it was a good landmark for her. Del found the place where the spier had fallen and dug around in the pine needles and dirt until she found the box. She'd hidden it long ago and sealed within it was a backpack with clothes, a fake ID, a pistol, and $200,000 in cash. After Del dressed, she checked the magazine in the gun, tucked it in the back of her jeans, then shouldered the backpack, and hiked down the mountain.

It was a lengthy walk to Aunt Jewel's place, and past midday by the time Del got there. The oppressive air caught in her lungs, and thick sweat poured from her. Del's head pounded from a lack of water and whiskey. She wiped the sweat from her face as she hunkered down in the woods across the road and watched. Aunt Jewel didn't own a car, but there was one parked in the drive with Maryland plates. It screamed rental car and Del's stomach lurched.

She ran across the road and up the little sidewalk. The screen door hung by one hinge and had a hole burnt in it. There was blood all over the porch, but no body. Aunt Jewel had finally blasted somebody. Del sniffed. Werewolves, and not hers. She growled and bared her teeth, then sniffed again. The scent of magic tickled her nose. That didn't surprise her, Aunt Jewel could sling curses with the best of them, and if she'd had to empty the shotgun, she wouldn't have hesitated to curse her unwanted visitors. The gun lay in the entryway. Once Aunt Jewel had emptied the barrels, she'd abandoned it.

The blood and magic trail led inside and down the hall. Aunt Jewel's old man was dead. A jagged fist-sized hole in his throat and the smell of wolf on him told Del all she needed to know about that.

The blood led away from him and down the hall, into the kitchen. She found the wolf there. He huddled in the corner by the refrigerator and whimpered. Blood soaked his middle from the gut wound. He'd heal from that, so that wasn't his chief problem. The bigger problem was that Aunt Jewel had hit him with at least three different curses.

His face sagged and drooped and looked like Silly Putty.

That was one of Aunt Jewel's specialties. The skin melted over his right eye, but Del could see that his eyes were milky green. She'd blinded him too. But the worst of all was the blood that dribbled from his mouth as he whimpered, burbling up from the space where his tongue used to be. He clutched the organ and when he heard Del, he looked around the room and mumble-cried, holding up his severed tongue in lament. The curse had made him rip it out himself. It was a vicious spell and one that she'd only heard old stories about. It was impressive that at 90, the old girl still had it in her.

Del didn't bother with the werewolf right away. He wasn't going anywhere, and she needed to find Jewel. Bloody footprints—three sets, one lug soled boots, one long-toed cowboy boots, and one that looked like little old lady Keds, all led outside. The screen door was missing. Del found it a few feet away, crumpled and mashed. She found the man wearing the lug soled boots-another wolf, unconscious. She kicked him over and saw white powder covering his face. A quick sniff told her it was the elephant tranquilizer. She left him and followed the scent trail and the other two sets of prints.

She found Aunt Jewel in her herb garden. They'd strung her up on her trellis. Thick black vines bound her to it, and the surrounding earth was black and scorched. The vines were slick with black ooze, and it trickled down Aunt Jewel's body from her binding. The old woman's eyes were gone. Great gaping holes were all that remained, and the inky tar

234

trickled down her cheeks. Her mouth was black from it too, as if it erupted from her guts.

Del fell to her knees and cried. Aunt Jewel had been her only surviving family and the last link she had to her gran. Even if Aunt Jewel had been a little crazy, she'd always been there, and her death reminded Del of the lonely black hole in her heart that she'd been trying to navigate around for a very long time. She cried until she felt something else, and that was her friend, the Rage, blossom in her guts. It bloomed and grew until it pushed the lonely sad back into its place.

Del growled and stood up. She sniffed around the area and gagged, overwhelmed by the smell of magic. She concentrated and realized she could pick out two distinct scents. One was positively Aunt Jewel. It smelled of ammonia and ozone and whiskey. The other one was ozone and prickly, but it smelled exotic, like spices. Del connected the dots and realized where she'd smelled it before. The Brujo she'd met in Laredo, Martin's pet witch. His footprints were the boots. Del followed them back through the grass to the front of the house. She found another set of tire tracks. The Brujo left in the second vehicle and abandoned the two wounded wolves to their fate, whatever it might be. Del was ready to resolve that question for them.

Her first stop was the garden shed. She selected the well-worn mattock from the pile of tools. Del went for the unconscious wolf first. He was just starting to blubber and moan as Aunt Jewel's tranquilizer wore off. Del considered letting him wake up and ask him some questions, but she knew who had ordered everything, and she knew where they would be, so she let her friend the Rage take control. She hacked off the Red Hand wolf's head with the flat side of the tool. The mattock wasn't as decisive as axe would have been and he struggled as she chopped, but the Rage loved it, and so did she.

When she finished with him, she went in the kitchen and drug the blind, tongueless wolf outside. He spit blood at her and mumbled as he kicked and wiggled, but Del had no trouble. It was as if he weighed nothing and his movements were wisps of a feather. She buried the pick side of the garden tool deep into his skull over and over until she was sure he couldn't heal from that. She left the mattock buried in his head mush.

With as much tenderness as Del had in her, she cut the vines that held the old woman, then laid her on the ground. The other two could rot in the summer heat, but she wouldn't leave Aunt Jewel to a mass of blowflies and maggots. She dug a hole in Aunt Jewel's sunflower patch. The big-faced flowers were in full summer bloom, and Aunt Jewel had always loved them. Del went to lift Jewel and noticed something in the pocket of her housecoat. It was a good-sized ginseng root, and it was out of place. Aunt Jewel didn't use ginseng, and she hadn't sold it for years. When Del was a kid, she'd gone with them back up in the woods to harvest the roots from her gran and Jewel's secret patch. It wasn't too far from the house, and it occurred to her that maybe the root wasn't random.

She stood at the edge of the woods and looked out through the trees as she turned the ginseng root over and over in her hand. It might be a clue, or it might just be a coincidence. Del's thirty years' experience in life and magic and crime had taught her coincidence was a fallacy, but she doubted that Aunt Jewel had meant for her to find the patch. The woman was old as dirt and likely couldn't have hiked out that far. It could be a distraction, a fruitless traipse back up in the woods that would cost her precious time. But then again, Aunt Jewel did pretty much whatever she was of a mind to do, sane or not, so it would be foolish for Del to doubt her.

The decision was made for her when she saw a white shimmer in the trees. It swirled around and twinkled in the afternoon sun, then formed up into a familiar figure.

In the last thirty years, Del had been shocked into awe maybe twice. That afternoon was the third. Her gran stood before in the woods. She looked younger, like Del's favorite picture of her, with the carefully coiffed beehive hair, colored bright red. She smiled at Del, and Del dropped to her knees and cried. When Del looked up, the apparition was still there, smiling down at her, a little closer. Del could feel the waves of magic and love pulsing from it. Then she heard the humming. It was the same tune her grandma always hummed, the old mountain ballad. It buoyed Del and comforted her, wrapping her in a cocoon of familiarity and love. She wiped her eyes and stood up. Her gran turned and floated through the woods.

Del followed her along the familiar path, and when they arrived at the ginseng patch, the humming got louder, and her gran came close. She reached out a shimmering hand and touched Del's cheek. Del tried to hold back the tears, but she sobbed, and they flowed again. She bowed her head. She was ashamed of herself. Of what she had become, what she did. She'd always hoped that her gran couldn't see it, but this apparition proved to Del that she could see it, and Del couldn't deny it or lie to herself any longer. She was paying for it all, and so was everyone around her.

Del jumped when she felt a light shock to her cheek. Her gran's hand tilted her chin up and caressed her face as she hummed. Del didn't feel disappointment from her; she felt that same thing she'd always felt. Love.

Del wiped the tears away and smiled at the ghost. Her gran smiled back, then stepped away. The tune faded out as she disappeared into the underbrush.

Next to an ancient Elm tree, Del found a spot of upturned earth. Buried about a foot down was a rusted Royal Dansk Danish cookie tin. Inside was a bunch of herbs and other ingredients and a letter from Aunt Jewel. In the old woman's shaky but careful cursive script, she'd detailed the binding spell.

Del put all the ingredients in her backpack, then hiked back to the house. She grabbed the shotgun and some shells, and a few bits of magic she thought might be useful. She also took the rest of Aunt Jewel's Old Grandad whiskey. The old woman wouldn't need it anymore and waste not, want not.

Del found the rental car keys on one of the werewolves, and she chucked her stuff in the passenger seat of the Nissan. It was getting late, and she needed a place to Turn. Del sped off toward one of her safe houses as she contemplated her next chess move.

CHAPTER 36

DEL MADE one of the boys take a message to Cal. She thought one of three things would happen. If Cal had not turned against her, he'd show up as asked. He'd always been loyal. If Del told him to do something; he did it, but in her heart, she knew that he was not with her anymore, if he had ever been. The light envelopes and the fact that he hadn't been the one to tell her about it told her that at the very least, he was skimming. She expected a little skim; it was the price of doing business. Guys kicked up what they thought they had to, and they never reported all of it. Del understood that. But light envelopes from everyone and a no-show on a Turn night signaled that Cal was gone, and he wasn't coming back.

The second possibility was that Martin's goons would be waiting for her. She'd kill them like she'd killed the others. The third possibility was that Cal had been working with the

Feds and instead of werewolves and demons, Federal agents would descend upon her. She had a police radio from the cruiser, and they hadn't been smart enough to change the channel, or at least, Jacob hadn't done it. She knew the locals and Fed were looking for her, and she couldn't stay in the area for much longer. Del prepared mentally and physically for either faction to be waiting for her in the morning.

When she woke up, she hiked back toward the Hollow following the trail of the boys. They were in fine spirits. Energized and refreshed, they teased and picked as they headed home. They had no idea Del trailed them, which disappointed her. She expected her people to be smarter.

When they got to the edge of the woods, the boys carried on as normal, but Del hung back. She circled around the hill and found the best observation spot. From there she could see the tree line and the road. The cop cars lined the dirt road just outside the Hollow, flashing their reds and blues. There were a few dark sedans—the FBI and state police. Jacob leaned against one of the trailers, sipping coffee, his arm in a sling. He looked bored. Del knew that it wasn't his idea to come out. He knew her well-enough to know that she wouldn't be stupid enough to show up there.

But somebody else didn't know that. For sure Cal hadn't known it, because he had called somebody and told them where she would be. Whether he called Martin or whether he called the Feds, Del didn't know.

Del laughed as the boys came out of the woods, and their moods went from swagger-happy to scared shitless when the cops put them all on the ground to arrest them. Del wasn't worried about them. She had good lawyers set up for these things, and they didn't really have anything on the boys. They'd all be out in a couple of hours. If any of them flipped on her, she wasn't worried about that either. The Feds already had dirt, and none of the boys could swear to as much as Cal could. Besides, it was past time for worrying about getting locked up for extortion and racketeering. Way past time.

Del circled back, then hiked out to where she'd hidden the rental car. Cal hadn't made the Turn at the Hollow, but he had to do it somewhere. She thought she knew where that would be. His family had a deer camp up in Morgan County. They all liked to turn there, but Cal didn't have but a few cousins left, so it would be sparse with folks. That suited Del just fine. The fewer people there, the better.

Everyone was gone by the time Del got there. She parked the car on a log trail and hid it with brush, then she hiked in. Their scent trail was easy to follow, and she knew about how far out they'd roamed the night before. Her main issue was that she couldn't control where she would end up in the morning. It was fine to turn out here, but there was no guarantee she'd be close when she woke up. She needed to catch Cal.

There was one person who could help her with that. She hesitated, thinking back to the last time, but if there was one thing Yella Boreman understood, it was money, and Del had

$200,000 in cash. She had time to make it out to Boreman Holler, just enough.

There was no way the Nissan was going down into the holler itself, so Del parked it a few miles out and walked the rest of the way. The first thing Del noticed was the lack of dogs. There wasn't a single dog running around the place and before, there had been upward of twenty. Nothing moved, nothing skittered in the trash, not even a rat. Del cocked the shotgun and hurried through the tangled mess of grass and garbage until she came to Yella's trailer.

She found Yella there, crying as she watched Dandy scream and throw himself against the side of the trailer over and over. He had angry scratches and festering bites all over him. Dandy got a running start every time, and he ran full tilt, then crashed his head against the side of the trailer, screaming nonsense. It was different from his normal gibberish and nonsense. In this, there was none of Dandy's signature pomp and Biblical diarrhea. This was the ravings of a person who had seen terror and couldn't stop seeing it.

Del lowered the shotgun. She knew who had been out there. The smell of fish and Sulphur remained.

"Yella," Del said.

Yella looked up at Del. Her tear-stained face was equal parts terrified and angry. "They sure are a hateful bunch, ain't they, Del."

Del looked about the place. "How many of your folks did they kill?"

"Not so many, but that man made 'em crazy. Made all the dogs go nuts, too. They all runned off in the hills."

Both Del and Yella jumped when Dandy landed a particularly loud whack against the trailer.

"He can't be fixed, can he, Del?"

Del shook her head. "No, Yella. He can't be fixed.

Yella broke down and cried. "I can't do it, Del."

Del patted the little goblin woman awkwardly and tried to hold her breath. Yella's smell had changed when she'd given up hope. She emitted a sour vomit stench. Del thought Boremans couldn't smell any worse, but she had been wrong.

"I'll do for him, Yella."

Yella sniffed and looked up. "You will?"

Del nodded. "And all your folks who need it too."

"Why? We waylaid you good. You're screwed now."

Del shrugged. "Business is business. It wasn't personal." Del looked around. "Where's all the rest?"

"Hiding under the trailers."

Del nodded. She went trailer by trailer. All in all, she found twenty-seven Boremans, all batshit crazy. They hissed and cried as they dug holes and shit themselves. Some of them were eating dogs. Del shot each one. It was easy. They didn't put up any fuss. When she got to Dandy, Yella cried and screamed. Del hauled him up, took him a ways up in the woods, and shot him in the head. She brought his body back to Yella and laid him at her feet.

"He looks like he's sleeping. I guess he's with Jesus, now. Like he always wanted." She broke down crying again.

"Yella, I got one last job for you."

"I-I don't know, Del. I'm thinking we steer clear of that bastard."

"It's best you do. I'll deal with him. I want you to snatch my guy, Cal." Del put down the gun and took off the backpack. She pulled out the cash. "I'll give you everything I got right now, 200 grand, to snatch him tomorrow morning."

When Yella saw the money, her eyes cleared up, and she sniffed. "That's a lot just to snatch one werewolf."

"Yeah, well, short notice. Can you do it? You got enough kin?"

"I'm Yella Boreman and I'm the biggest, baddest motherfucker of all the Boremans and you better believe that." Yella didn't scream it this time. She said it softly, and Del thought it was more to convince herself than anyone else. Maybe it always had been. Del knew the feeling.

"That's why I come out here. Will you do it?"

Yella straightened her squat little shoulders and screwed up her face in reckless determination. She spit a green wad into her hand and held it out for Del. "I'll do it, but I don't want no money. I want you to send that demon shitbird straight back to Hell."

Del spit in her palm, then slapped it into Yella's as they shook on it.

CHAPTER 37

WHEN DEL WOKE UP, she was clean, and she was close to where she'd stashed her things. She washed off in a little creek, then dressed, and headed to Boreman Hollow. She had to walk, and it was far, but she'd wanted to be far enough away not to run in to any other wolves, and she'd told Yella she'd be there by noon.

The position of the sun in the sky showed her she was right on schedule. When she walked out of the woods into the hollow, she saw several more Boremans than she'd seen yesterday. They were cleaner, less albino, and they smelled different from the rest. She found Yella smoking a cigarette and sitting on an old porch swing that wasn't hanging on anything. It was propped up between a garbage can and a couple of car fenders. It was too high for Yella and her legs dangled like a kid's, which gave a more whimsical sense to the scene than it deserved.

"Who's all them folks?" Del asked, nodding to the cleaner goblins.

"Some relations from Porter. I called 'em up. They was keen to help."

"You get him?" Del asked.

"Does a bear shit in the woods?" Yella stubbed out the cigarette and jumped down from the swing seat. "I got him in the shed."

"Good, that's perfect," Del said.

She heard tires and saw a black SUV roll into the hollow. Del narrowed her eyes and furrowed her brow. She wasn't confused as to who it was, she was annoyed.

"How the fuck did you find your way out here?" Del yelled to Elizabeth Barton-Carr, who stepped out of the passenger side of the Escalade.

Elizabeth looked around at the squalor and goblins, wrinkled her nose, and gave Del a dirty look.

"Somebody thought you could use some help." She looked down at Yella and her lip wrinkled up like she'd smelled something bad.

"I don't like how she's a lookin' at me," Yella growled. The little woman balled up her fists and hissed. "I'm Yella Boreman and I'm the biggest and the baddest—"

"Yeah, I know. Calm your tits, Yella. She don't mean no harm." Del put her hand on Yella's shoulder and patted it. She then took Elizabeth's elbow and led her off a few feet from the Boremans. "Unless you wanna be an accessory to murder, you best turn that Escalade around and get on back to Columbus."

Elizabeth shook her head. "Avoiding that is precisely why I am here, Delilah. I'm not the help. She is." Elizabeth waved at the vehicle.

Del's jaw dropped when the back door opened, and Davida Barker stepped out.

Del had only a few lines and wrinkles and had aged slowly and finely. Davi hadn't aged a day. She was well over forty, but she looked exactly the same as Del remembered her, a girl of only twenty-two. Her shoulder length chestnut hair gleamed in the midday sun and she looked fit and wholesome, no different to Del than when she'd last seen her drive away in a Honda Civic with her seven-year-old son, twenty years before.

Del grabbed Elizabeth's suit jacket and growled. "What are you playing at, bringing her to me?"

"Well, I can see that time has done nothing for your anger management skills, Delilah," Davi said. She walked over and crossed her arms. "You're in trouble, and I came to help."

"I don't want your help, Davida," Del said. "Best you leave. You don't need mixed up in this."

"As I've told you many times, you are not the boss of me. I say who I help and when I do it," Davi said.

"You're short on time, options, and friends, Delilah. Davida can speed this up and maybe, you know, she's the better way," Elizabeth said.

"Davida, we talked about this way back. You helping me, that ain't good for you. I'm dealing with some things I don't think... well, I don't want you mixed up with them. It's dangerous."

Davi rolled her eyes at Del. "Not to get cocky, but not much can hurt me," Davi said. "Now show me to the guy and let's figure this crap out." Davi looked around the holler. "I think it's better to leave these folks be as soon as possible."

Yella stared up at Davi with a rapt, loving look on her face. "Who's she, Del? Is she an angel? I can see her halo, I think."

"Naw, Yella. You probably just smoked too much," Del said. "She's just a regular..." Del stumbled a minute over the description of Davi and then shrugged. "I don't know exactly what she is, but I reckon it don't matter, because I know what she come out here to do." Del needed the help. Davi was the right kind of help, at the right time, which was kind of a miracle, all things considered.

They walked back up in the woods to the Boreman's kidnap shack. It still smelled of the goatsucker and burnt hair. Elizabeth gagged.

"What is that smell?" she yelled.

"Burnt Chupacabra hair," Del said.

Cal was passed out cold and restrained with the thick log chain. Yella had taken no chances with his bonds. His hands and feet were shackled too, and the filthy gag was held in place by the pink cameo duct tape wound around his head.

He looked dead. She checked his pulse and found it beating steadily. "How much did you dope him with?"

"Not as much as I used on you, but a solid whack," Yella said.

"I need him awake. This ain't no good." Del kicked Cal hard in the side and he didn't move.

"Well, I had to dose him real good, because he was mean," Yella said. "The bites didn't slow him down none. We just thought that was you, Del."

"No, they wouldn't work on werewolves too good. We heal fast. Goddamit, Yella, I ain't got time to—"

"For Pete's sake, Delilah." Davi sighed as she bent down and touched Cal with her finger. His eyes opened and when he saw Del, he scrambled around and scooted back against the rusted corrugated metal of the shed. He mumbled at her and cowered against the wall.

"Yeah, you're right to be scared," Del said. She growled and covered the distance between them, then picked Cal up and slammed him against the wall.

"Delilah, if you beat him to death, it kind of defeats the purpose, don't you think?" Davi said.

"He deserves it," Del snarled. She showed him her teeth. The big canines pushed down through her gums as her old friend, the Rage built up and circulated through her. But she still needed some information. She pushed back the anger and took a deep breath. "I got questions and you're gonna answer." Del ripped off the filthy gag and tossed Cal back on the ground.

"Go fuck yourself, Del." Cal returned her growl and snarled.

Del growled louder than him and went to punch him, but a warm hand on her back stopped her. She felt a little of the rage dissipate and looked over at Davi. "Is that a new trick of yours?"

Davi nodded. "Let me try him." She stood in front of Cal and cocked her head at him for a few seconds, seeming to measure him, then Davi smiled and touched his forehead with two fingers.

Cal stopped snarling and struggling. His face relaxed and so did his body. Davi turned to Del. "Ask him whatever you want. He'll tell you."

"You been practicing," Del said. She stared down at Cal and let a little hate build back up. "Are you working with the Feds or Martin?"

"Martin," he said. His face showed no emotion at all.

"How long?"

"From the first. After that first meeting."

Del felt her face flush. How had she missed that?

"Did they glamour you?"

Cal shook his head. "No. They paid me. You left so much money on the table, Del. They promised me everything. Nothing left behind."

"And what did they want you to do?"

"Help them figure out the cloaking spells and set you up. It was way too easy."

The set up, he meant. Del had to agree. She had walked into that one.

"We got you all riled up about the murders. Who cares about some stupid whores and those trailer trash kids? You. It was so easy. I seen you do some crazy shit in this Valley for these idiots. I knew it wouldn't be hard."

"You helped them. The goatsucker and that fucking vamp." Del balled up her fists as she thought about Astrid, and Misty-Dawn, and those little girls.

"And that old lady. Fucking trailer Jesus lady," he said. "All of them."

Del nodded. "Just cause you're a greedy fuck. You had everything you wanted. I paid you good."

"They paid better. And Martin said there'd be none of your stupid fucking rules. We'd get to hunt and not be boxed in at the Turn. Free, like nature meant for us to be."

"Uh huh. How much do they know about the spell?"

"They got nothing. That Mexican witch guy can't figure it out. He's pissed about it."

Del smiled. A glimmer of hope threatened. She reached over and patted Cal's cheek. "Thanks, bub. That's all I really needed." Del looked over at Davi. "You learn any tricks to explode his head or anything good?"

Davi shook her head. "Afraid not. He can't hurt you anymore, Del."

"Oh, he can tell them I know. It's been my experience you can't leave his kind hanging. Best break his neck and be done." Del went to grab him, but Davi stopped her. Her hand was firm and hot on Del's arm. Del let out a troubled grumble growl, and she felt a cramp hit her.

"Don't kill him, Del." Davi said.

She let go of Del, and Del felt the cramps subside. She shook herself and nodded at Davi.

"Alright, then Davida. I won't kill him. But he can't go nowhere. Not until this business is finished." Del looked over at Yella. "You think you can keep him?"

"He helped that sonofabitch find us?" Yella asked.

Del looked over at Cal. "Did you?"

He nodded. "Yep. Told him to hire you and get rid of you after."

Yella's face flushed, and she screeched. Her mouth erupted in jagged shark teeth and she launched herself at Cal. She latched on to his shoulder and bit down, her jaw muscles strained, and she shook her head, like a terrier with a rat. Cal screamed, and Del pulled Yella off him. She held him back and looked at Davi.

"He gave the idea to kill her whole family."

Yella's mouth dripped blood. "That demon made 'em all crazy. I'll keep him. Point of fact, I demand it, Del!"

"What is she talking about? A demon?" Davi asked.

"Head of the Cartel is a demon. An old one. He's behind all this. All these killings, fucking my shit up, made Yella's clan batshit and couldn't be saved."

Davi nodded. "Yeah, he's an old demon if he did all that. Look, Del, you can't handle this."

"Of course I can."

Davi shook her head. "No, you can't. I bet you think binding him will fix him?"

"Yeah. Then I'll rip him to bits or bury him so deep he won't get out. Or I'll die. Either way, I'm gonna get mine before I go."

"That's an idiotic plan. You can't bind him. I mean, you can, but it won't stop him for more than a few minutes and he's invulnerable, anyway. You can't kill him."

"Fucking great. Well, so what? I'm gonna take my ass to California, and I'm gonna kill every last fucker of his I find until I come to him, then I'm gonna spit in his face before he kills me."

"That's very cinematic, but even you don't have that kind of muscle. Be smart."

"Well, you just told me I got no chance, so I figure I might as well have some fun before I go."

"I said your plan was idiotic, but I didn't say you had no chance."

"What do you mean?"

"I mean, he can be dealt with, just not by binding him, and not by you."

Del looked at Davi for a few seconds, then shook her head. "Absolutely not, Davida. You got a kid."

"He's safe at Stanford. As safe as I can make him, but with those kinds of demons in the world, that isn't very safe. I'm the only one who can help you and I'll do it, this one last time," Davi said.

"And how you figure on doing it?" Del asked. "If I can't bind him or kill him, what are we gonna do?"

"We're gonna send him back where he came from," Davi said. "But I'll need time, and I'll have to get close."

Del nodded. "I think I know a way." She looked down at Yella. "He's yours. Keep him here until the next moon. He'll heal on you after that and them chains won't hold him, unless you drug the shit out of him with Wolfsbane."

"Oh, I reckon I know just what to do with him, Del," Yella said. She grinned and showed him her teeth again. "When he heals, do he grow stuff back?"

Del laughed. "No, he sure don't." She left Yella to it and walked back down the hill with Elizabeth and Davi. "How long you need to get ready, Davida?"

"A week," Davi said.

"I reckon I can last that long," Del said. "Lizzy, I'm gonna need a clean car and some more cash."

CHAPTER 38

DEL CROSSED the border at San Diego with no problems, however, if she thought she went unnoticed, she would have been wrong. Martin's goons got to her before she even got to a hotel.

They crashed their truck into hers and shoved it off the side of the road, then screamed at her in screeching Spanish. They were dressed like cops, but the lumps and black, wiry hair of the Chupacabra stood out at odd angles from beneath the starched blue of the police officers' uniforms. "I don't know why you're wearing cop clothes, you're obviously not fucking cops, dipshits," Del said. They slammed her against the side of the truck and bashed her head against the doorframe. Del growled but didn't fight them. Their acid spit would burn, and anyway, she wanted caught. That was the point. They put a black hood over her head and shoved her in a vehicle. After a few hours, they stopped.

Even with the hood on, Del could smell the sea. She'd never been to the ocean, never smelled it before, but she knew what the scent was, salty and alive, and for a brief second, she let herself feel excited about that. They pulled her out of the vehicle, then walked her outside for a bit. The sounds and smells and temperature changed from outside to inside. They dragged her around a bit inside, then shoved her down in a chair and pulled the hood off.

Martin Price smiled at Del as he leaned against a massive mahogany desk. Again, he was over-dressed for the occasion in a tuxedo shirt and jacket, sans tie. His black hair shone in the afternoon light as it filtered in through the huge stained-glass windows and his black eyes danced. The luxe, mahogany furniture, and leather-bound books screamed expensive, traditional study. Every book, every knick-knack in the place was intentionally placed to give the impression of cultured intelligence, but it smelled new. There was none of the tart, mildew smell of old paper or any layers of living smells of tobacco and sweat that characterized old rooms. This place was brand new and had yet to see any intelligent discourse. Del doubted it would now either.

"Delilah, welcome to Mexico. I wish you would have phoned to tell me of your visit, but I am so happy to see you."

Del looked around. She didn't return the smile. "I doubt it was a surprise. You been tailing me since Vegas."

"You've come, and I'm so glad. I'd like for us to work out

our differences." Martin snapped to one of the Chupacabra who pulled a chair over and set it in front of Del. Martin sat down and crossed his legs.

"Nah, that ain't what you want," Del said.

"Of course it is. What is it that you think I want?"

"The only difference you wanna work out is why I can move millions of dollars of shit around, and you can't move a dog turd with without cops on your ass."

"Delilah, we've made a lot of money together. Everyone benefited. You are the one who severed our partnership, not me."

"Don't."

"Don't what?" Martin asked.

"Don't fucking play pretend now. We both know what's what, so let's just get on with it."

The side door of the study opened, and Olivia walked in, followed by the witch, Lalo. Olivia stood next to Martin and crossed her arms. She didn't smile. When she looked at Del, Del thought she saw a bit of sadness in her eyes. That sudden sadness enraged Del. She growled.

Martin looked between them and laughed. "Hell hath no fury, Olivia."

He motioned to the witch. Lalo toddled forward on his short legs and ridiculous, long-toed boots. He began a chant and waved his hands as he walked around Del. She felt as if the air thickened and closed in on her, and when he finished, he smiled at her and winked.

Del lunged for him, but she was held in place by the very

air pushing back against her. She growled at him. "Oh, don't think we're done, Short Stuff. Me and you got unfinished business." She let the image of Aunt Jewel roll through her mind and her canines pushed down through her gums. Del snarled and smiled at the little man, showing him her teeth. He winked at her again, then left the room.

"Well, that's interesting," Martin said. "I didn't know werewolves could do that." He looked at Del and tilted his head, then shrugged. "Let's see what treasures you brought." He snapped at the Chupacabra, and one of them brought over Del's backpack. Olivia rummaged through it and pulled out the materials for the binding spell. She handed it to Martin.

Martin turned the worn zip-loc baggie around in his hands and laughed. "How cute! You thought you could bind me."

Olivia narrowed her eyes and looked at Del, then at Martin. From her pursed lips, Del could tell that Olivia knew something she wasn't saying. And she wasn't saying it to Martin.

"That's what you do to demons, ain't it?"

"That's what you do to lesser demons. That isn't what you do to me."

"You got a high opinion of yourself," Del said. "You'll die. Same as everyone else."

"You're an ignorant hillbilly. I'm unamused by it now. You're going to tell me what spell you're using. You're going to set it up down here."

"I'm not telling you shit," Del said. "Except that you fucking stink. You smell like if a mermaid's twat queefed rotten eggs. Even a human could smell it. Sorry, if nobody ever told you before."

Martin's smile didn't fade, but his eyes darkened and Del gagged as the fishy Sulphur smell got stronger. Del laughed.

"Ah, so when you get mad, you stink worse. That's a shitty power. You got anything else, sport?"

"She excels at making you angry," Olivia said. "She's stalling."

"For some master plan, I'm sure," Martin said. He took a deep breath and sighed. "Well, we will have to try a different means of persuasion, since I asked politely, and you answered impolitely."

"Your demon whammy? Go on," Del sat back in the chair and relaxed.

"I tried at that first meeting, but it had no effect on you at all. It's curious. I was told you were an ordinary werewolf."

"I ain't all ordinary," Del growled.

"Now who has a high opinion of themselves?" Martin laughed, then smiled and leaned forward, close to Del's face. "You are a run of the mill, garden variety, unremarkable werewolf. Although it is rare to find females. Most don't make it past the first year."

"Are you gonna torture me with werewolf trivia? Cause I still ain't gonna tell you shit."

Martin motioned to the Chupacabra, and they left the room. When they returned, they drug a large, burly man in a sheriff's uniform. They threw him on the floor at Martin's feet. Del growled and lunged for Martin, but the bonds held her tight in a cocoon of magic and space.

"He's important to you? That is a terrible shame," Martin said.

Jacob was conscious. His face was bloody and bruised, and blood from his nose had dribbled down onto his shirt. He looked up at Del and blinked.

"Del?"

"It'll be all right, Jake."

Jacob looked up at Martin and shook his head. Dark energy swirled around them. Del could smell it, and from the look of fear and confusion on Jacob's face, he could feel it.

"I think this is a tough spot, Del," he said. "You gotta do what you gotta do. Don't worry none about me."

"I've always worried some," Del said. "But this is fine." She looked at Martin. "Call your dumbass witch in. I'll give him a list of shit."

Martin clapped. "There. See? Was that so difficult?"

Olivia got the brujo and Del gave him a list. He eyed Del. When she told him the spell to use, he scoffed. "That's it? That's... basic."

"I like to keep shit simple," Del said.

Lalo shook his head and looked to Martin. "She's lying. There is no way this would work. I saw the markings. It's more complicated."

"She isn't lying," Olivia said. "She knew we'd be expecting complex witchcraft."

Martin shrugged. "Well, we will try it and see. That's all we can do. Delilah, you will remain my guest until Lalo confirms the spell works."

"Let Jacob go. You got what you wanted."

"I suppose I did. Although," Martin tapped his finger to his lips in thought. "There was one thing I wanted that I did not get. Do you know what it is, Delilah?"

"I really don't fucking care," Del said. She looked at Jacob, who looked woozy from the head trauma. He swayed and could barely sit upright. "Just let him go."

"I wanted to hear you scream."

Martin smiled and put his hands on either side of Jacob's face, forcing him to stare into his. Del smelled a whiff of ozone and heard a crisp crackle of electricity, then Jacob shrieked.

The enormous man screamed and cried as he scrambled around on the floor, unable to get his feet under him and stand. He bashed around, crashing into furniture, and sending books and curios flying as he tried to squeeze himself into any nook he could find. He fit in nothing and he bawled like a baby until he got the hiccups. He drooled and spit and made awful retching noises as he looked around the room, every few seconds finding something horrific and invisible to scream about.

Inside her magic cocoon, Del screamed along with him. Hers was of rage and horror. She banged herself against the confines that held her, but she couldn't move. She never stopped trying and the rage ball in her gut exploded. Her skin bubbled and stretched, bones broke and grew, and she let it come. She welcomed the pain because it brought the Turn and when she Turned, she'd kill them all.

"She's changing, not at a moon. Isn't that interesting?" Martin peered at Del curiously, then motioned to the brujo.

Del snarled and snapped at him, and the bubble that held her was loosening. She gave a great, murderous growl, and pushed harder. She burst through it and lunged at him, but he blew something in her face and said an incantation. Del collapsed to the ground and twitched, unable to control herself. She shifted back. The pain was excruciating, and she couldn't make a sound, but she could still hear, and Jacob's screams were loud in her ears. Her vision blurred and darkened. Del felt heavy and slow as she lost consciousness. Martin knelt in front of her and smiled.

"It's okay. He's screaming for you."

CHAPTER 39

"Sissy, wake up. Your eggs is done."

Del opened her eyes and sat up. Adrenaline pumped through her veins and her heart pounded. That voice was familiar and yet, it could not be. Del looked around the room and her heart skipped and beat harder as she realized it was the place she'd woken up in countless times, and yet, it could not be. Crisp white sheets that smelled of being hung to dry in summer sunshine lined the bed. Del touched the soft, well-worn quilt that had kept her warm on many a night. It should now be on her bed at home, not here on this bed. It could not be.

Yet it was.

"Delilah Elizabeth Monroe! Get up now! You're going to be late to catch the bus!"

The voice was firm now, but not angry. It was just past

time to get up, and the use of the whole name told Del that she'd be wise to comply. Not because she was afraid of getting the belt. Never once in her whole life had that voice been paired with an angry blow. Her failure to comply would just disappoint, not anger, and to Del, for that voice, disappointment was far worse than ire.

She pulled back the bedclothes and when her feet hit the floorboards, the old wood gave a familiar groan. Del shifted around and the floor creaked and moaned, the same conversation with her weight that it had had over a good many years, just of varying intensities. She padded down the hallway, stopping to touch the pictures on the walls. A picture of her as a baby, in a pink dress, grinning and bald. Her kindergarten picture, the one where she'd crossed her eyes for fun. Her mom had been unable to get her money back for it, and she'd screamed and beaten Del black and blue. Gran had laughed at the cross-eyed photo and loved it. The picture of her taken on her thirteenth birthday, all knees and elbows and attitude, with a half-smile on her face and a homemade birthday cake in front of her. Del recalled it was chocolate. Her favorite. All of those pictures she'd seen a thousand times, but they had been packed up. Gone where it is old pictures go when nobody cares. Not here and not now. It could not be.

When she got to the kitchen, she stopped and fingered the herbs drying and breathed in the good smell of earth and magic and love. She choked back a sob. Her breakfast waited for her on the kitchen table. Two eggs, sunny side up with a little black pepper dotting the yolks. A slice of red tomato from the garden. Two thick pieces of the home-cured bacon, and toast, two slices, with homemade butter and cut on the diagonal, because Gran called that "fancy." There was a short glass of orange juice and tall class of cold milk. The silver-ware was laid out with care and precision on gingham patterned napkin, cut up from an old table cloth and hand sewn. The smell of the bacon grease lingered in the air and mixed with the herbs and bubbling potions. To Del, it smelled like love.

Her Gran puttered at the sink, humming one of her murder ballads, "In the Pines." She washed the dishes, then cleaned and seasoned the big cast-iron skillet. Del had seen her do it a million times. If you skipped a step or left that skillet wet, all the heavens couldn't help you. Her gran had thumped Jerry solid once when he'd left it to rust. Del had never dared be so lax.

Gran worked and hummed, and every so often, she'd sing in her pleasant contralto.

In the Pines, in the pines, where the
Sun never shines,
And we shivered when the cold winds blow...

She looked up from the dish pan and smiled at Del. Del's gran wasn't as she'd been at the end, frail, stooped, and shaky from the cancer that ate her insides. She was straight and strong, with her perfectly done up make-up and hair, ready to head to town. It was how she remained always in Del's mind, with the coral lipstick and the auburn hair swept up into the beehive, and the lingering smell of herbs and magic.

"Sit down and eat, Sis. That bus will be here before long." Her grand walked over and kissed Del on top of the head. Del knew the act happened, but she couldn't feel it.

Del couldn't speak. She went to say something, and the sound caught in her throat. She touched the hollow place and tried to clear it, but nothing came out, and she couldn't feel it either, not even a tickle. She sat down anyway, and her gran went back to humming her song. Del picked up the fork and broke into her eggs, mushing them around and mixing up the runny yellow yolks. When she went to put the egg in her mouth, it was gone. All the food on her plate was gone, the only thing left were a few tomato seeds, and the scraped around egg yolk mixed with toast crumbs.

The humming had stopped, and it was replaced by a different music, classical this time, and also familiar to Del. Her heart skipped several beats, and she felt her stomach roll when Nina sat down at the table with a cup of coffee.

"You're about healed up. Shouldn't be but a few more days."

Del stared at her, open mouthed, then looked around the kitchen. It was the same space, her gran's space, but Gran was gone. The smells remained, then she got a whiff of something new, Nina's shampoo. She'd always loved that smell. Fresh, clean, with just a kiss of tropical something else. Her favorite way to wake up had been to roll over and smell that on the pillow next to hers. She hadn't smelled it well over thirty years, but it was as beautiful and familiar to her as it had been the first time she'd smelled it.

Del tried to say something, to answer Nina back, but just like before, her voice wouldn't come. She motioned to her throat, but Nina ignored her.

"When you're healed, don't go to him. You don't have to do it," Nina said.

Del knew what she was talking about; they'd had the same conversation at a different kitchen table. Nina's face was sad. Her eyes looked tired, and she cracked her neck in that way that meant she'd stayed up too late the night before. In spite of the weariness, she looked beautiful to Del. Her dark brown hair was upswept into a messy bun, with little tendrils of it wisping around her face, each one begging Del to reach out and tuck behind an ear.

"You're not gonna drink the shake? You'll heal faster if you do," Nina said, sliding the tall glass of brown liquid closer.

She reached out her hand and entwined her fingers with Del's. Del could see it, she knew they were locked, but she couldn't feel it. Her guts lurched again, and she tried to squeeze Nina's hand. She wanted so desperately to feel those fingers. A sob caught in her throat as she remembered what they'd looked like after Nina died—broken, mangled, bloody.

The glass was frosty, and the rich, delicious smell wafted up from it. Del's stomach grumbled, and she was suddenly hungry again. She knew what was in the shake now. Nina left her the recipe. If she had known back then, would she have drank it, she wondered? Would knowing it was herbs and human flesh have made her turn it away, even though it was the very thing that strengthened her? Her hands shook as she reached out for it, but when she went to put it to her lips, the shake was gone. Just a few frothy bits remained in the glass, not even a sip.

Del set the glass down on the table and looked over at Nina, but Nina was gone.

Davida Barker sat in her place. Davi drummed her fingers and looked bored. The other hand propped her head up. Del could smell the magic rolling off Davi. It rippled and shimmered all around her and tickled Del's nose. When they made eye contact, Davi puffed out a sigh.

"Finally. You dream long," Davi said.

Del tried to retort and ask a question, but Davi went on.

"You can't talk. Don't bother. I probably should have prepared you for this part before, but I kind of forgot. Oh well. Look, Del. This is me, no dream. I'm coming. You just have to stay alive a little longer."

Stay alive a little longer? How was she supposed to do that? Once they had confirmation that the cloaking spell worked, Del would be unnecessary. She had hours, if that, when she woke up. Del shrugged and shook her head at Davi as she scrunched up her face in angry question.

"Yeah, I know, that seems hard, but I'm close. I'll be there in just a little bit. But I'm not the only one coming, Del. Cops are coming too." Davi smiled, "It complicates things and also provides a distraction, which I'm sure you knew about when you called them."

Del flopped her hands up then back on the table again in a whatever gesture.

"Just keep stalling them. Try and maybe get them all in one place. When I get there, you'll know it's me. Just don't... don't die if I'm not there. I can't help from away. I mean, you can be your asshole self, just don't make them so mad they kill you quick. Okay? Got it? Good. Time for you to wakey-wakey." Davi snapped her fingers and a great whooshing sound filled Del's ears, then everything was gone.

DEL OPENED her eyes and saw dirt floor. It was dry and sandy and smelled of rat piss and rotting meat. Chained next to her, a bloated corpse slumped and rotted. Sleek, fat rats eeked and skittered and screamed at each other as they worried and gnashed their way through the dead man. A big, bold one came for Del. She grabbed it and broke its neck, then threw it at the rest, who scattered for a second before going back to the body.

"Little bastards," Del said. She stood up, then kicked another one into the concrete wall. He made a satisfying splat when he hit. The walls were earthen and had several holes in them. Del knew rat holes when she saw them. She also knew how bold the little bastards could be and while a couple of growls and kicks sent them running now, she knew their numbers would win the battle, eventually. She didn't intend to stay put long enough to be overwhelmed.

Davi's foray into her dream asked for time or a distraction. Del was certain that there was no good way out now. They had what they wanted. When the spell was verified, they'd kill her. Her death had been a long time coming. She'd done things, not so different from Martin, that were just about money. She'd profited from misery, but she'd been so miserable herself that she hadn't cared. That wasn't true. She'd cared, but she'd kicked the emotions out and done it anyway. Every day, it poked at her, some days more than others. But in her later years, she'd tried to make a little peace with it and do a little less harm, or at least control the harm.

But that had been a lie she told herself. Harm was harm. Crime was crime. No amount of charity work or keeping criminals in check made up for all the pain and violence she'd dealt in the past thirty years. She could take care of single moms and give old ladies free rent. She could pay for upkeep of playgrounds and make sure every kid in Denton county had a laptop computer and free lunch. She could make donations to the cancer ward and outfit the local volunteer fire department. She could do all things she did, and none of it would erase the pain and misery that she'd doled out. That bill was always going to come due, and it was ready to be paid right now.

Del squared her shoulders and kicked another rat. It gave her a bit of happiness, then she thought of Astrid and

Glenna, of Misty-Dawn, those three little girls, Ginny, and Aunt Jewel. Last, she thought of Jacob and the sound of his hysterical, terrified screams. She let her old friend, Rage, burble up from the hole he lived in, and she welcomed him. She felt the power course through her, pushing out any wolfsbane or tranquilizer they had given her. It was all gone, replaced by the white-hot fire of hate. She let it flow freely, and when she grabbed the heavy oak door, she ripped it off the hinges and threw it at the rats. They screeched and squeaked as some lay dying. The rest hissed and squalled at her, angry and defiant. Del soaked up their hatred. She added it to her own as she stalked out the door and sniffed. She caught the scent trail she was after and smiled as she growled and followed it.

CHAPTER 40

As DEL NAVIGATED the breezeways and halls of the massive compound, the smells of the age and magic on the place bombarded her senses—the scent of ozone mixed with mildew and life. It smelled different from the one room she'd been in. That room had been new smelling, as if it were an addition. Every other place smelled like it had been around since the beginning of time, filled with memory and life and death.

She skulked around and followed her nose. It led her to a spindly stairwell that wound around and up to a round tower room. Del sniffed the door and growled. She knocked on the door, three light raps. Nobody answered. When Del entered, the room was empty, but Olivia's scent was every-where. Del sat and watched the door.

If Olivia knew Del was waiting for her, she gave no sign

of it when she opened the door. Del grabbed her by the throat and slammed her against the wall.

"Where's Jacob?"

Olivia clutched her throat and Del tightened her grip, then released her, and let her drop to the floor.

"They locked him in one of the cellar rooms." Olivia coughed a few times but stood still. She made no move toward the door or window. "You can't help him. Leave while you can." She sighed and looked at Del. "But that isn't what you're going to do. They're testing your spell this morning. If it works, he'll kill you right after."

"We'll see about that."

"You can't hurt him. Your binding spell won't work either."

Del concentrated and let the magic flow right along with the Rage. It was an interesting combination—powerful and wild. Del grinned at the fear on Olivia's face as she said the binding incantation Aunt Jewel left for her. She hadn't needed the herbs. Aunt Jewel had left instructions and said that it was easier with them, but once Del had seen Olivia bind the French-Canadian without the herbs, she'd known it was possible and for Del, just knowing a thing was possible was sometimes all she needed.

Olivia's eyes went white. She collapsed to the floor and held her head. When Del finished, Olivia was out of breath, but her eyes returned to their normal brown color. She got to her feet and winced.

"How did you learn to do that?"

Del smiled. "It was a long drive. I had me a book on tape."

Olivia sat down in a chair. "Are you going to kill me?"

Del shook her head. "No. Least ways not right away."

"If you think I had a choice in any of this, you're wrong."

"One thing I learned in this whole fucked up life of mine, is that we all got choices. We might not like the outcomes from them, but we got 'em. You're gonna pay for yours, same as I'm gonna pay for mine."

"You don't know what happens to a para-demon if we disobey."

"Uh, you die? Get sent back to Hell? Torture?" Del scoffed and shook her head. "Same as anybody else. You ain't special. I would have thought being alive so long you would have come to terms with that."

"It's unending torture until he raises me again. Pain you can't even begin to imagine. And he'll never let me go."

"If he's done it before, he'll do it again. And again. And again," Del said. "Time to stop him."

"And how are you going to do that?" Olivia laughed. "Martin is a demon as old as time itself. He has his own Hell Dimension. Unless you're capable of sending him back..." Olivia paused. She cocked her head and looked at Del. "You think you're capable."

"Oh I ain't. All I'm good for is a distraction."

"Delilah, I only know of one kind being capable of doing that. How would you have crossed paths with one?"

"You don't know as much as you think you know. Until a

few months ago, I hadn't crossed paths with some asshole king of a hell dimension. Life's exciting."

"If you send him back, I go back too."

"Seems fair," Del said. "But what if you was bound in that body?"

Olivia's face got red, and she sputtered a moment, then she sighed. "If it doesn't work, I'll be stuck inside a rotting corpse in a place so vile you cannot imagine its filth and torment."

"Liv, you seen where I'm from. I know an awful lot about filth and torment. Look, you're fucked either way. If you're gonna go out, make the right choice and go."

"It would be smart of you to just kill me now. What if I'm not willing to bet on your plan?"

She leaned down in Olivia's space and stared into her face. "You can go on and raise the alarm. Won't hurt a bit. I ain't gonna be subtle. When the time is right, you'll either help me, or you won't." Their faces were so close that their noses could touch. Del wanted to choke Olivia to death, and she could do it now. She could do it for all her dead and for all the betrayal, but Del knew all that death was as much her fault as anyone's. Olivia had only been the gun. Del had pulled the trigger a long time ago.

She kissed her instead. Hard and fast. When Del pulled away, she went to the door. "Help or don't."

"Wait," Olivia said. She got up and went to the desk in the corner. She pulled a pistol and two full clips from the drawer. She checked them, then held them out to Del. "You might need these."

Del took the gun and chambered a round. "Thanks."

"Go left after the stairs. There's another entrance to the cellar. Your sheriff will be there."

Del nodded. She closed the door behind her and went left.

CHAPTER 41

JACOB STOOD IN THE DOORFRAME, *blocking all the light, and taking up all the space, yet he didn't seem out of place or in the way.*

"You ain't been to school in three days," he said. He crossed his beefy arms against his burly sixteen-year-old's chest and scowled down at Del as she lay on her bed.

Del rolled over, biting back a cry as her abused body protested any movement. She looked up at him and returned his scowl.

"What are you, the school police?"

"They call 'em Truancy Officers," Jacob said. "And they're layin' out for you at your place."

Del was staying at her gran's, as she always did after Turns. Her mom was no use at all, and Del would rather die than be out at the Holler with Galen and Junior.

"Congratulations on your A plus in vocabulary," Del said. "Now how about you fuck off, Jake."

"Delilah Elizabeth Monroe, I will wash your mouth out with soap!" Del's gran yelled. She came around the doorframe with a wooden spoon and pushed past Jacob's bulk. "Let me hear you say that word again and you'll wish you hadn't!" She looked up at Jacob and smiled. "You all come on out here, and I'll cut a cake." She patted Jacob on his broad shoulder and went back out to the kitchen.

"I guess she told you," Jacob said.

"You just wait til we get outside." Del heaved herself up off the bed. She wobbled when she stood, and Jacob caught her. For a big boy, he was quick and graceful. Del shoved him off her. He flew backward; big as he was, Del was stronger. "I can do it my own self."

"No, you can't. You're hurt. Let me help."

He was right back at her side, despite her surly mood. He put his arms around her and steadied her, and Del's heart and mood calmed. She leaned into him and breathed in the smell of his teen cologne and slight funk. It was him, and it was comforting. Jacob led her out to the kitchen and her gran smiled at the two of them. She had two big slices of chocolate cake cut and two glasses of cold milk poured.

Del and Jacob sat down at the little kitchen table and demolished the cake.

"Why don't the two of you go get some sunshine," Gran said. "You'll feel better, Sissy, if you get moving."

Del nodded and followed Jacob outside. They hiked a ways back up in the woods, to the spot where their old clubhouse stood. They'd carted discarded plywood and lumber up the hill and built a little *shed when they were five and full of imagination and possibilities. It hadn't been well-constructed to start with, and time hadn't been kind to the old structure. It drooped and had collapsed in on itself from the rot, a haven for spiders and mice. Del could hear them and smell them as they scurried around in the wreckage of her childhood.*

They sat against an enormous oak tree, side-by-side in the leaf litter. Del leaned against both Jacob and the tree. Jacob wrapped an arm around her, and she let him.

"You wanna tell me what run you over?" he asked.

"Not really," Del said.

"Did Galen do this to you?" Jacob asked. There was an angry edge in his normally calm voice, and Del felt his arm tense around her.

In fact, Galen had done it to her, in a roundabout way, but he hadn't beaten her. Del shook her head and snuggled in against him.

"No, he don't beat me."

"Junior do it? I'll kill him."

Del shook her head again. "That pussy can't do shit to me." She looked up at Jacob. "He'd fuck you up though, so don't mess at him."

"He can't hurt me," Jacob said, puffing up a little.

Bravado wasn't his natural state, and it amused Del. She laughed. "The fuck he can't. He'd beat your ass and make you like it."

"I don't care what he'd do to me. If he hurts you, I'll kill him."

"Don't nobody hurt me but me," Del said. She pulled away and

squinted her eyes at him. *"You promise me you'll keep clear of me and this shit."*

"Keep clear of what shit?"

"You know what. Galen's shit. I know you know."

"Your daddy is just a meth dealer, Del. He'll get his someday." Jacob puffed up again. *"If we had a sheriff that had any sack at all. Old Stew don't do shit about it. If I was the sheriff, I'd–"*

"You wouldn't do shit because Galen would skin you alive," Del said. She reached up and turned Jacob's face to hers. She stared into his eyes and felt his breath catch and his heart pound when she touched him. *"He ain't just a drug dealer. He's dangerous and so am I. You promise me you'll keep clear of us."*

"Delilah, there's no power in this world that will ever make me keep clear of you. I can't. I won't."

"Jake. You know it can't be like that with us. We talked about it."

He nodded and blushed. She could see in his face that he both knew that she could never be with him, and yet he knew she loved him. Still, he ducked his head and kissed her. Del let him for a second, then she pushed him back.

"No. It can't ever be Jake. I love your big dumb ass, but not like that."

"You can have your girlfriends too. I won't mind." He cupped her face in his huge hand. *"I just want to keep you safe."*

Del pulled back. She grimaced and got to her feet. *"I don't need you to keep me safe. Truth is, you ain't safe with me."*

Jacob shifted from foot to foot and jammed his hands in his pockets. *"Of course I am. What are you talking about?"*

"When it comes, I don't know nothin'. I'd hurt you and I wouldn't know it. You can't stop me."

"I'd stop you." Jacob enveloped her in a bear hug. He squeezed her tight, but gently to his immense body. "You'll be alright with me."

Del sighed and hugged him back. "I ain't ever gonna be alright with nobody." She buried her face in his chest and breathed in deep, then she let go of him and shoved him back. "Promise me you won't get in the way of me. Swear it or I'll never talk to you again."

"You will so. You'll—" He reached for her.

Del stepped backward and avoided him. "No. I won't. You swear to me you'll keep clear of Galen, of Junior, and you won't come looking for me when I'm gone."

Jacob looked down at his shoes, and Del thought he was going to cry. He stood there for a moment, then he looked up at her and nodded. "Alright. I won't. But I ain't gonna stop looking out for you, Delilah."

"It'll be a thankless job, son," Del said. "Frustrating as fuck, I reckon."

Jacob nodded. "It's been thataway since we was five. I don't guess you've gotten no smarter in ten years, and I doubt you'll make much progress in the next ten."

Del laughed and took his hand. "You're smarter than you look," she said as she leaned against him and they walked back to the house where they both hoped to steal another slice of the chocolate cake.

CHAPTER 42

THE LABYRINTH SPANNED the whole of the hacienda. As she navigated the dark corridors, she realized that it wasn't a cellar, but another structure. The new had been built on top of it. The walls down here had hundreds, maybe a thousand years on the ones upstairs.

Jacob's room was on the opposite end from where she's been held. The door was thick, heavy oak, but she could hear Jacob screaming behind it. Del growled, channeled the Rage and kicked hard at the door. She growled again, punched through the ruined lock, and ripped it out.

Jacob huddled in a corner of the filthy room. The rats had him pinned down. The hateful bastards would dart in and take a hunk out of him. He screamed and slapped at them, but they didn't seem to be his chief concern. Every so often, he'd look up at the corner of the ceiling, point, and scream louder. Del couldn't see anything, but she felt something in that room—a cold, heaviness hanging in the corner. She growled at it but left it be to deal with Jacob.

When he saw Del, Jacob backed away and flattened himself against the wall. His clothes were soaked with blood from the beatings and the rat bites, and he'd been crying so much that his eyes were red-rimmed and almost swollen shut.

"Easy, Jake. It's me." Del grabbed a bold, fat rat that had just taken a chunk out of Jacob's forearm, snapped its neck, then hurled it at the hole where the rest were. They screeched and hissed at her, then pounced on their dead brother. Jacob's eyes were vacant of recognition. She saw only terror in them. He blubbered and cried at her and hid his face. When he looked to the corner, he wailed.

She grabbed him and tried to stand him up. He ran from her to another corner. "Come on, bud, we gotta go." She grabbed him again to lead him to the door, but he pounded her with his meaty fists. He got a lucky punch in, an uppercut that sent her to her ass in the rat corner. One bit her. She growled and ripped its head off. Jacob scrambled to his feet and was now screeching and sobbing as he ran himself repeatedly into the wall, just like Dandy had done, only Jacob's mass was making the carnage a whole lot worse, a whole lot faster. Del grabbed him and threw him in his corner. He huddled there and keened as he rocked and beat his head against the wall.

Del pulled out the pistol. A deep sob welled up in her

throat. She pushed it back and aimed the gun at Jacob's head. The sob came out anyway. Del lowered the gun and let it come, then she vomited. She spit a few times to clear her mouth and cried as the weight of the task crashed down on her. She gathered herself, squinted her eyes, then screamed. Del aimed the gun at the base of Jacob's head, and she shot him.

The noise inside the chamber deafened her. The air seemed to shake, and Del let the pain of it cut through her. After a bit, the ringing cleared, and her hearing returned. There was still a slight buzz in her ears, but she didn't need hearing as much as she need her other senses at the moment.

She looked over at Jacob and she let out a cry of such pain and rage that it could be heard miles away. She cried as she remembered the boy she'd first met-fat and awkward, but gentle. The gigantic teen who'd dwarfed her and followed her everywhere. The bear of a man with a steady voice and steadier heart who'd loved her through the years. She remembered his calming presence, the love that never wavered, not even when she'd told him they couldn't date anymore, not even when he'd known she'd killed people. All the memories from over forty years of love and friendship washed over her in waves, and Del sobbed. Jacob had never left her, and she wouldn't leave him. She certainly wouldn't leave him for the fat corpse rats and whatever it was that lurked in the corner. Del picked up the big man and put him on her shoulder. She held him there with one arm and kept the pistol ready in the other.

The first werewolf found her at the top of the steps. She shot him in the face and kicked him down the stairs. She shot two more wolves. One she caught in the leg, the other in the gut. She'd put another bullet in each of their heads and growled at the satisfying splatter.

She found a spot in a corner of the courtyard. There was a nice shade tree and a fountain with a statue of St. Francis, the one with all the animals. She propped Jacob up there, under the tree, in the warm morning sunshine with the soothing sounds of the water, amidst the chirps of little birds.

"I'm sorry, Jake. I wish I could do better by you. Wish that we were back up in our place, behind Gran's. But we ain't. I love you." Del kissed his cheek, then stood up. She sniffed the air and growled.

"Do you know what he saw before he died?" Lalo's voice was quiet and reverent as he asked the question. "He saw every terrible thing you ever did to him."

Del turned and shot him in the gut. The little man fell backward onto his butt. He hissed a curse at her, but Del uttered a counter and the spell bounced off her harmlessly. Lalo go to his feet, holding his stomach as he tried more curses, but Del deflected them with the protective spell Aunt Jewel had left for her. Lalo was livid at his impotence. He spit and cursed at her. Del laughed at him, then uttered a curse of her own.

As soon as he heard the words, Lalo's face went from angry red to white, drained of all color. His hands shook and the muscles in his arm tensed as he tried to stop his hand. His fingers flexed and moved closer to his face. He clenched his jaw and strained as he fought to keep his mouth closed, but when his hand came near, he opened his mouth, reached in, and ripped out his own tongue.

Del knelt down next to him and smiled at the blood gurgling from the jagged wound in his mouth. "It'd be nice to have you back at my holler. It's quiet there, and I coulda took my time with you, but you get what you get, I reckon." Del reached out and jammed her fingers into his gut wound. She twisted them around the bloody flesh. Lalo screamed and spit blood everywhere. Del didn't shy away from it. She let it hit her and didn't wipe it off her face. She was used to it.

She pulled her fingers from the hole and wiped it on his vest. "Gonna take a while to die from that, but you will die." She shot him in both kneecaps, so he couldn't walk, then in both elbows, so he couldn't crawl. "Sure wish I could stay and watch you grub around, but I got shit to do." Del reached out and patted his cheek, then she stood up, kicked him in the gut, and left him writhing and whimpering in the bright morning sunshine.

CHAPTER 43

WHEN SHE FOUND THE KITCHEN, Del turned on all the burners on the huge gas stove, then tossed towels on them. She rummaged through the cabinets and found a few aerosol cans of cleaning supplies. She put them in the microwave, added time, then left the kitchen to explode.

The fire in the kitchen had spread and alarms whirled and whined. It hurt her ears, but she let the Rage deal with it and added the pain to her guts to fuel her fury. Above them, Del could make out the sounds of helicopter rotors and automatic gunfire. Del grinned. The Feds. That meant Davi was close. Del just had to hold on a bit longer.

She wound around through the compound, killing anyone she found. When she ran out of bullets, she punched and tore through them with a smile on her face and a hateful purpose.

The two Chupacabra found her in the fancy study. She dodged the first's acid spit ball and when he slashed at her with his claw, Del grabbed his hand and yanked the claw out. He screamed, then dropped to the ground, holding his hand. Del tossed the bloody claw in his face. She stomped his head, then turned to the other one. A big glob of his spit hit her in the shoulder and splashed her cheek. It sizzled and smoked as it burned her flesh. Del let the pain help and channeled it into more power. He came for her with his big, black claw and she sidestepped, grabbed it, and swiped his hand across his belly, growling and laughing as she gutted him with his own claw.

More came—the Red Hand werewolves, a few vampires —she fought them as best she could until they overwhelmed her. They held her as Martin swept into the room, with Olivia on his heels. His face was red and angry, and he clenched and unclenched his fists as the stench of rotten fish and eggs rolled off him and filled the room, choking everyone.

Del spat a mouthful of blood into the face of a short vampire and pulled herself free. They ringed her and growled, but Martin held up a hand and they kept their distance.

Del looked at Martin and made a disgusted face. "Whew. That queef power you got is terrible. You should call up Hell and ask them to give you a different one."

"Multi-National Crime Task Force?" Martin said. "How did you manage that, Delilah?"

"I got friends in low places," Del grabbed one wolf's arm and gave a mighty yank. It pulled from his body like a chicken wing, and Del hit one of the others with it. They all backed off her.

"They're all going to die screaming. That will be on your conscience," Martin said.

"Well, we ain't that good of friends," Del said. She looked to Olivia. Olivia made eye contact with Del but didn't move toward Martin. Del felt a double-cross coming on. She threw the bloody arm at Martin's feet. "What's the matter? Don't like getting your hands dirty? Gotta have all these puke wolves and goatsuckers do everything for you?"

Martin smiled. "You're baiting me. Stalling. For what, I wonder? Your Federale friends?" Martin held a palm up and one of the werewolves levitated off the ground. He cried and pleaded as Martin moved him close. Martin closed his fist and the wolf's eyes went white, then he collapsed to the ground, screaming. Martin raised both hands and everyone in the room, except for Del and Olivia suffered the same fate, all at once. "It's a blink for me. No effort at all."

"I don't know why you don't just get on with it then," Del said. "Big talker, keeps talking, I reckon. That's all you can do."

"You're right, enough is enough." Martin held up both palms and closed his eyes.

A rush of air and energy hit Del, and the air crackled with magic, but it wasn't coming from Martin. The side of the room blew apart, and Davi levitated through the opening. She pushed out with her hands and everyone in the room went flying.

CHAPTER 44

DEL STUMBLED TO HER FEET. The magic swirled around her. Davi touched down next to Del, and the force of it knocked Del off her feet again.

"Good job on not dying," Davi said. "Yet." She kept her eyes on Martin, who had just gotten to his feet, with Olivia's help. "That is an ancient and powerful demon, Del."

"Ah, yup. He can make a whole crowd of people go batshit. I think he can explode their brains too."

Martin's face was black with rage. He lost control for a second and sent a hateful, hissing scream in Davi's direction. "Half-breed. Abomination." He pointed at Del. "I can see your mark on her now. I'm not sure how I missed it before. That handprint, right in the middle of her back."

"Why don't you just stand down? No one else needs to be harmed today." Davi took a step forward.

Martin smirked. "Half-breed scum. You and your pet wolf can scream together forever in a pit of filth and misery." He motioned with his hand and hunks of the wall flew at Del and Davi. Davi deflected them as if they were gnats. A chunk of stucco hit Del, and she yelped. Martin continued to throw chunks of architecture and screech at them. Davi deflected and Del dodged.

"When I open it, we're going to shove her through and close it quick," Davi said.

Del dodged another huge chunk of the structure. Martin hurled them as easily as if he were playing toss with a wiffle ball. "Can't nobody hold him."

Davi smiled. "You can. But not like you are."

Del shook her head. "I can't just turn, unless you do it to me. And even then, I won't be able to control myself."

"Yes, you can. You just need to control it a little bit."

"Easy for you to say, Davi." Del lowered her head and let out a long, slow breath. She could transform. She'd done it before in limited amounts, and she might hold control for a few seconds, but after that... she'd be gone. But the alternative was dead.

"All right, but she's gonna see this coming," Del said.

Davi wasn't paying attention, she was looking at Olivia. Olivia had picked up a chair and held it behind Martin. "Maybe not," Davi said. "On three."

Del growled and crouched. She let the Rage bubble, pop, and fester. The fiery anger percolated and pulsed through her, out from her guts, and her muscles swelled, ready to rip and engorge. In her brain, the pain began and there was a foggy haze as rational thought receded and the desire to rip and tear threatened to take over. She concentrated and forced it back on the edge, ready when she needed it.

When Davi yelled three, Olivia hit Martin with the chair. Martin turned and looked at Olivia. He picked her up and slammed her down against the ground, bashing her skull until she lay still. Olivia's body turned black and rotted in seconds as one hundred and forty-five years caught up with her. Del's heart caught for a moment as she looked at the mangled mess that had been Olivia.

"Was that your plan? Pathetic." Martin laughed and pointed to Davi. "You're going to scream, half-breed." He pointed to Del. "I'm going to skin you and keep your pelt on my wall."

Del jumped, growled, and sprinted for Martin. Del's bones broke and her muscles ripped. The pain was white hot and seemed unmanageable, but the rage did it somehow. She used it to hold back the full transformation and grabbed Martin. Through hazy vision, Del saw Davi rise levitate. Davi chanted and the ground in front of them shimmered. The magic smell was choking, a gaseous ammonia cloud that burned Del's eyes and stopped her breath.

"I go, you go," Martin smiled. He latched on to Del and they grappled as Davi finished the spell. The ground swirled, blood red, then fiery orange. Screams and pleas for help found her ears as the heat of hellfire and the stench of a world full of hot rot and burning putrescence gushed through the hole. Del gagged and almost lost her grip. The heat rushed up and the side of Del's face burned and sizzled. She ignored the searing pain and strained every muscle in her body as she held Martin fast.

"Now, Del!" Davi yelled.

"In we go, huh?" Martin said. "Or... throw the Half-breed in." He nodded toward Davi. "I'll make you rich. I'll give you everything you could ever want."

When Del's voice came out, it was low and garbled, more growl than anything else. "I'm already rich and all I'm ever gonna want is for you to rot in that stinking hole."

She let the rip and tear and Rage out as she bit down into Martin's neck. Del strained her jaw muscles as hard as she could and let her big canines dig deep into the flesh. She couldn't taste blood, just a disgusting mixture of fish and rotten eggs, but she fought the urge to vomit. She thought of Ginny and the little girls. Of Aunt Jewel, with her eyes burned out, strung up in her own garden. And she thought of Jacob. The Rage strengthened her jaw muscles and Del bit down harder as shook her head from side to side and growled. Martin yelped and let her go for just a second, and when he did, Del released him, then shoved him into the fetid, swirling hole.

She heard Davi say something, and the hole shimmered and closed up. Where it had been opened, the floor was scorched and stank of rot. Del looked to Olivia's body. It was a black mess. She looked over at Davi, who grinned at her. She couldn't make out the words Davi was saying, though.

Del's vision blurred, and the pain exploded behind her eyes. She dropped to the ground and screamed. She couldn't hold it back any longer. The Rage would have its day. The rest of her muscles popped, and her bones broke as she finished her transformation. The last thing she saw before she was gone was Davi, smiling at her, mouthing the word, "Good. Now, run."

CHAPTER 45

"SONOFABITCH," Del murmured as she woke up and pressed her hands into the soft sand. She was naked and the morning sun burned hot on her sensitive skin. The smell of the salt-water tickled her nose as the waves crashed against the shore in a soothing, hypnotic cadence. She didn't try to get up just yet. She lay there in the unfamiliar sand and surf. The water rolled up and tickled her feet, then washed out. It was the most pleasant way to wake up after a Turn Del had ever experienced, and she smiled, content to lay still and let the water and sounds and sun calm her.

She was raised out of her meditation by someone clearing their throat.

"I'm sure that does feel great and all, but you're naked and people are just down the beach."

Del sat up and stretched. She bit back a scream. Her arms and legs were black and blue all over, and every muscle in her body cried out in pain when she moved. The right side of her face burned and when she reached up and touched it, it was raw. It hadn't healed in the Turn.

"I think it's going to take a while for that to heal. I tried while you were asleep, but it seems hellfire is the one thing I can't overcome." Davida Barker sat next to her in the sand. She smiled and handed Del a bottle of mezcal. "I couldn't get pickle juice or whiskey on such short notice."

Del took the bottle and downed it. It had a smoky flavor, and Del thought it tasted wonderful. She drank half the bottle.

"How'd you find me?"

"Well, a werewolf isn't exactly stealthy," Davi said. "You're easy to track. Besides, I'll always be able to find you."

"Your mark." Del shifted her shoulders as the space in the middle of her back tingled when Davi nodded.

"I didn't know that would happen. When I learned what I did, I never thought I'd have cause to use it. I guess I was wrong."

"Guess you were," Del said. She took another long swig of mezcal and looked out at the ocean. The gigantic waves of the Pacific rolled and crashed against the sandy shore. Del drank in the sight. The water was dark blue, and it stretched as far as Del could see. She'd never seen anything so beautiful. "Now that's something to see."

Davi nodded. "It is. It's a big wide world, Delilah. Maybe it's time you see it."

Del heard a car door open, and Elizabeth Barton-Carr stumbled out of the black SUV and onto the sand. She threw a large backpack at Del. "Clothes. Money. The magic items you requested. Also, I threw in some passports and bank documents. All your accounts are set up. I think you're going to have some trouble with those FBI agents. They're pretty pissed they got nothing in the raid."

"Everybody can't win," Del said. She pulled on a pair of jeans and a t-shirt, then pulled her hair back in a low ponytail.

"No. They can't, but you did," Elizabeth said. "Well played, Delilah."

"A lot of people died in that game."

"But not you. You live to fight another day." Elizabeth smiled at her and Davi. "Shall we?"

Davi stood up, but Del shook her head. "I ain't going with you."

"What? There's nothing here. Let us at least drop you off in a town."

"I don't want no town. Just leave me be." Del turned to Davi and shouldered the backpack. "Thanks for the assistance, Davida. I'm grateful, but please, don't ever find me again."

"You're lucky that I could," Davi said.

"I know. But nothing has changed for us, so please, don't ever do it again."

"A lot has changed, for both of use, but I get it, and I won't. Not unless you ask."

"I ain't never gonna ask."

Davi smiled. "No, Del, I don't think you will." Davi looked Del up and down a few times. She grinned at whatever she saw. "I think you're going to be okay."

EPILOGUE

DELILAH MONROE WIPED down the bar. She stopped and cussed when the old jukebox got stuck and the music slowed —distorted and pained. Del walked over and gave it a good whack. It evened out and resumed playing "Coal Miner's Daughter." Satisfied, she went back behind the bar.

"No mas Loretty," The little man at the end of the bar slammed his beer bottle down and flipped off the jukebox. Del scowled at him and answered him in English.

"Fuck off, Jose. It's my goddamn bar. I played that accordion Tejano shit for you last night."

"Fuck the Coal Miner's Daughter!" he screamed.

Del growled at him, then came from behind the bar. He yelped when she snatched him up and tossed him outside into the sand. She walked back inside and went back to cleaning as Loretta played on. After a few seconds, Jose shuffled back inside and climbed on to his stool. He huffed and scowled as he looked over at Del, but he kept quiet. Del pulled another beer from the cooler, opened it, and set it in front of him. She growled at him, then gave him a half-smile. She tossed him out two or three times a day. He always came back. They both seemed to enjoy it.

The dive bar sat on the beach just outside a sleepy little port town on the Bay of Campeche. Del had switched the Pacific view for the Caribbean, one she'd wanted since she was small—her blue teacup realized. Del opened the roll-up windows, breathed in deeply as the ocean breeze ruffled her bleached hair and the wonderful bite of the salt tickled her nose. It was hot and the little bar had no air conditioning. She preferred it that way. Her one requirement was that the jukebox work. And that the old lady who ran her kitchen learn to make fried mushrooms.

Everyone in the bar looked up when the two Americans walked in. The man spoke Spanish with a flat accent and fake smile. He walked up to the bar and handed Del a picture of herself. His partner, a disapproving short woman with gray hair and gray skin, haunted the area behind him. The man flashed her an FBI badge.

"Hola, senorita. Buscando a la mujer."

Del shook her head. "Nope. Ain't seen her."

He looked at her, perplexed, cocking his head. He continued in Spanish.

"Estas Seguro? Mire de nuevo."

"Real sure, bub, I think you all best leave."

The surrounding air shimmered. Their eyes glazed over, then the two agents nodded in unison. "Okay, yeah, I think we'd better leave."

Del held the door for them and waved.

"Fucking dumbasses," she said under her breath. She leaned in the doorway and laughed as she watched them wobble and weave through the sand. The spell would keep them confused for a while.

Del caught a whiff of a familiar scent as a tall, auburn-haired woman in a stylish caftan and wide-brimmed hat rolled in off the beach. She sat down at one of the outside tables and smiled at Del. She twitched a little as she waited.

Del rolled her eyes. She went behind the bar and grabbed the bottle of tequila and two glasses. She sat down at the table with the woman and poured the drinks.

"The glamour is very good. The Spanish is a nice touch."

Del nodded. "Thanks. I see you found yourself a new body."

Olivia smiled. She twitched a bit, then motioned down her body. "Yes. You like?"

"I ain't noticing you ever take over no ugly girls."

"We all have our vices, Delilah." The woman clinked her glass against Del's and sipped her drink.

Del relaxed back into the chair and watched the clear blue water glimmer and glint in the sun.

"Yeah. I reckon we do."

ACKNOWLEDGMENTS

This book is dedicated to the memory of my Nan. I usually dedicate books to her but this one is special. Everyone needs a cheerleader in life. Somebody who thinks you breathe art and believes you can do anything. My Nan was that person to me. She loved me and encouraged me to be anything I wanted. When I lost her, I didn't know a person could hurt that much. In writing this book, I drew on my memories of her, and I felt her with me as I put the words on the page. I miss her every day, but the parts of this book I know came from her make me happy and that's a good thing.

Thank you for taking the journey with me and Del. We hope you enjoyed the ride.

ABOUT THE AUTHOR

Jessica Raney is the author of seven books. Her latest, *Rack and Ruin* is the final book in her Appalachian-Supernatural-Noir series. Her other works include a zombie Apocalypse adventure, *These Violent Delights*, and two collections of short stories, *Oddballs* and *Dreadful Pennies*. She has also co-written a collection of short, dark fiction, *Tales from the Den: Volume I*. She loves all things quirky and spooky, and her style could be best described as the intersection of dark comedy, horror, and the fantastical. Originally from southern Ohio, Jessica now lives in Houston, Texas and is active in the Houston Writer's Guild and Writespace organizations. When not writing or navigating Houston traffic, she's enjoying the Gulf Coast with friends and her cat/dog/demon/baby, Gimli.

Also by Jessica Raney

Oddballs: A collection of Short Fiction

Dreadful Pennies: A collection of Short Things

Tooth and Nail

These Violent Delights

The Hard Truth

Rack and Ruin

Co-Authored with Jae Mazer

Tales from the Den, Dark Fiction, Volume I

www.ingramcontent.com/pod-product-compliance
Lightning Source LLC
Chambersburg PA
CBHW060951030726
47503CB00003B/818